MICHAEL I. SILBERKLEIT
Chairman and Co-Publisher

RICHARD H. GOLDWATER
President and Co-Publisher

VICTOR GORELICK
Vice President / Managing Editor

FRED MAUSSER
Vice President / Director of Circulation

Compilation Editor:
PAUL CASTIGLIA

Production Editor:
NELSON RIBEIRO

Art Director:
JOE PEP

Cover Art
JEFF SHULTZ
& BOB SMITH

Production Manager &
Front Cover Coloring:
ROBBIE O'QUINN

Production:
CARLOS ANTUNES
PAUL d'ONOFRIO
MIKE PELLERITO
ROSARIO "TITO" PEÑA

Archie characters created by JOHN L. GOLDWATER
The likenesses of the original Archie characters
were created by BOB MONTANA

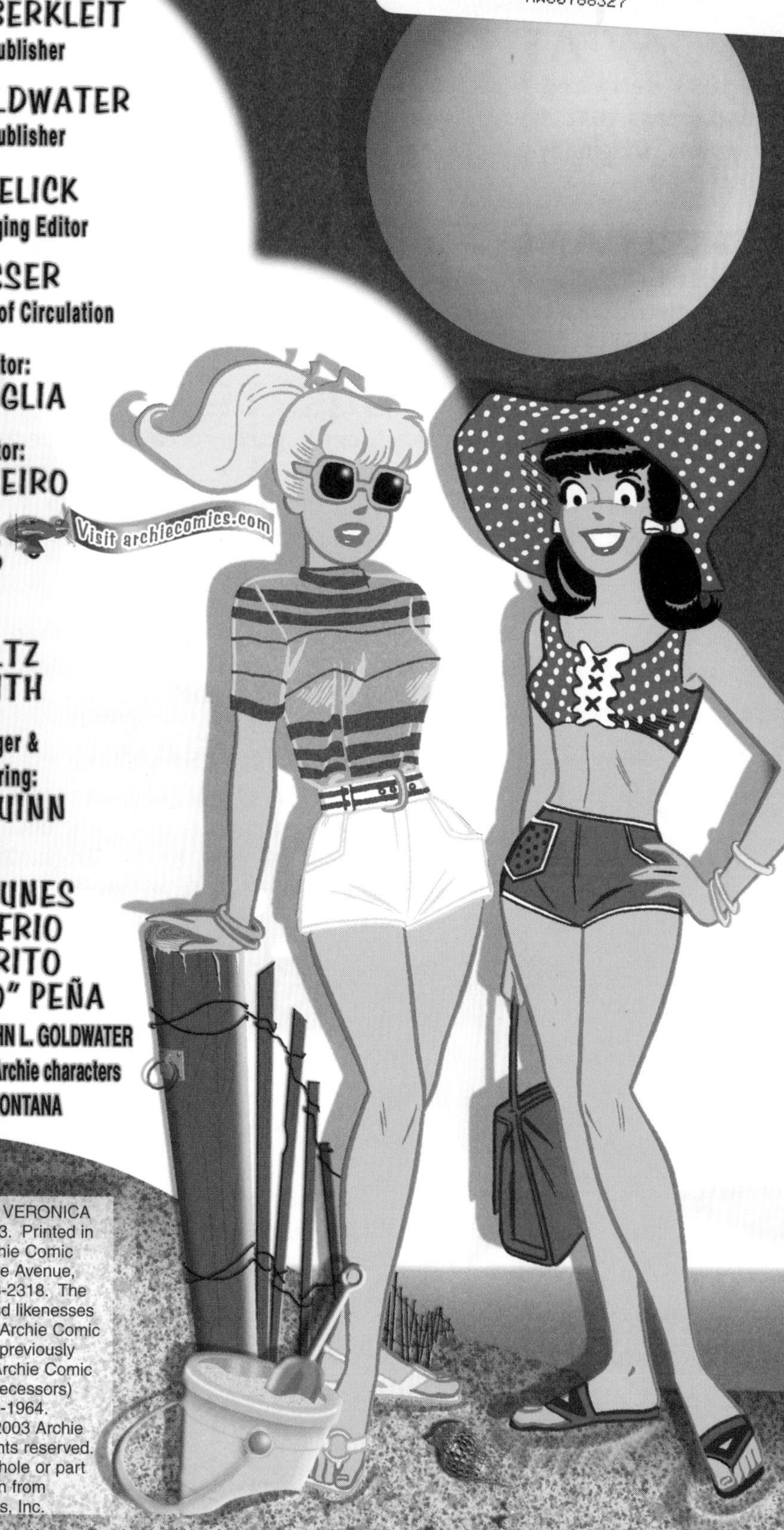
Visit archiecomics.com

ARCHIE CLASSICS-BETTY & VERONICA SUMMER FUN, Volume 1, 2003. Printed in CANADA. Published by Archie Comic Publications, Inc., 325 Fayette Avenue, Mamaroneck, New York 10543-2318.

ISBN 1-879794-13-6

TABLE OF CONTENTS

4 FOREWORD by DAWN WELLS "MARY ANN" FROM GILLIGAN'S ISLAND

6 A DAY AT THE BEACH

Archie takes Betty and Veronica to the beach so they can relax before the big dance, but soon learns that it's anything but relaxing, as he ends up catering to the girls' every whim! Originally presented in BETTY & VERONICA SUMMER FUN #8, October, 1960

16 FISH AND FLIPS

Reggie tries to take a bite out of lifeguard Archie's popularity-literally-by donning a shark suit to embarrass him in front of the girls! Originally presented in BETTY & VERONICA SUMMER FUN #8, October, 1960

18 MUSCLE AND BUSTLE

Betty and Veronica get to the beach extra early to catch Archie and Reggie's morning workout, but when the boys insist they join in on their exercise, the girls wish they had stayed in bed! Originally presented in BETTY & VERONICA SUMMER FUN #8, October, 1960

23 THE PLUNGERS

Having your own pool is great, but when the water looks cold, it's hard to take that first plunge! Originally presented in BETTY & VERONICA SUMMER FUN #13, October, 1961

29 FOUL BAWL

When Archie leaves for summer vacation, Veronica is heartbroken-at least until she meets up with her substitute boyfriend, Bert! Originally presented in BETTY & VERONICA SUMMER FUN #13, October, 1961

39 BETTY'S SUMMER FASHIONS

Paper doll cut-out page originally presented in BETTY & VERONICA SUMMER FUN #8, October,1960

40 READERS CHOICE

Veronica sees her dating life flash before her eyes when Archie gets a hold of her secret guidebook for women! Originally presented in BETTY & VERONICA SUMMER FUN #13, October, 1961

46 HERE'S HEALTH

Veronica's love life gets a workout-and so does she-when she falls for a health-obsessed lifeguard. Originally presented in BETTY & VERONICA SUMMER FUN #13, October, 1961

SKIN DEEP 52

The girls get under Archie's skin when they ask him to judge who's got the best tan.
Originally presented in BETTY & VERONICA SUMMER FUN #18, September, 1962

THE BOAT BUILDER 58

Reggie and Veronica make waves in a speedboat, but Archie and Betty
are lucky to keep their heap afloat! Originally presented in
BETTY & VERONICA SUMMER FUN #18, September, 1962

MUSCLE HUSTLE 64

Betty and Veronica go gaga over the new lifeguard, but is he more...
or less... than meets the eye?! Originally presented in
BETTY & VERONICA SUMMER FUN #18, September, 1962

VERONICA'S FASHIONS 70

Paper doll cut-out page originally presented in
BETTY & VERONICA SUMMER FUN #8, October, 1960

THE WADING GAME 71

Archie has a tough choice to make-keep a
tennis date with Veronica, or cool off
with Betty in the pool? Originally presented in
BETTY & VERONICA SUMMER FUN #18, September, 1962

ALL ABOUT ARCHIE 77

Jughead pits Veronica against Betty... so he can make several pit
stops at the poolside barbecue! Originally presented in BETTY
& VERONICA SUMMER FUN #28, September, 1964

COMPLETE CIRCLE 83

Veronica abandons a sinking ship-literally-
when she leaves Archie floundering on
his raft to join Reggie on his speedboat!
Originally presented in BETTY & VERONICA
SUMMER FUN #28, September, 1964

FLY BOY 89

Today's "Extreme Sports" stars have
nothing on Archie and Mr. Lodge.
Wait till you see the "splash" they
make! Originally presented in
BETTY & VERONICA SUMMER FUN
#28, September, 1964

*A note about BETTY & VERONICA SUMMER FUN. You may
notice a disparity of dates between issues, such as #8 being
released in 1960, #13 in 1961 and #18 in 1962. This is because
BETTY & VERONICA SUMMER FUN was part of the ARCHIE GIANT SERIES
which included other titles like ARCHIE'S JOKES and THE WORLD OF
JUGHEAD. BETTY & VERONICA SUMMER FUN alternated with these titles.
Therefore, if ARCHIE'S JOKES #17 was the ARCHIE GIANT SERIES preceding
BETTY & VERONICA SUMMER FUN, the SUMMER FUN issue was #18.
Each year, there was one BETTY & VERONICA SUMMER FUN in the ARCHIE GIANT SERIES.*

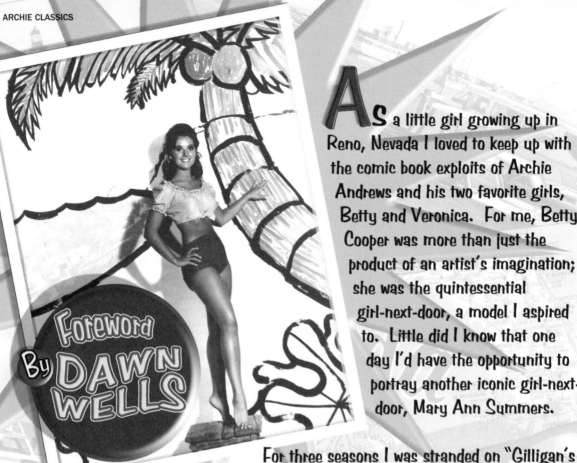

Foreword By DAWN WELLS

As a little girl growing up in Reno, Nevada I loved to keep up with the comic book exploits of Archie Andrews and his two favorite girls, Betty and Veronica. For me, Betty Cooper was more than just the product of an artist's imagination; she was the quintessential girl-next-door, a model I aspired to. Little did I know that one day I'd have the opportunity to portray another iconic girl-next-door, Mary Ann Summers.

For three seasons I was stranded on "Gilligan's Island" with the most famous castaways in television history. Mary Ann has remained a very important part of, not only my life, but also the lives of fans all over the world. Both Mary Ann and Betty Cooper have been popular for decades, and when one compares the two, it's easy to see why.

The most obvious connection between Mary Ann and Betty is the fact that they are forever engaged in friendships/rivalries with the glamour queens, Ginger Grant and Veronica Lodge, respectively. Ginger and Veronica represent the "fantasy" sex symbols—the unattainable girls most guys know they don't have a shot at marrying. They are constantly pushing the envelope, using their beauty to get their way.

While the Gingers and Veronicas of the world intimidate them, men know they can count on the Mary Anns and Bettys. Loyal, sweet, trustworthy and sensible, Mary Ann and Betty are highly approachable. Unlike Ginger and Veronica, Mary Ann and Betty do not "use" men or let jealously lead their hearts. Most men want to spend their lives with someone like that—a best friend who is nice, ethical and will help you through life.

Mary Ann acted as one of the rudders of the ship on "Gilligan's Island." She was an enthusiastic leader, effective at getting everyone to do his or her part. In the same way, Betty Cooper is a stabilizing influence in Archie and the gang's lives. It is a Midwestern, small-town ethic that Mary Ann, Betty and myself share—a patriotic, never-give-up approach to life.

When it came time to develop my character, I knew that in order for the contrasting personalities of Mary Ann and Ginger to work, I had to play Mary Ann completely "apple pie." Growing up, I didn't really drink or have any drug problems. I was well behaved, which at that time was considered by some to be "square." No doubt the sincerity and gumption I'd seen Betty display in those comics sunk into my subconscious! I applied those same positive attributes to Mary Ann.

Both Mary Ann and Betty Cooper blazed trails in their respective mediums. I consider Mary Ann to be among the first "women's lib" characters on television. As an independent, fair, handy and organized leader, she often showed the men how to get things done. Likewise, it is Betty who is most likely to get under the hood of Archie's car to get it started again so they can continue their date! Sadly, I feel that while Mary Ann and Betty were among the first positive female role models in popular entertainment, they are rapidly becoming an endangered species in popular entertainment. Producers take note: during "Gilligan's Island's" heyday, my Mary Ann character received much more fan mail than Ginger did (in fact, more than any other character including Gilligan!), and my fan mail was from boys and girls alike! Likewise, in popularity polls Betty Cooper often comes out on top with both boys and girls. There is still a place for the "good girl" in entertainment and I am thankful the images of Mary Ann and Betty endure to influence new generations today.

There's a lot of me in Mary Ann, and rereading the wonderful stories in this volume, I've also discovered there's a lot of Betty Cooper, too. So sit right back and you'll hear some tales, some tales of teenage girls, who hit the surf to impress Archie, riding waves and curls!

Since her classic role on "Gilligan's Island," Dawn Wells has kept busy doing theater, television, feature films and commercials. She also co-executive produced two hit TV-movies for CBS, "Surviving Gilligan's Island" and "Return to the Batcave: the Adventures of Adam & Burt" and operates a film school, The Actor's Boot Camp. She developed the "Wishing Wells" line of clothing designed for the elderly and disabled, colorful fashions incorporating easy-to-use Velcro fasteners instead of zippers and buttons. An avid world traveler, Dawn has climbed the mountains in Rwanda to view the mountain gorillas, gone on four Safaris, flown around the world on the Concorde, and in some trail-blazing of her own, canoed in the Solomon Islands where women had never been before!

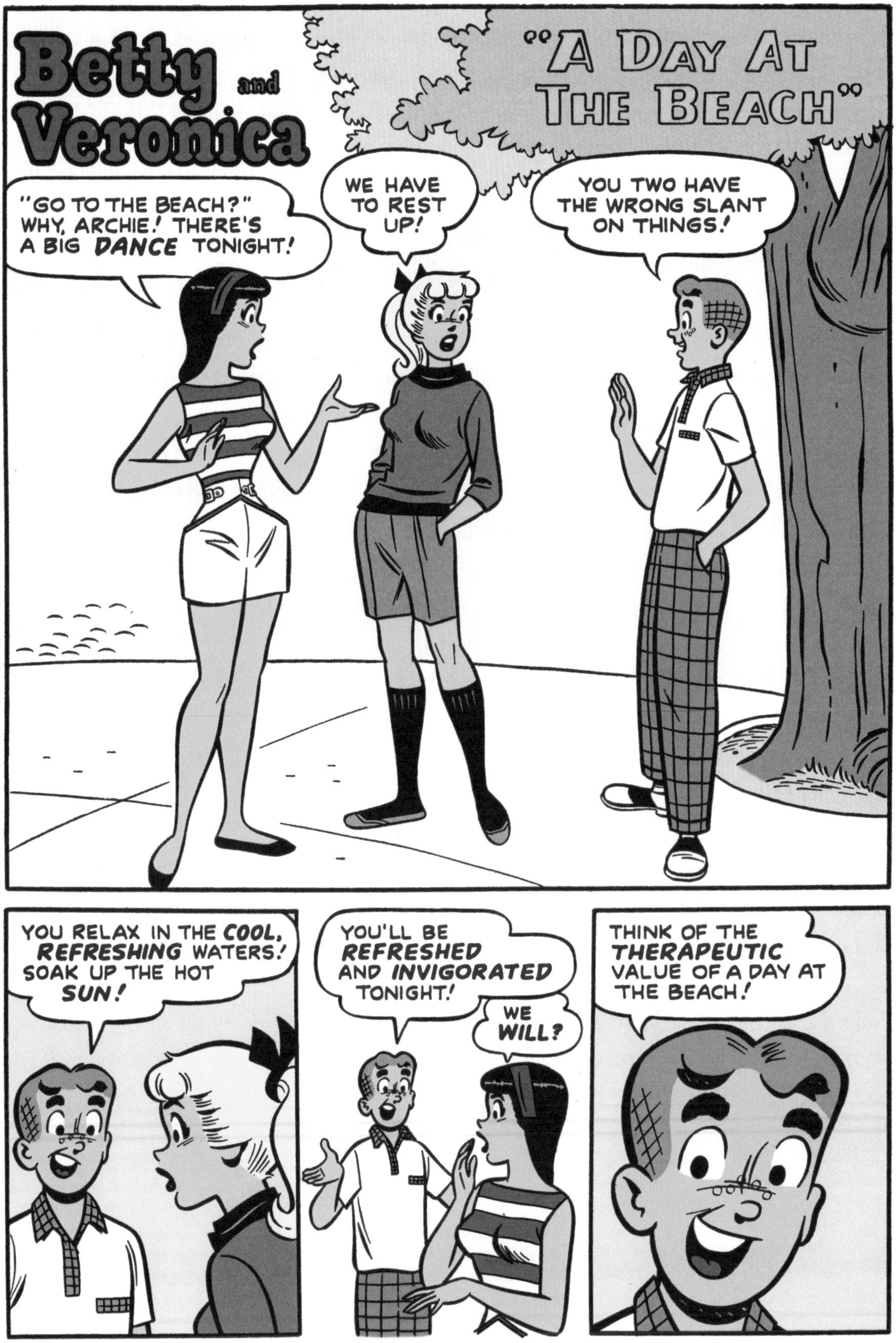
Betty and Veronica
"A DAY AT THE BEACH"
"GO TO THE BEACH?" WHY, ARCHIE! THERE'S A BIG DANCE TONIGHT!
WE HAVE TO REST UP!
YOU TWO HAVE THE WRONG SLANT ON THINGS!
YOU RELAX IN THE COOL, REFRESHING WATERS! SOAK UP THE HOT SUN!
YOU'LL BE REFRESHED AND INVIGORATED TONIGHT!
WE WILL?
THINK OF THE THERAPEUTIC VALUE OF A DAY AT THE BEACH!

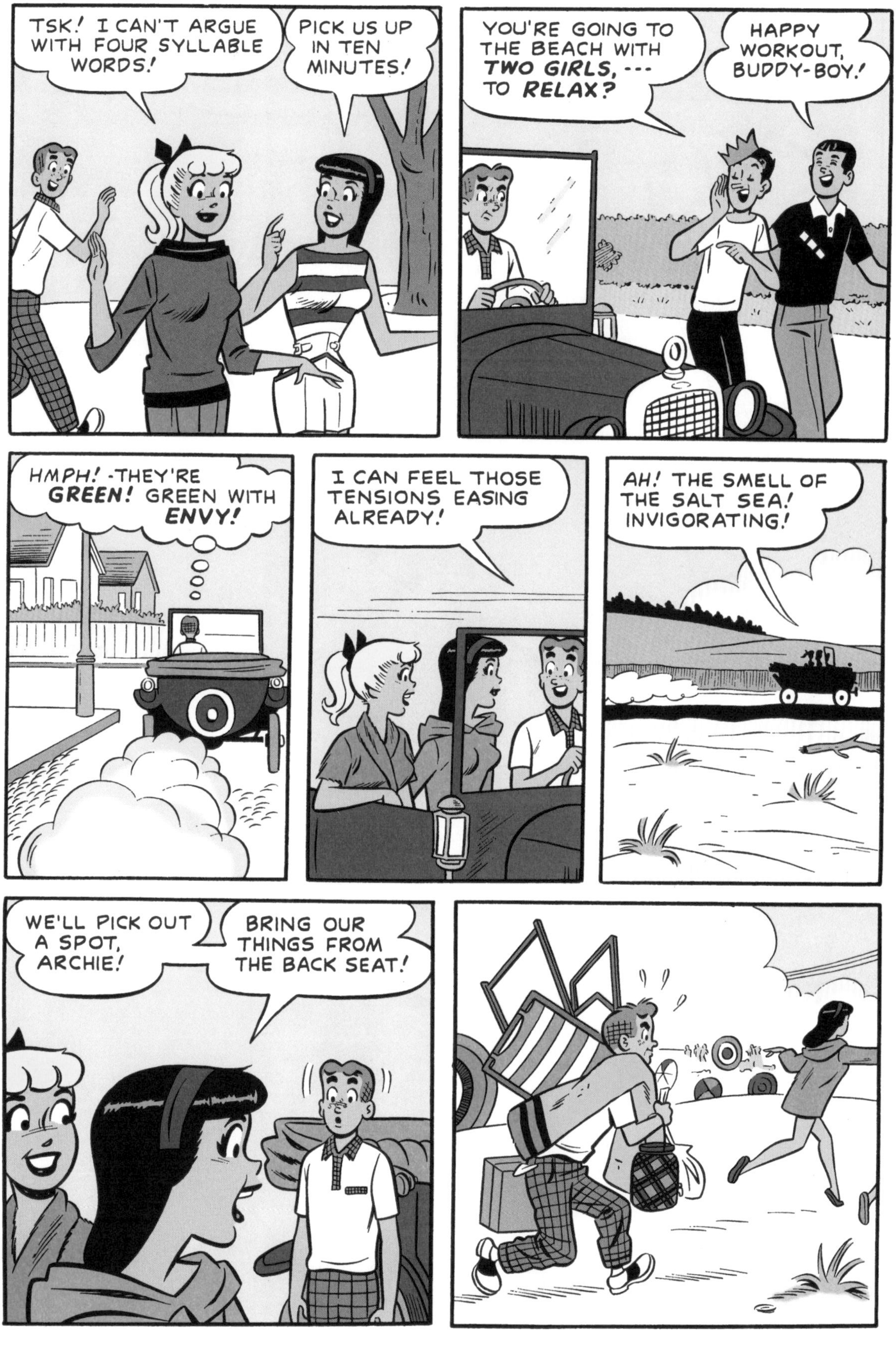
TSK! I CAN'T ARGUE WITH FOUR SYLLABLE WORDS!
PICK US UP IN TEN MINUTES!
YOU'RE GOING TO THE BEACH WITH TWO GIRLS, --- TO RELAX?
HAPPY WORKOUT, BUDDY-BOY!
HMPH! -THEY'RE GREEN! GREEN WITH ENVY!
I CAN FEEL THOSE TENSIONS EASING ALREADY!
AH! THE SMELL OF THE SALT SEA! INVIGORATING!
WE'LL PICK OUT A SPOT, ARCHIE!
BRING OUR THINGS FROM THE BACK SEAT!

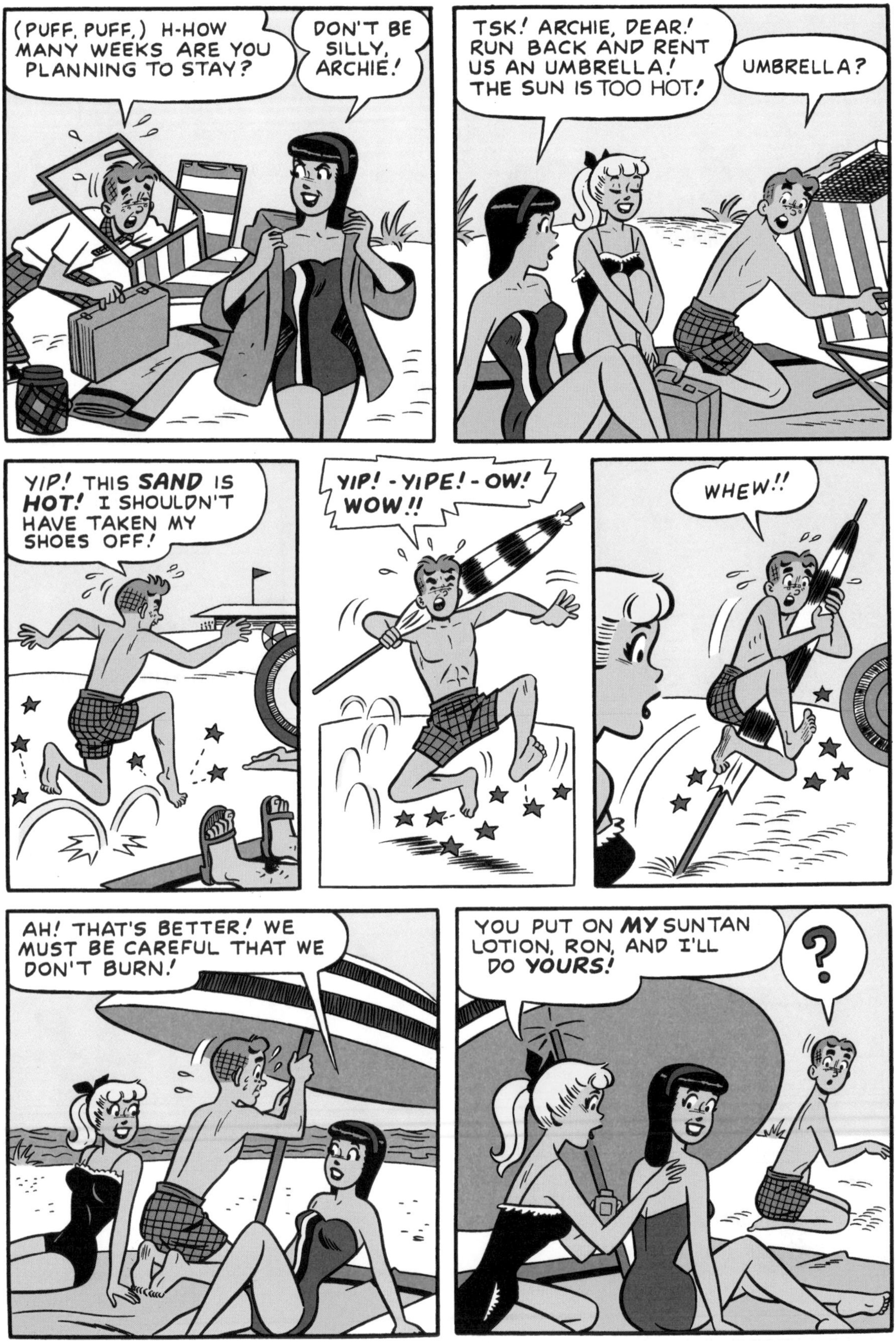
(PUFF, PUFF,) H-HOW MANY WEEKS ARE YOU PLANNING TO STAY?
DON'T BE SILLY, ARCHIE!
TSK! ARCHIE, DEAR! RUN BACK AND RENT US AN UMBRELLA! THE SUN IS TOO HOT!
UMBRELLA?
YIP! THIS SAND IS HOT! I SHOULDN'T HAVE TAKEN MY SHOES OFF!
YIP! -YIPE! -OW! WOW!!
WHEW!!
AH! THAT'S BETTER! WE MUST BE CAREFUL THAT WE DON'T BURN!
YOU PUT ON MY SUNTAN LOTION, RON, AND I'LL DO YOURS!
?

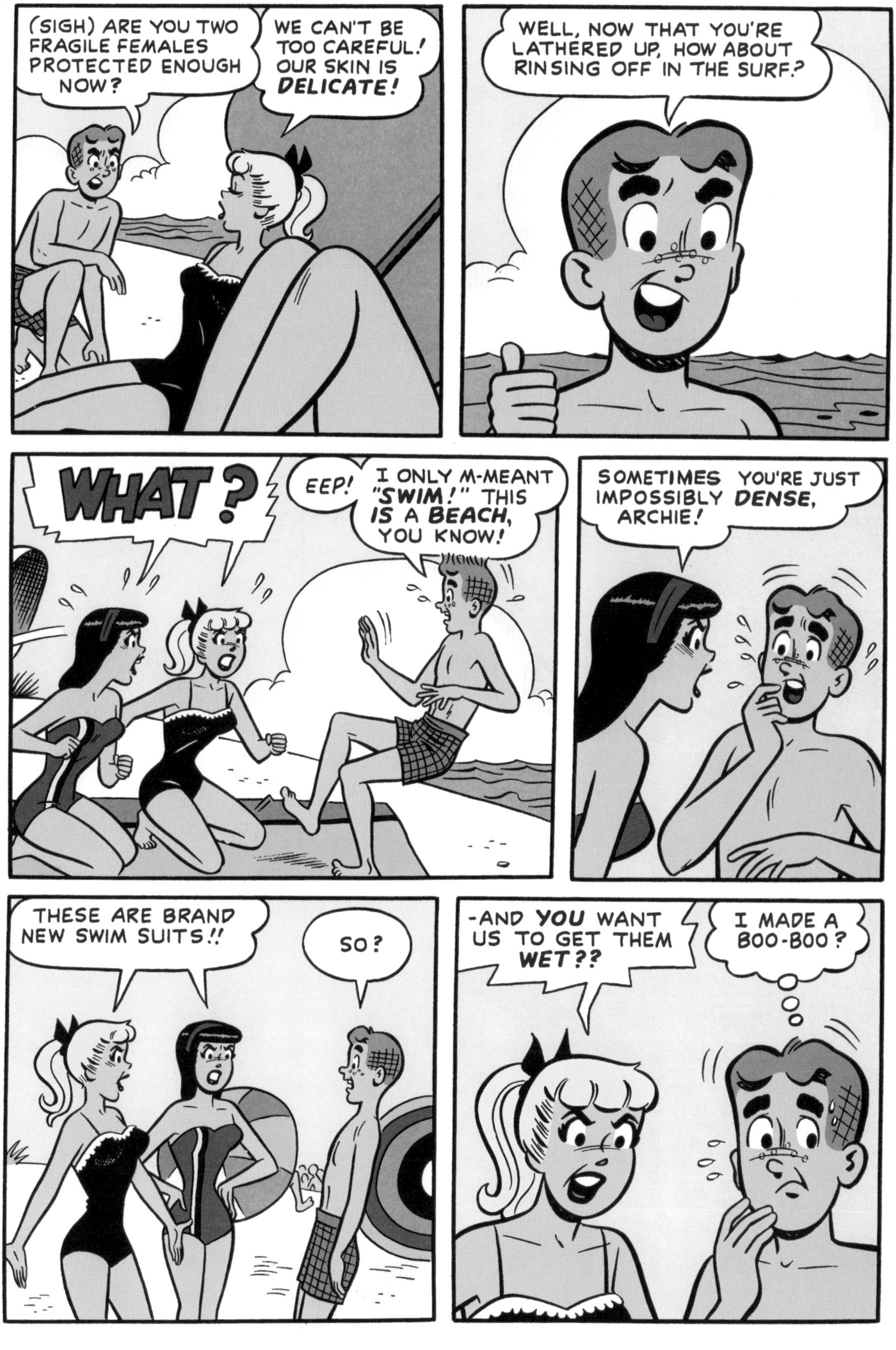
(SIGH) ARE YOU TWO FRAGILE FEMALES PROTECTED ENOUGH NOW?
WE CAN'T BE TOO CAREFUL! OUR SKIN IS DELICATE!
WELL, NOW THAT YOU'RE LATHERED UP, HOW ABOUT RINSING OFF IN THE SURF?
WHAT?
EEP!
I ONLY M-MEANT "SWIM!" THIS IS A BEACH, YOU KNOW!
SOMETIMES YOU'RE JUST IMPOSSIBLY DENSE, ARCHIE!
THESE ARE BRAND NEW SWIM SUITS!!
SO?
-AND YOU WANT US TO GET THEM WET??
I MADE A BOO-BOO?

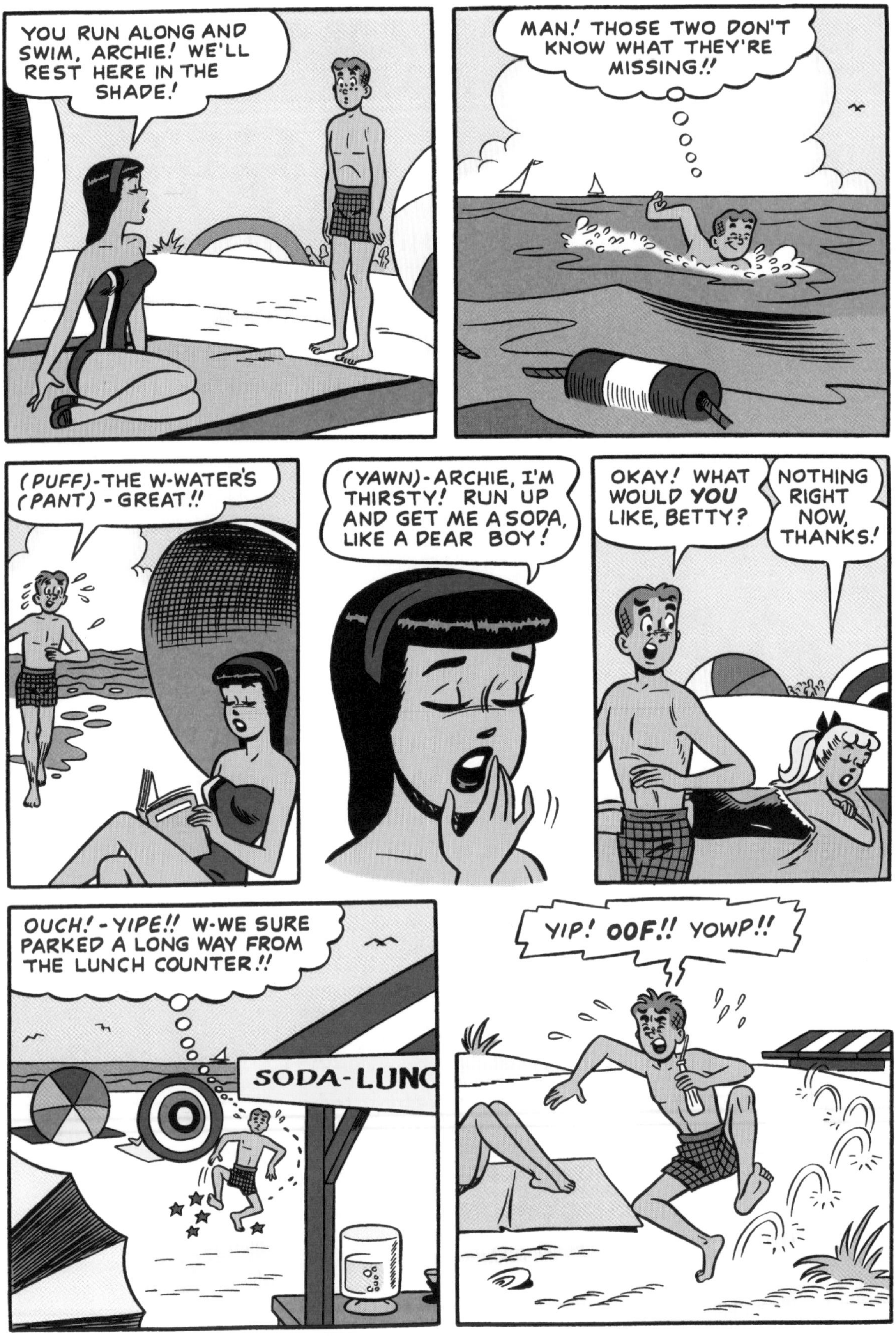
YOU RUN ALONG AND SWIM, ARCHIE! WE'LL REST HERE IN THE SHADE!
MAN! THOSE TWO DON'T KNOW WHAT THEY'RE MISSING!!
(PUFF)-THE W-WATER'S (PANT)-GREAT!!
(YAWN)-ARCHIE, I'M THIRSTY! RUN UP AND GET ME A SODA, LIKE A DEAR BOY!
OKAY! WHAT WOULD YOU LIKE, BETTY?
NOTHING RIGHT NOW, THANKS!
OUCH!-YIPE!! W-WE SURE PARKED A LONG WAY FROM THE LUNCH COUNTER!!
SODA-LUNC
YIP! OOF!! YOWP!!

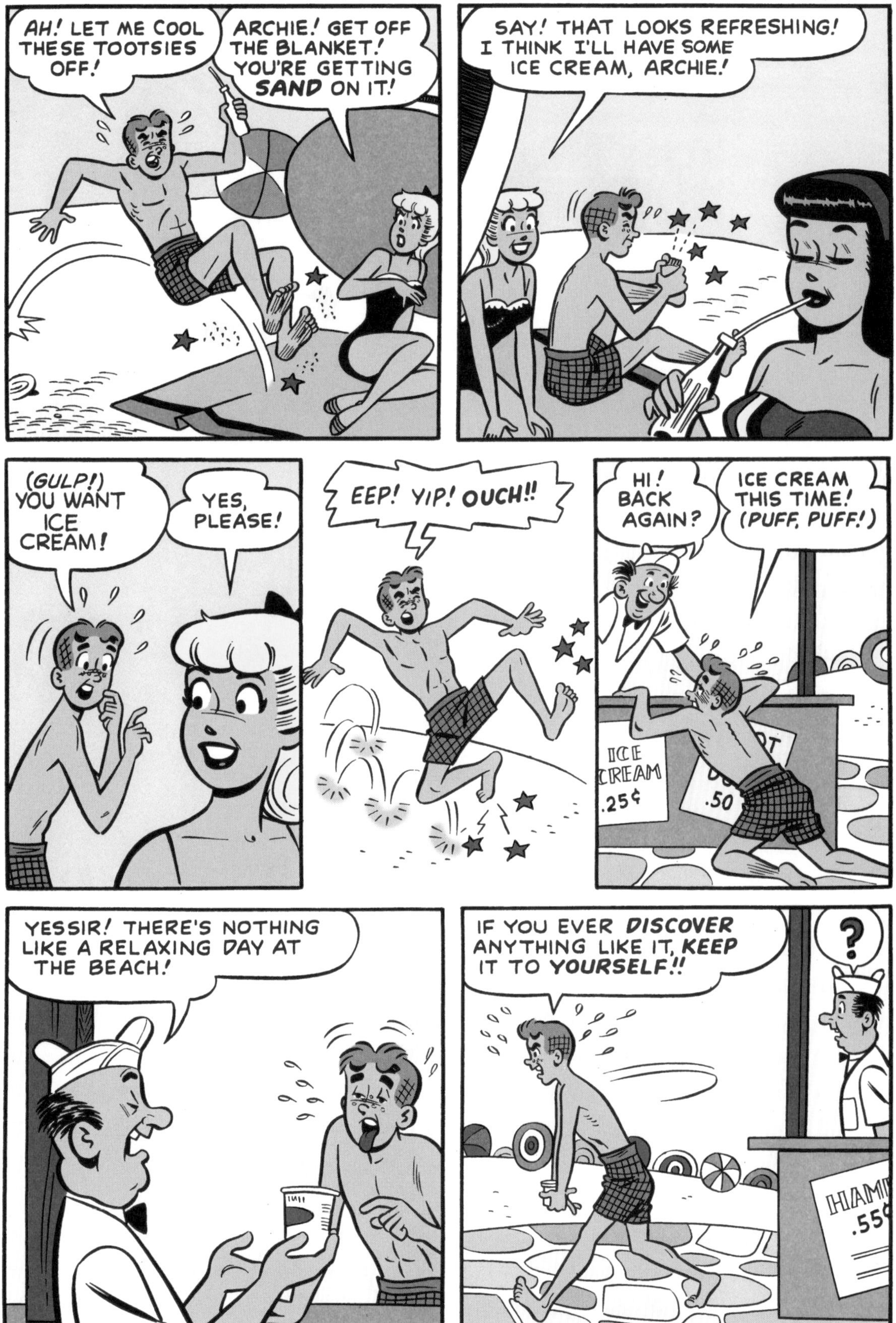
AH! LET ME COOL THESE TOOTSIES OFF!
ARCHIE! GET OFF THE BLANKET! YOU'RE GETTING SAND ON IT!
SAY! THAT LOOKS REFRESHING! I THINK I'LL HAVE SOME ICE CREAM, ARCHIE!
(GULP!) YOU WANT ICE CREAM!
YES, PLEASE!
EEP! YIP! OUCH!!
HI! BACK AGAIN?
ICE CREAM THIS TIME! (PUFF, PUFF!)
ICE CREAM .25¢
.50
YESSIR! THERE'S NOTHING LIKE A RELAXING DAY AT THE BEACH!
IF YOU EVER DISCOVER ANYTHING LIKE IT, KEEP IT TO YOURSELF!!
?
.55¢

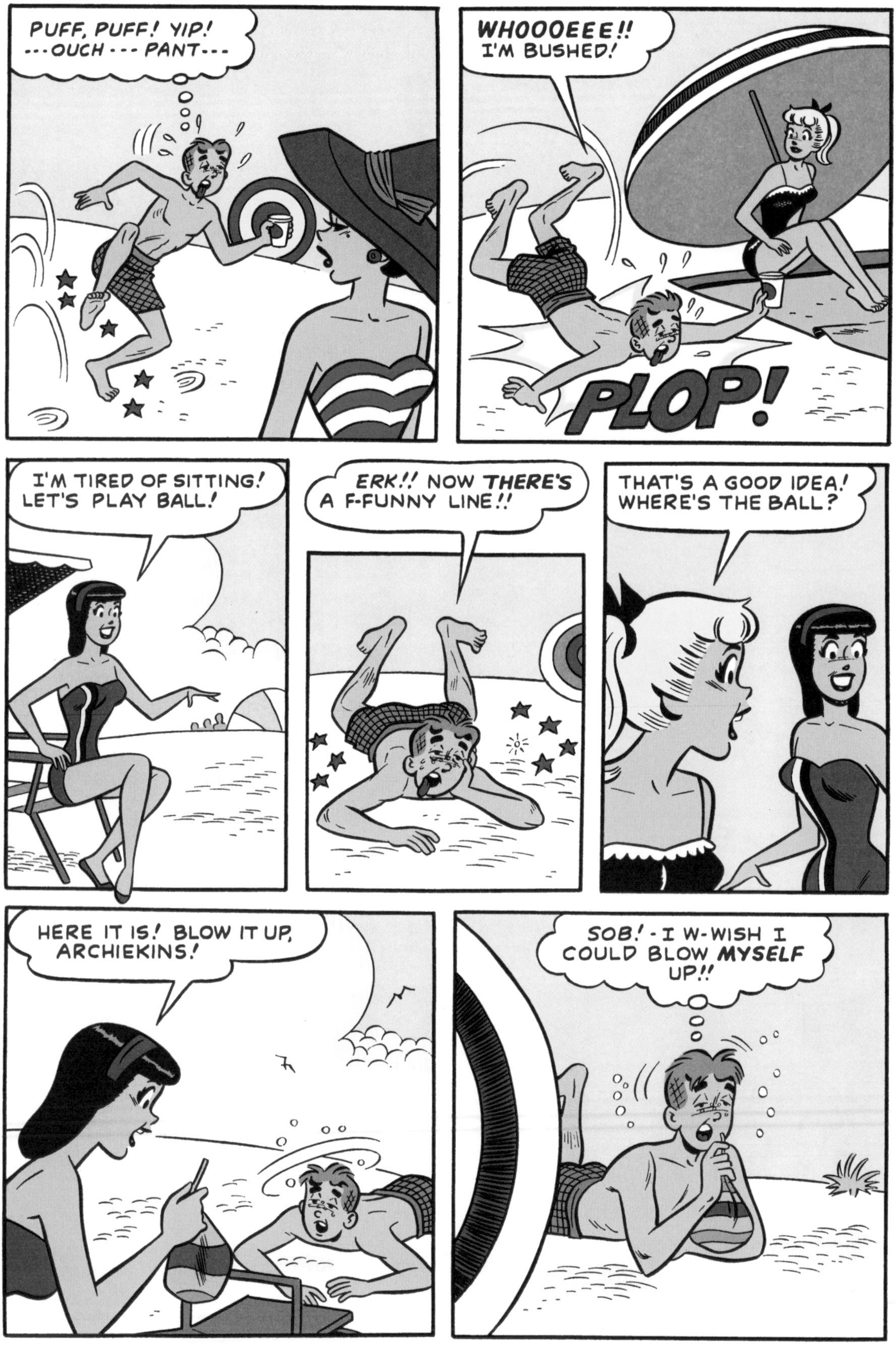
PUFF, PUFF! YIP! ---OUCH --- PANT---
WHOOOEEE!! I'M BUSHED!
PLOP!
I'M TIRED OF SITTING! LET'S PLAY BALL!
ERK!! NOW THERE'S A F-FUNNY LINE!!
THAT'S A GOOD IDEA! WHERE'S THE BALL?
HERE IT IS! BLOW IT UP, ARCHIEKINS!
SOB! - I W-WISH I COULD BLOW MYSELF UP!!

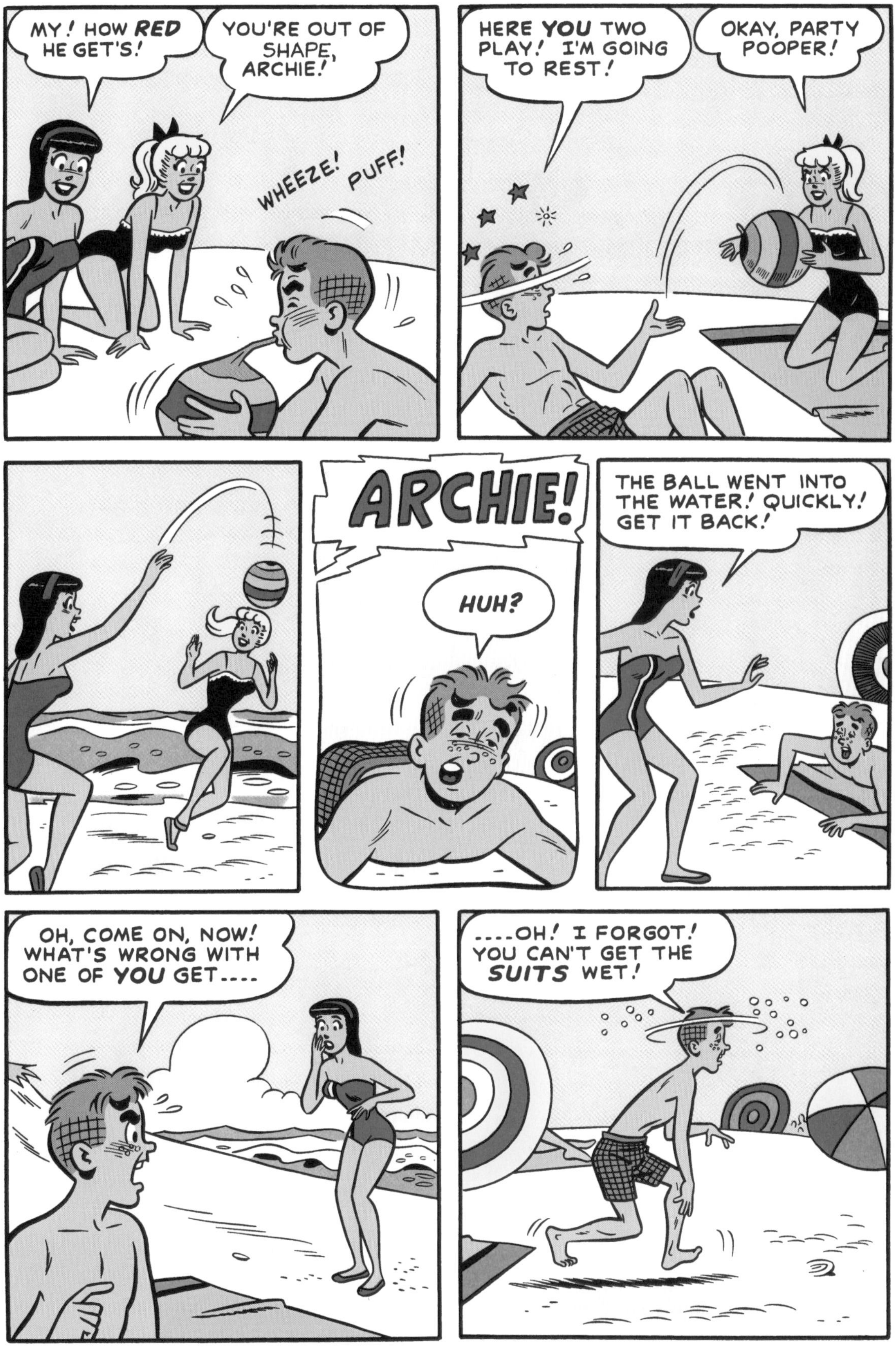
MY! HOW RED HE GET'S!
YOU'RE OUT OF SHAPE, ARCHIE!
WHEEZE! PUFF!
HERE YOU TWO PLAY! I'M GOING TO REST!
OKAY, PARTY POOPER!
ARCHIE!
HUH?
THE BALL WENT INTO THE WATER! QUICKLY! GET IT BACK!
OH, COME ON, NOW! WHAT'S WRONG WITH ONE OF YOU GET....
....OH! I FORGOT! YOU CAN'T GET THE SUITS WET!

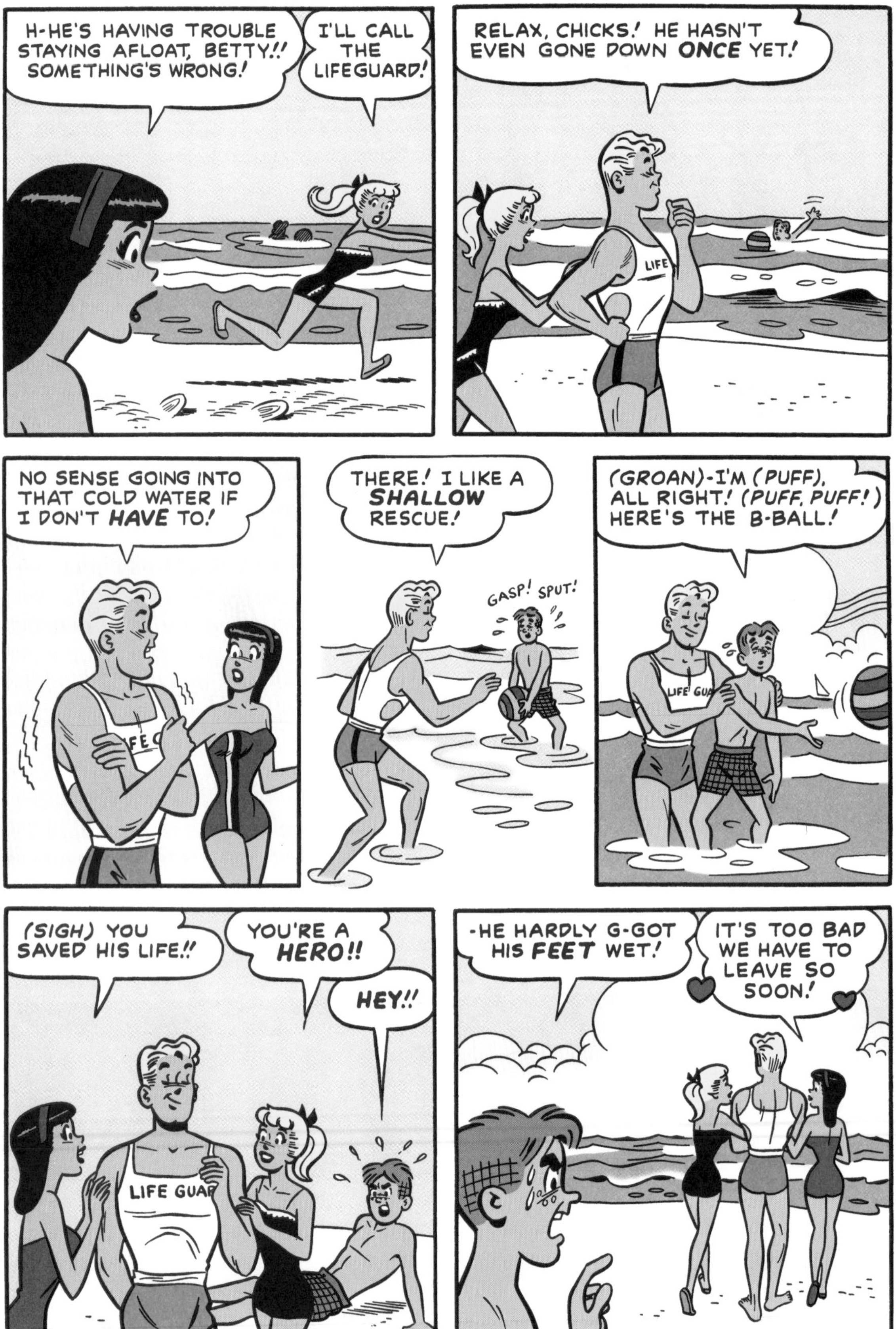
H-HE'S HAVING TROUBLE STAYING AFLOAT, BETTY!! SOMETHING'S WRONG!
I'LL CALL THE LIFEGUARD!
RELAX, CHICKS! HE HASN'T EVEN GONE DOWN ONCE YET!
LIFE
NO SENSE GOING INTO THAT COLD WATER IF I DON'T HAVE TO!
THERE! I LIKE A SHALLOW RESCUE!
GASP! SPUT!
(GROAN)-I'M (PUFF), ALL RIGHT! (PUFF, PUFF!) HERE'S THE B-BALL!
(SIGH) YOU SAVED HIS LIFE!!
YOU'RE A HERO!!
HEY!!
LIFE GUAR
-HE HARDLY G-GOT HIS FEET WET!
IT'S TOO BAD WE HAVE TO LEAVE SO SOON!

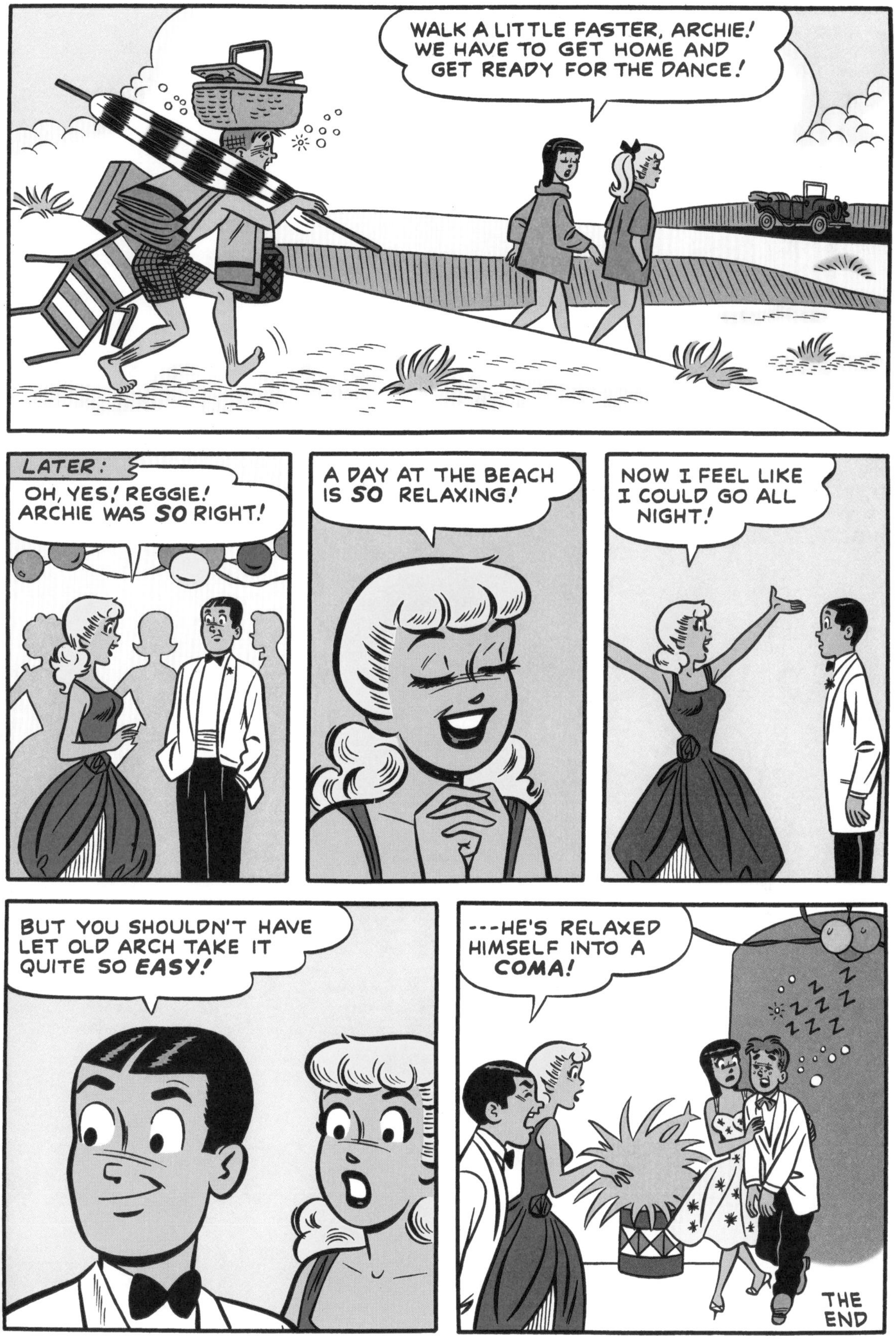
WALK A LITTLE FASTER, ARCHIE! WE HAVE TO GET HOME AND GET READY FOR THE DANCE!
LATER:
OH, YES, REGGIE! ARCHIE WAS SO RIGHT!
A DAY AT THE BEACH IS SO RELAXING!
NOW I FEEL LIKE I COULD GO ALL NIGHT!
BUT YOU SHOULDN'T HAVE LET OLD ARCH TAKE IT QUITE SO EASY!
---HE'S RELAXED HIMSELF INTO A COMA!
Z Z Z Z Z Z Z
THE END

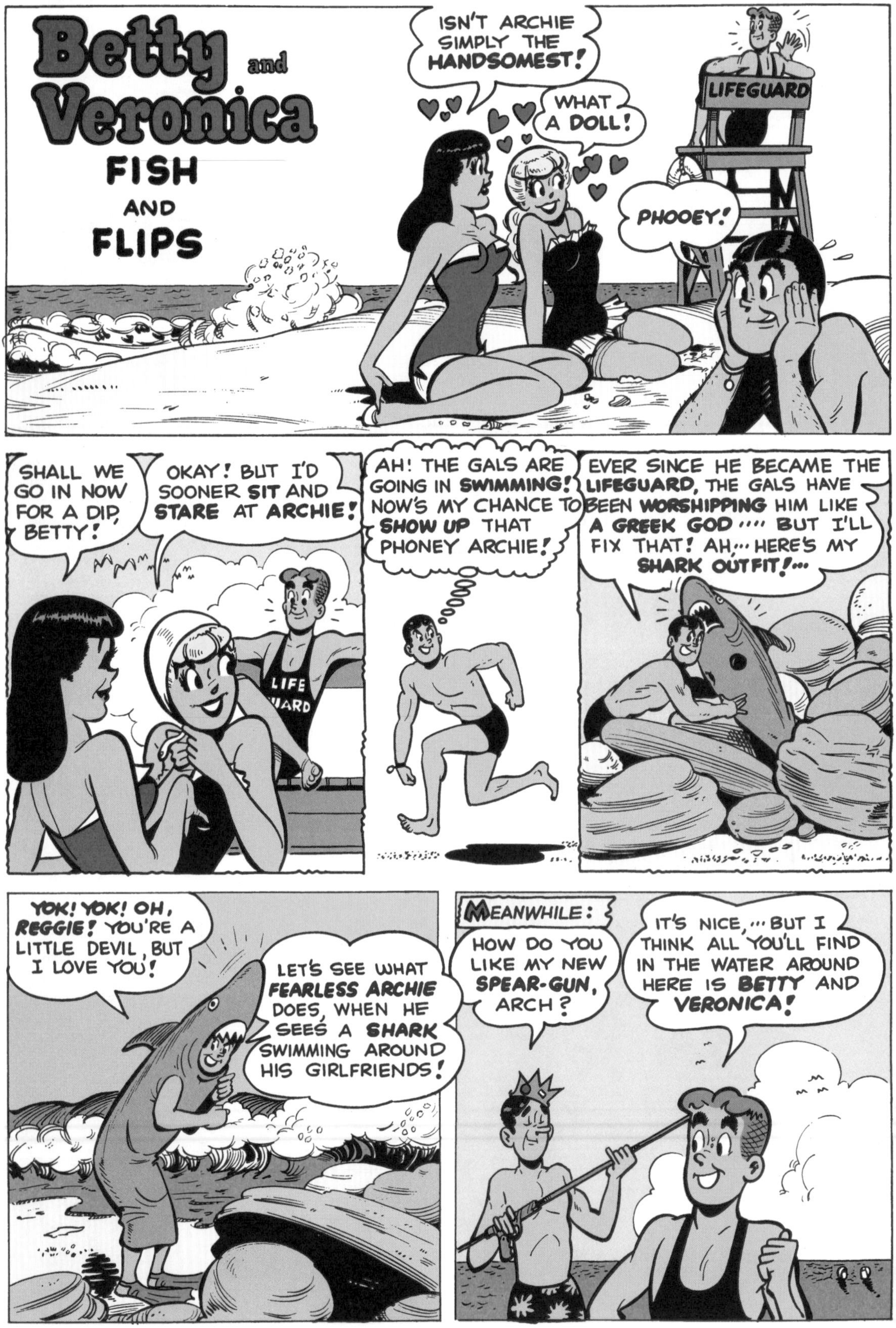

Betty and Veronica
FISH AND FLIPS
ISN'T ARCHIE SIMPLY THE HANDSOMEST!
WHAT A DOLL!
LIFEGUARD
PHOOEY!
SHALL WE GO IN NOW FOR A DIP, BETTY!
OKAY! BUT I'D SOONER SIT AND STARE AT ARCHIE!
LIFE GUARD
AH! THE GALS ARE GOING IN SWIMMING! NOW'S MY CHANCE TO SHOW UP THAT PHONEY ARCHIE!
EVER SINCE HE BECAME THE LIFEGUARD, THE GALS HAVE BEEN WORSHIPPING HIM LIKE A GREEK GOD.... BUT I'LL FIX THAT! AH,... HERE'S MY SHARK OUTFIT!...
YOK! YOK! OH, REGGIE! YOU'RE A LITTLE DEVIL, BUT I LOVE YOU!
LET'S SEE WHAT FEARLESS ARCHIE DOES, WHEN HE SEES A SHARK SWIMMING AROUND HIS GIRLFRIENDS!
MEANWHILE:
HOW DO YOU LIKE MY NEW SPEAR-GUN, ARCH?
IT'S NICE,... BUT I THINK ALL YOU'LL FIND IN THE WATER AROUND HERE IS BETTY AND VERONICA!

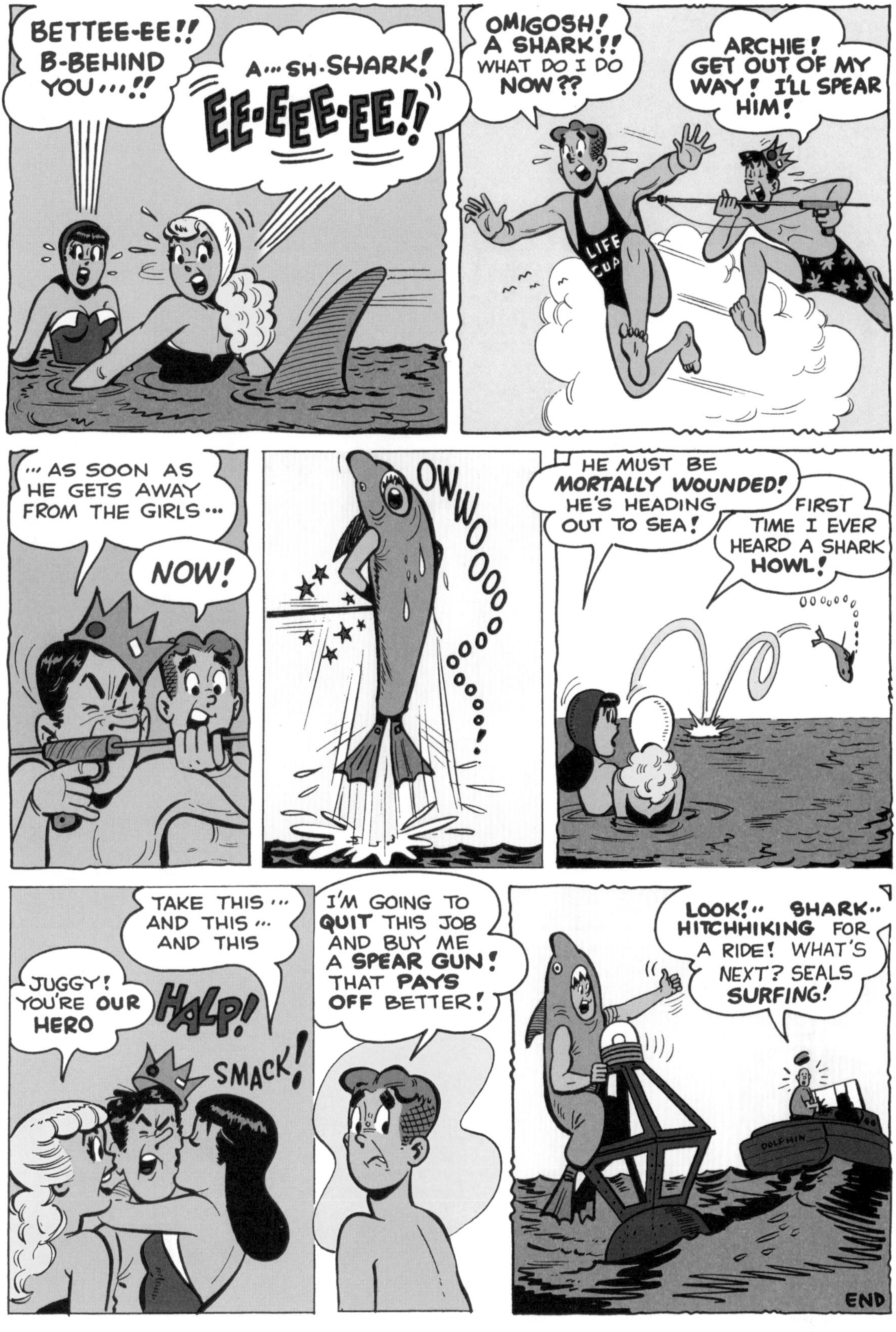
BETTEE-EE!! B-BEHIND YOU....!!
A... SH-SHARK! EE-EEE-EE!!
OMIGOSH! A SHARK!! WHAT DO I DO NOW??
ARCHIE! GET OUT OF MY WAY! I'LL SPEAR HIM!
LIFE GUA
...AS SOON AS HE GETS AWAY FROM THE GIRLS...
NOW!
OWWOOOOOOOOOOOO!
HE MUST BE MORTALLY WOUNDED! HE'S HEADING OUT TO SEA!
FIRST TIME I EVER HEARD A SHARK HOWL!
TAKE THIS... AND THIS... AND THIS
JUGGY! YOU'RE OUR HERO
HALP!
SMACK!
I'M GOING TO QUIT THIS JOB AND BUY ME A SPEAR GUN! THAT PAYS OFF BETTER!
LOOK!.. SHARK.. HITCHHIKING FOR A RIDE! WHAT'S NEXT? SEALS SURFING!
DOLPHIN
END

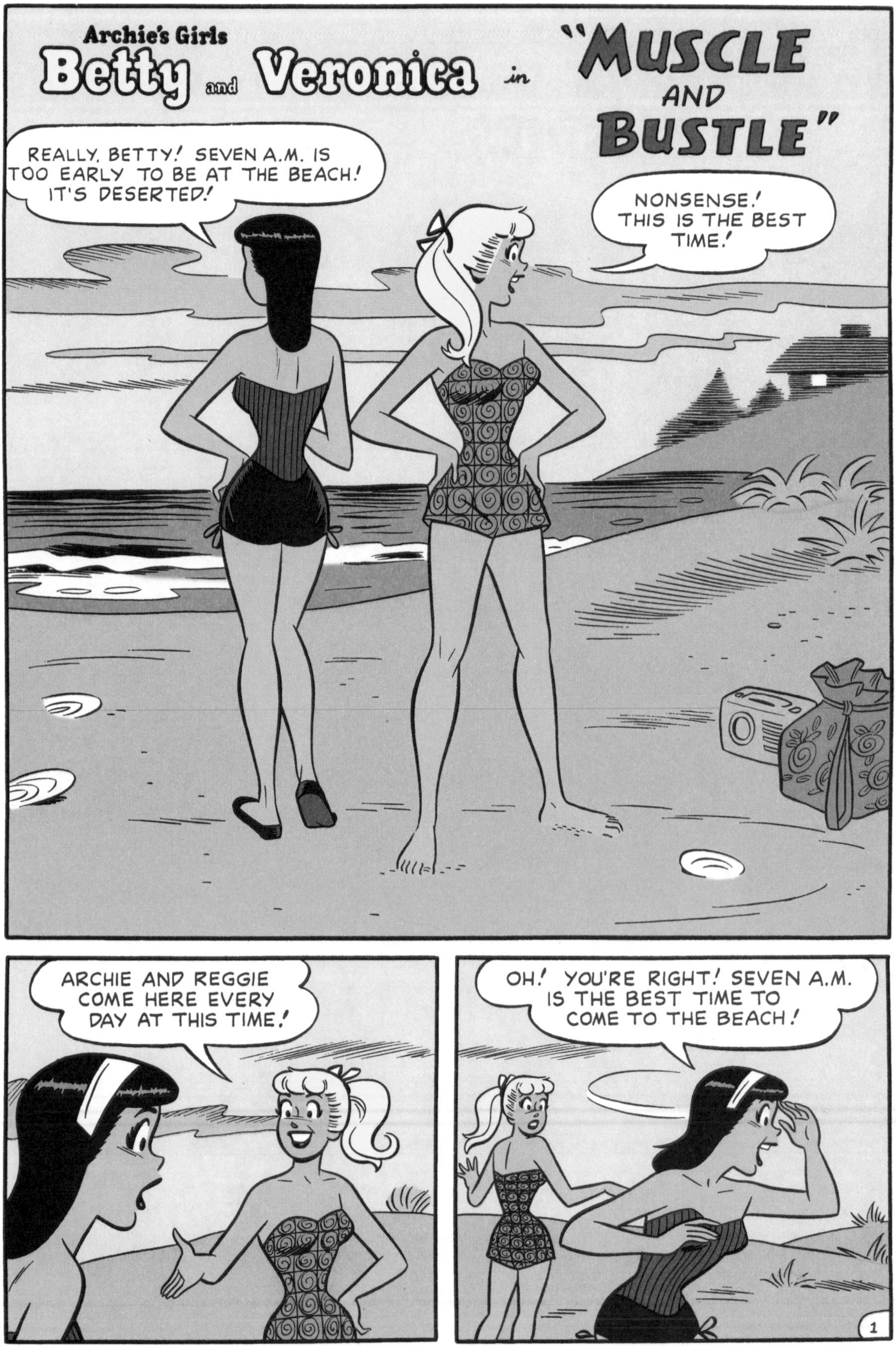
Archie's Girls Betty and Veronica in "MUSCLE AND BUSTLE"
REALLY, BETTY! SEVEN A.M. IS TOO EARLY TO BE AT THE BEACH! IT'S DESERTED!
NONSENSE! THIS IS THE BEST TIME!
ARCHIE AND REGGIE COME HERE EVERY DAY AT THIS TIME!
OH! YOU'RE RIGHT! SEVEN A.M. IS THE BEST TIME TO COME TO THE BEACH!
1

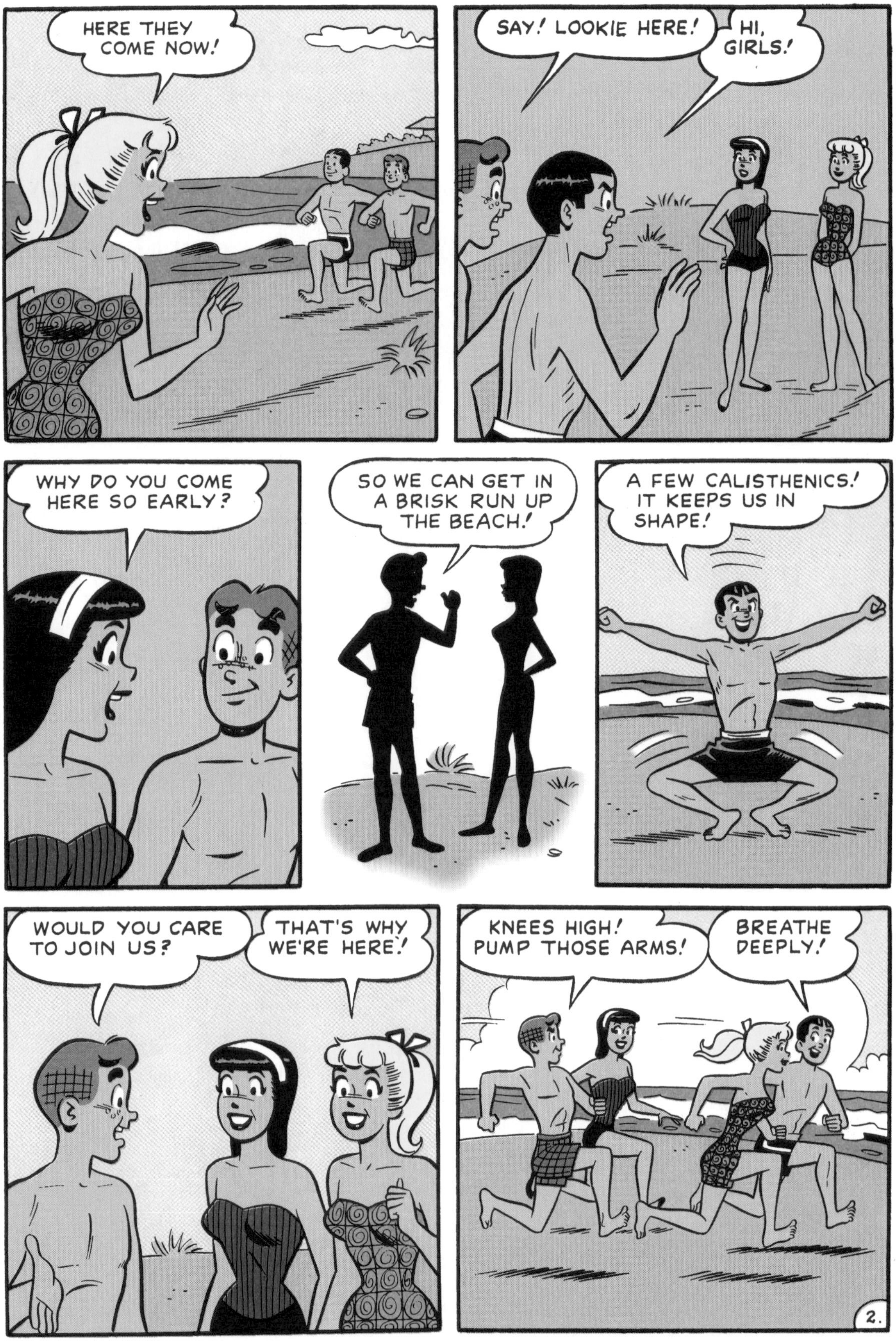
HERE THEY COME NOW!
SAY! LOOKIE HERE!
HI, GIRLS!
WHY DO YOU COME HERE SO EARLY?
SO WE CAN GET IN A BRISK RUN UP THE BEACH!
A FEW CALISTHENICS! IT KEEPS US IN SHAPE!
WOULD YOU CARE TO JOIN US?
THAT'S WHY WE'RE HERE!
KNEES HIGH! PUMP THOSE ARMS!
BREATHE DEEPLY!
2.

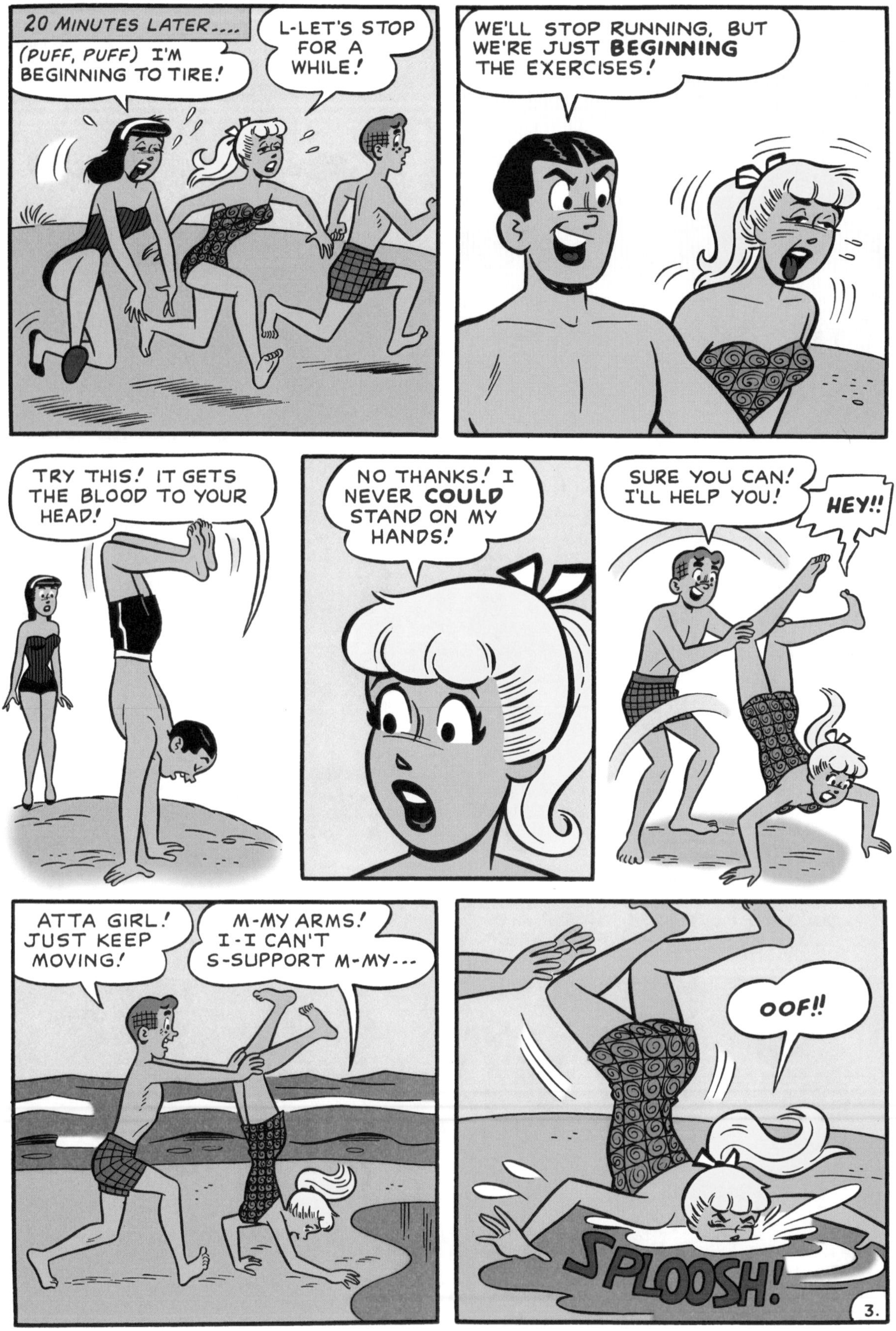
20 MINUTES LATER....
(PUFF, PUFF) I'M BEGINNING TO TIRE!
L-LET'S STOP FOR A WHILE!
WE'LL STOP RUNNING, BUT WE'RE JUST **BEGINNING** THE EXERCISES!
TRY THIS! IT GETS THE BLOOD TO YOUR HEAD!
NO THANKS! I NEVER **COULD** STAND ON MY HANDS!
SURE YOU CAN! I'LL HELP YOU!
HEY!!
ATTA GIRL! JUST KEEP MOVING!
M-MY ARMS! I-I CAN'T S-SUPPORT M-MY---
OOF!!
SPLOOSH!
3.

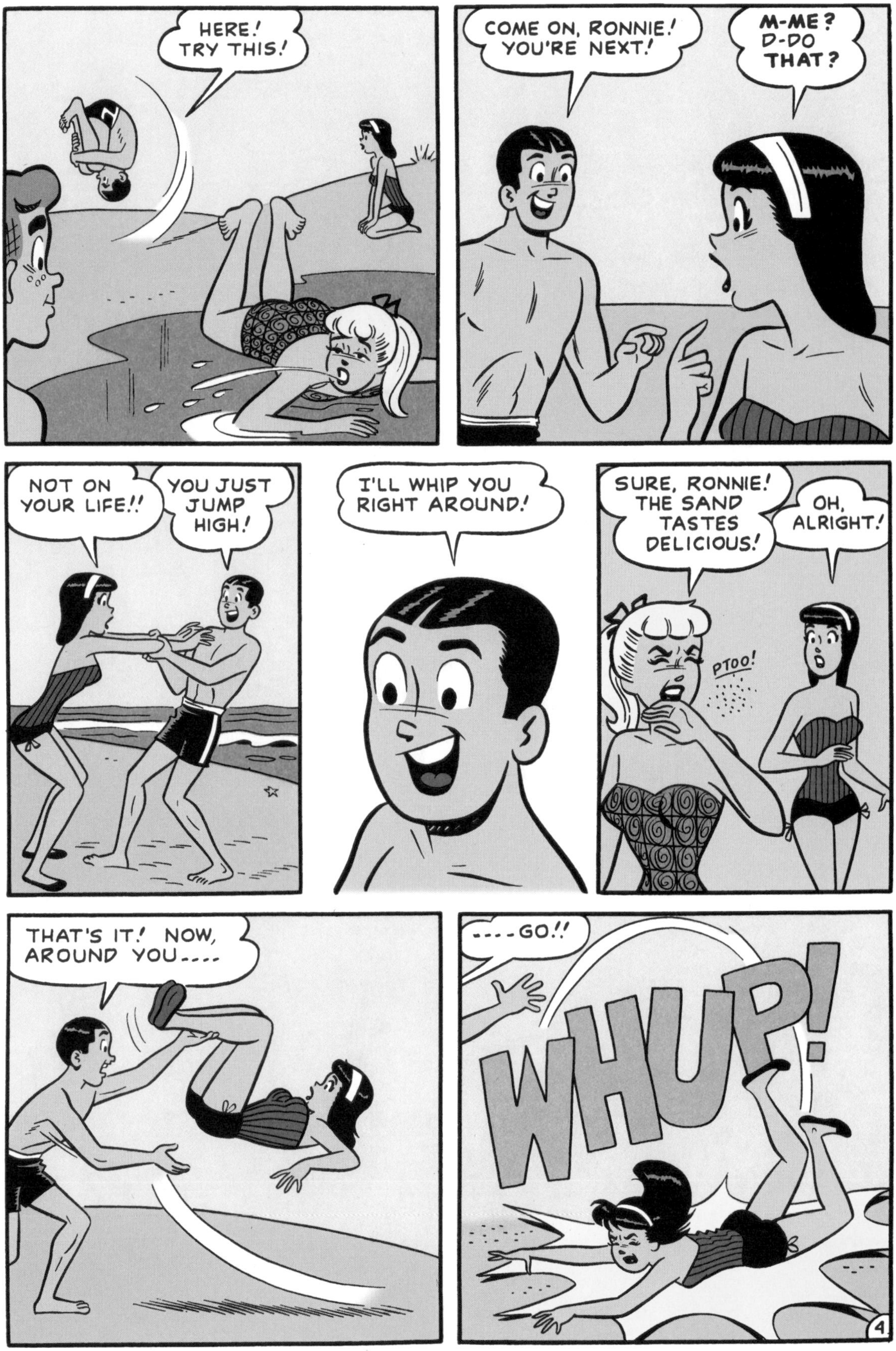
HERE! TRY THIS!
COME ON, RONNIE! YOU'RE NEXT!
M-ME? D-DO THAT?
NOT ON YOUR LIFE!!
YOU JUST JUMP HIGH!
I'LL WHIP YOU RIGHT AROUND!
SURE, RONNIE! THE SAND TASTES DELICIOUS!
PTOO!
OH, ALRIGHT!
THAT'S IT! NOW, AROUND YOU----
----GO!!
WHUP!
4

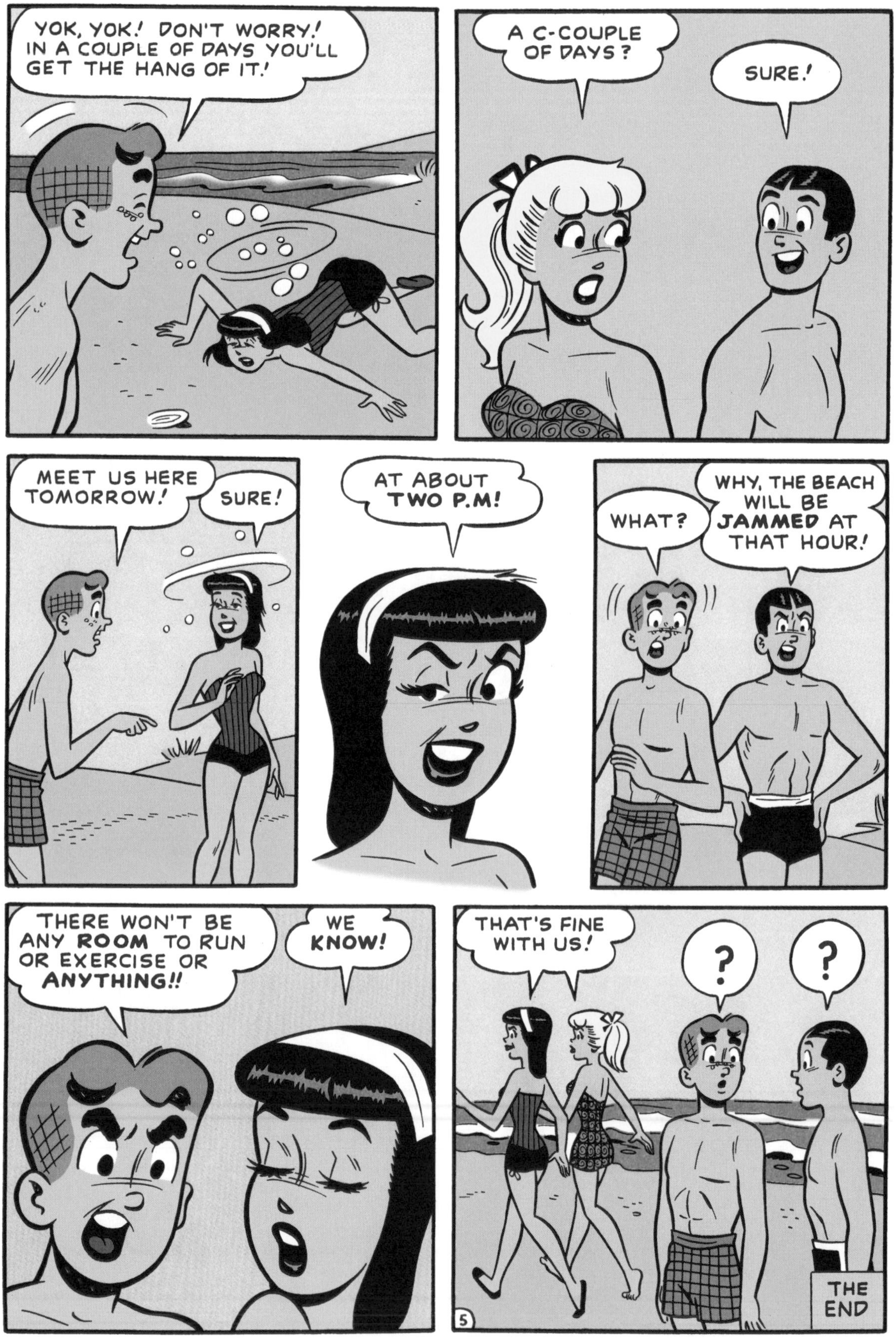
YOK, YOK! DON'T WORRY! IN A COUPLE OF DAYS YOU'LL GET THE HANG OF IT!
A C-COUPLE OF DAYS?
SURE!
MEET US HERE TOMORROW!
SURE!
AT ABOUT TWO P.M!
WHAT?
WHY, THE BEACH WILL BE JAMMED AT THAT HOUR!
THERE WON'T BE ANY ROOM TO RUN OR EXERCISE OR ANYTHING!!
WE KNOW!
THAT'S FINE WITH US!
?
?
5
THE END

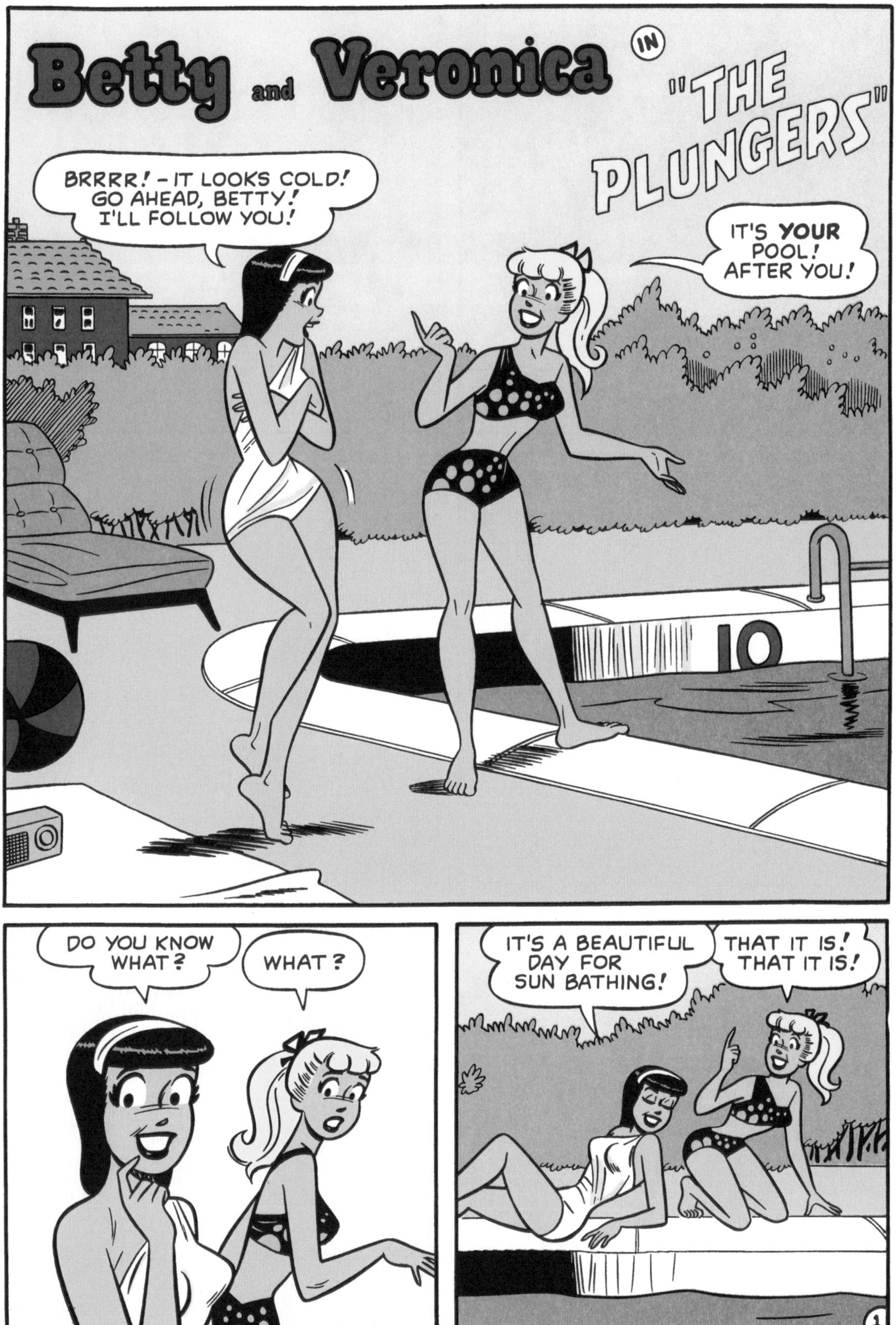
Betty and Veronica
IN
"THE PLUNGERS"
BRRRR! - IT LOOKS COLD! GO AHEAD, BETTY! I'LL FOLLOW YOU!
IT'S YOUR POOL! AFTER YOU!
10
DO YOU KNOW WHAT?
WHAT?
IT'S A BEAUTIFUL DAY FOR SUN BATHING!
THAT IT IS! THAT IT IS!
1

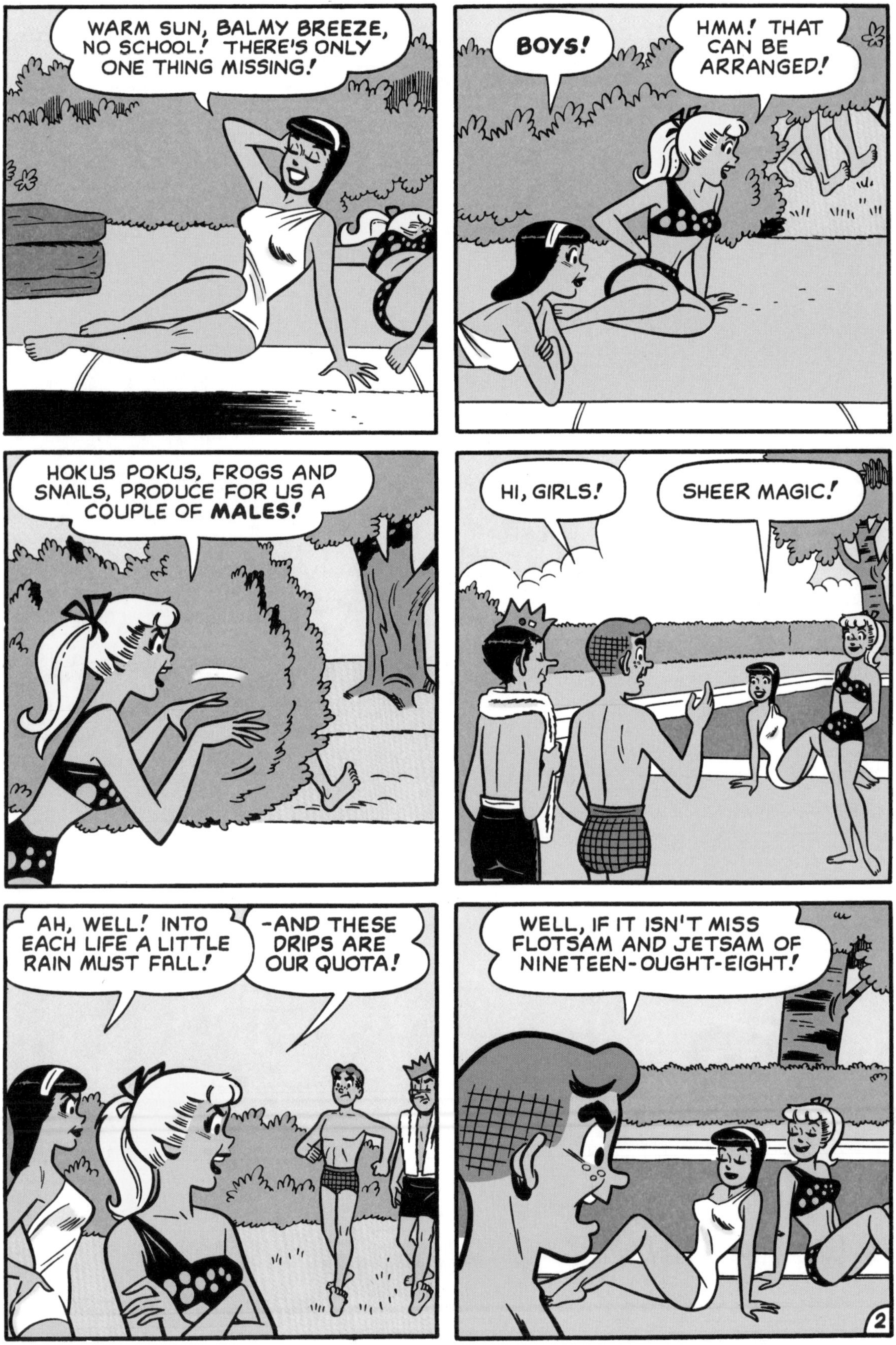
WARM SUN, BALMY BREEZE, NO SCHOOL! THERE'S ONLY ONE THING MISSING!
BOYS!
HMM! THAT CAN BE ARRANGED!
HOKUS POKUS, FROGS AND SNAILS, PRODUCE FOR US A COUPLE OF MALES!
HI, GIRLS!
SHEER MAGIC!
AH, WELL! INTO EACH LIFE A LITTLE RAIN MUST FALL!
-AND THESE DRIPS ARE OUR QUOTA!
WELL, IF IT ISN'T MISS FLOTSAM AND JETSAM OF NINETEEN-OUGHT-EIGHT!

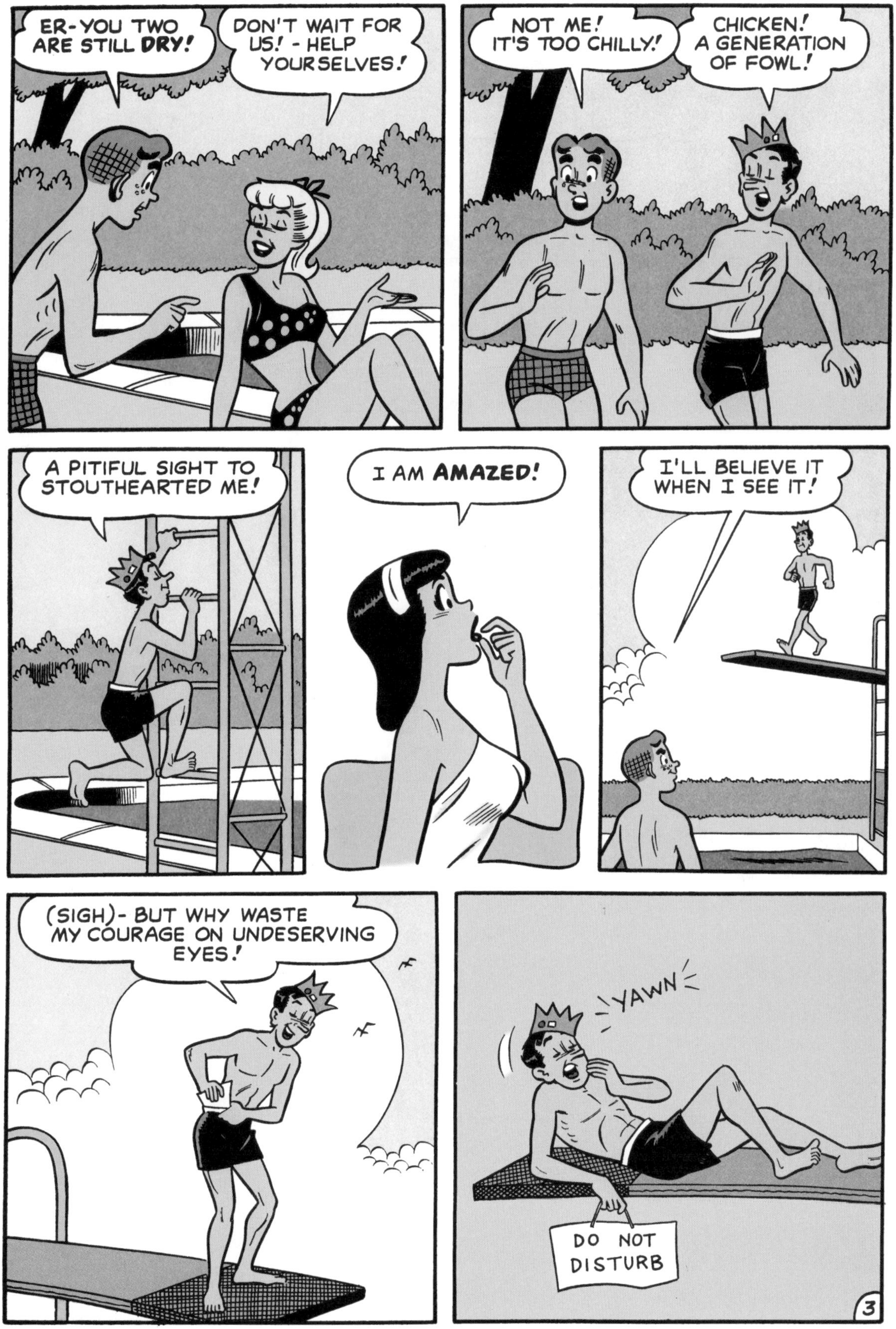
ER-YOU TWO ARE STILL DRY!
DON'T WAIT FOR US! - HELP YOURSELVES!
NOT ME! IT'S TOO CHILLY!
CHICKEN! A GENERATION OF FOWL!
A PITIFUL SIGHT TO STOUTHEARTED ME!
I AM AMAZED!
I'LL BELIEVE IT WHEN I SEE IT!
(SIGH)- BUT WHY WASTE MY COURAGE ON UNDESERVING EYES!
YAWN
DO NOT DISTURB
3

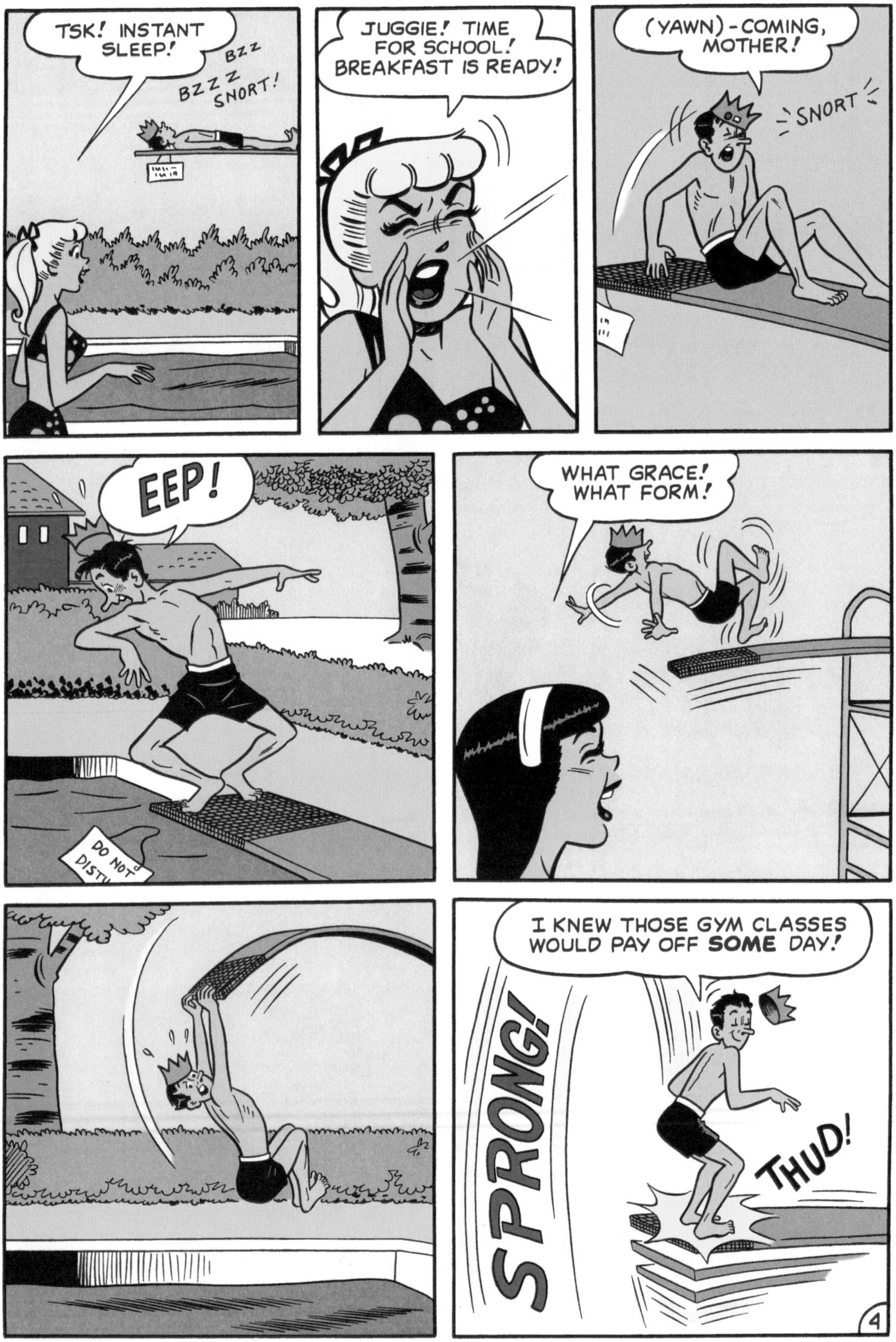
TSK! INSTANT SLEEP!
BZZ BZZZ SNORT!
JUGGIE! TIME FOR SCHOOL! BREAKFAST IS READY!
(YAWN)-COMING, MOTHER!
SNORT
EEP!
DO NOT DISTU
WHAT GRACE! WHAT FORM!
I KNEW THOSE GYM CLASSES WOULD PAY OFF SOME DAY!
SPRONG!
THUD!
4

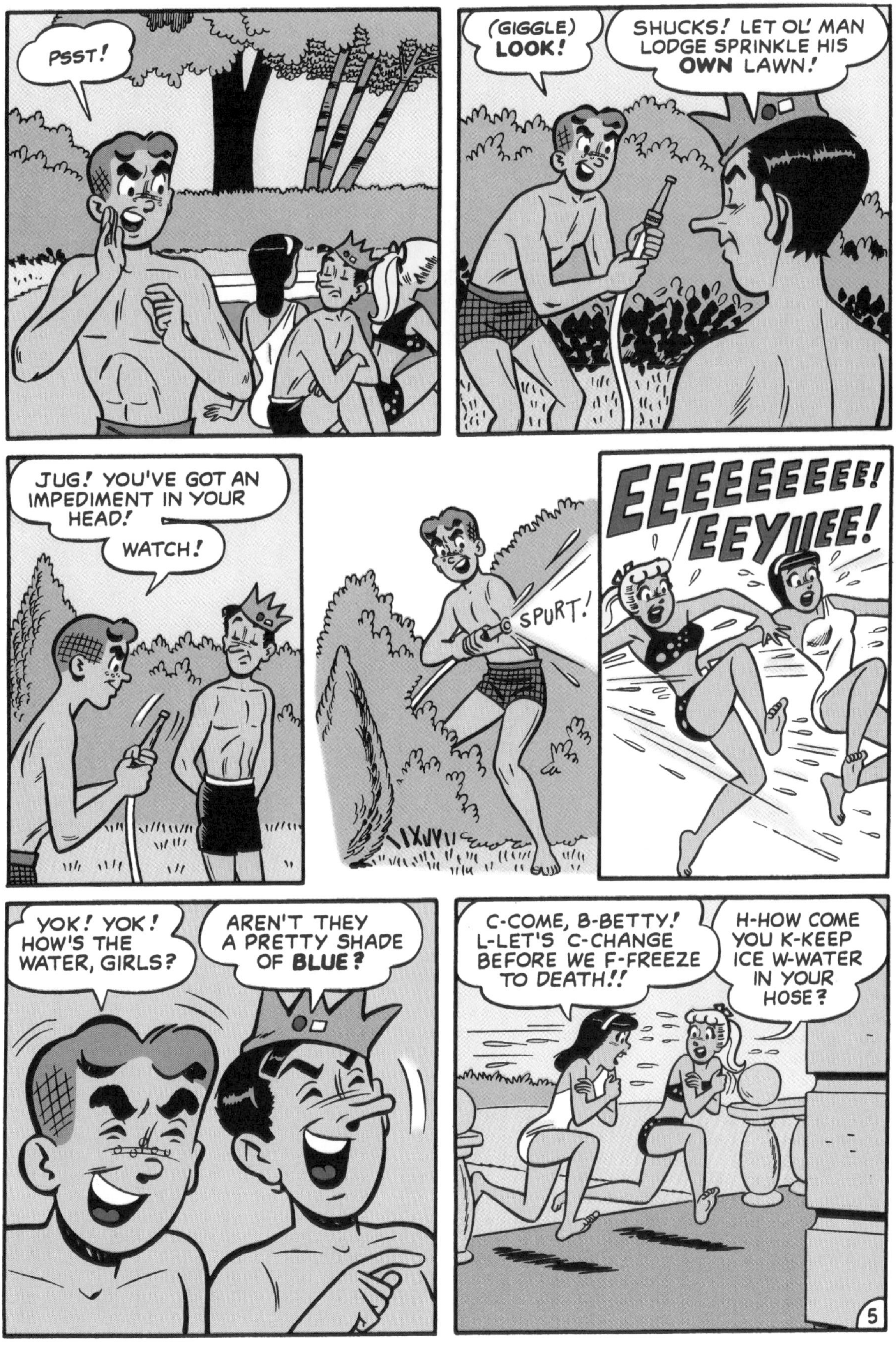
PSST!
(GIGGLE) LOOK!
SHUCKS! LET OL' MAN LODGE SPRINKLE HIS OWN LAWN!
JUG! YOU'VE GOT AN IMPEDIMENT IN YOUR HEAD!
WATCH!
SPURT!
EEEEEEEEE! EEYIIEE!
YOK! YOK! HOW'S THE WATER, GIRLS?
AREN'T THEY A PRETTY SHADE OF BLUE?
C-COME, B-BETTY! L-LET'S C-CHANGE BEFORE WE F-FREEZE TO DEATH!!
H-HOW COME YOU K-KEEP ICE W-WATER IN YOUR HOSE?
5

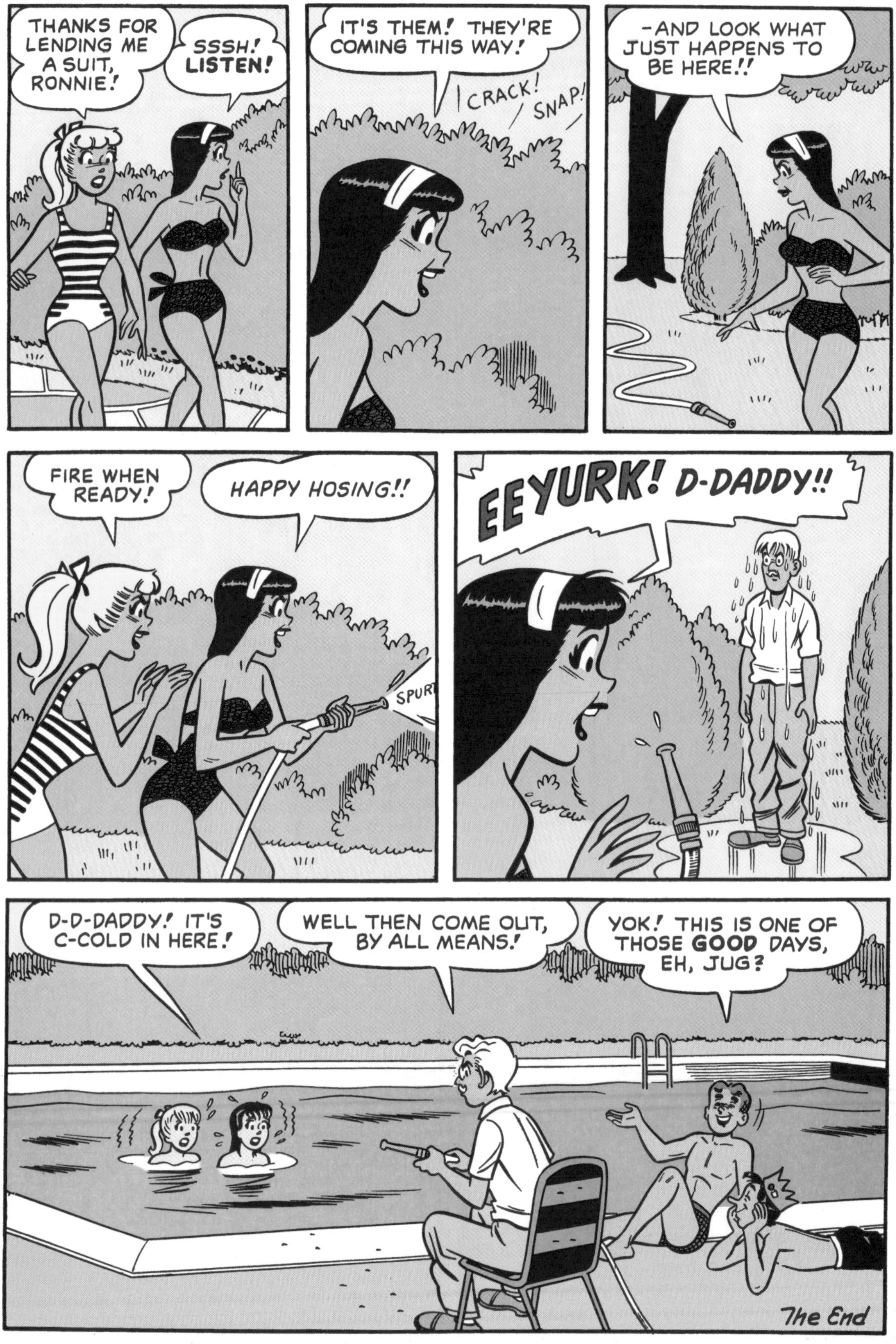
THANKS FOR LENDING ME A SUIT, RONNIE!
SSSH! LISTEN!
IT'S THEM! THEY'RE COMING THIS WAY!
CRACK!
SNAP!
-AND LOOK WHAT JUST HAPPENS TO BE HERE!!
FIRE WHEN READY!
HAPPY HOSING!!
SPURT
EEYURK! D-DADDY!!
D-D-DADDY! IT'S C-COLD IN HERE!
WELL THEN COME OUT, BY ALL MEANS!
YOK! THIS IS ONE OF THOSE GOOD DAYS, EH, JUG?
The End

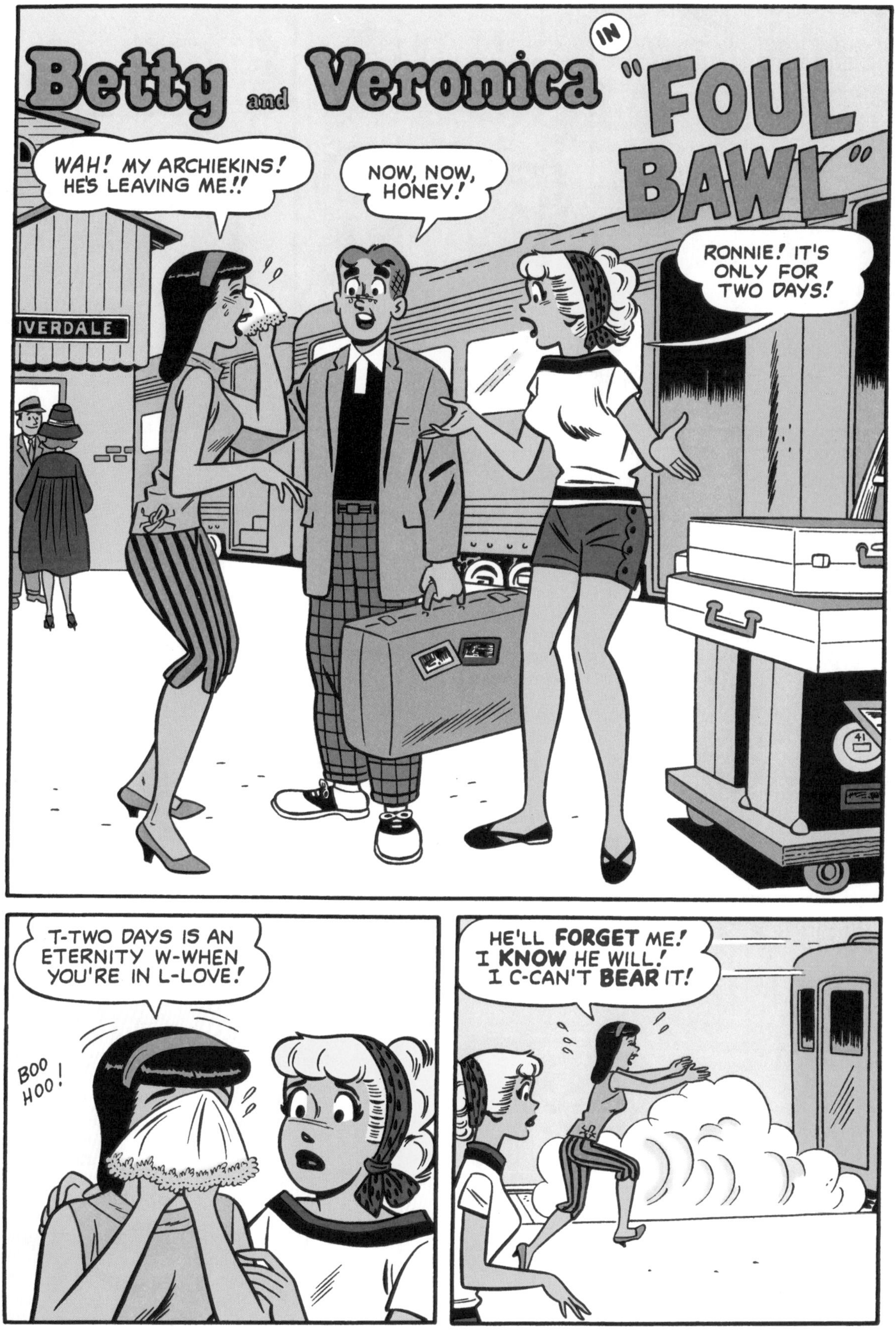
Betty and Veronica in "FOUL BAWL"
WAH! MY ARCHIEKINS! HE'S LEAVING ME!!
NOW, NOW, HONEY!
RONNIE! IT'S ONLY FOR TWO DAYS!
IVERDALE
T-TWO DAYS IS AN ETERNITY W-WHEN YOU'RE IN L-LOVE!
BOO HOO!
HE'LL FORGET ME! I KNOW HE WILL! I C-CAN'T BEAR IT!

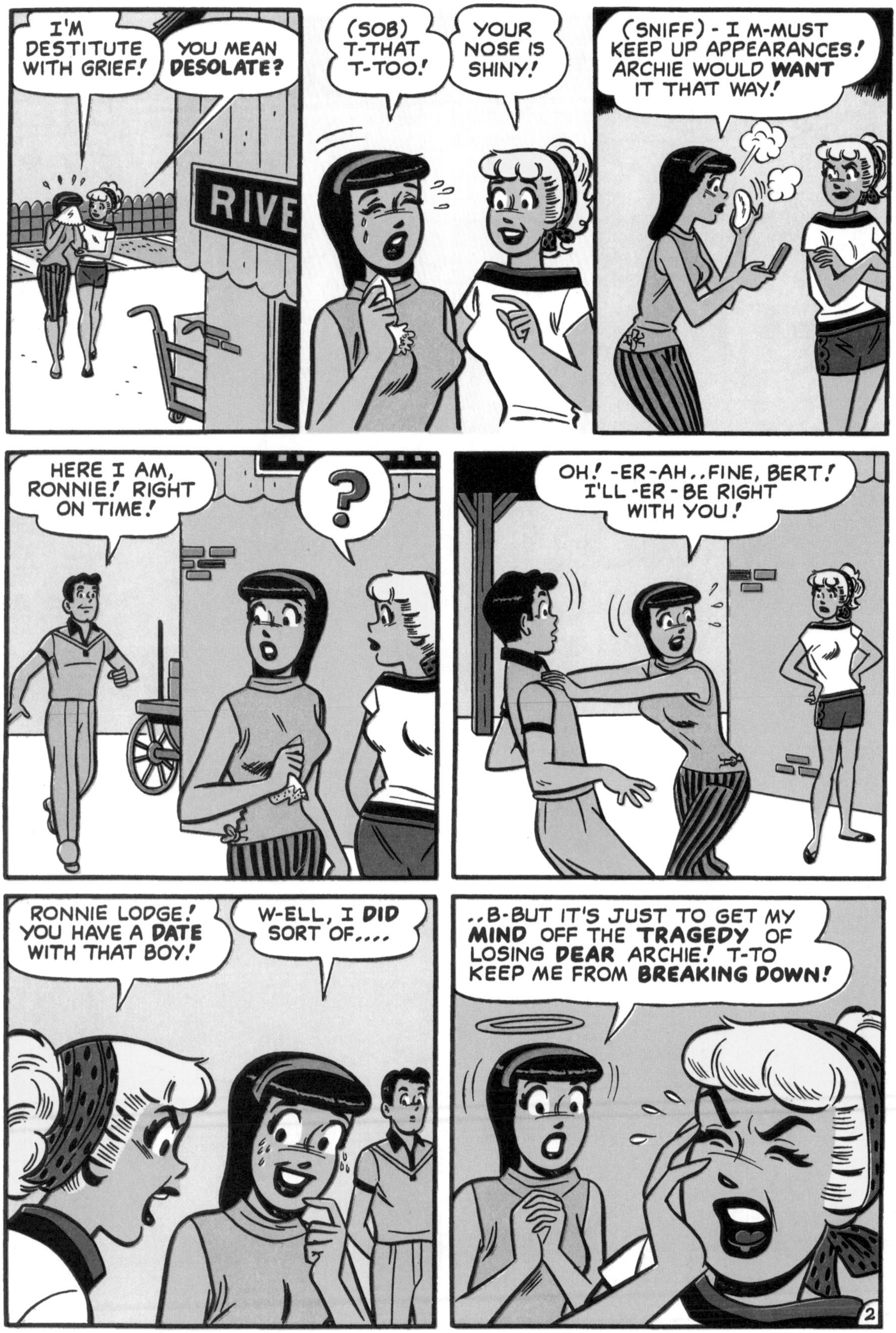
I'M DESTITUTE WITH GRIEF!
YOU MEAN DESOLATE?
RIVE
(SOB) T-THAT T-TOO!
YOUR NOSE IS SHINY!
(SNIFF) - I M-MUST KEEP UP APPEARANCES! ARCHIE WOULD WANT IT THAT WAY!
HERE I AM, RONNIE! RIGHT ON TIME!
?
OH! -ER-AH..FINE, BERT! I'LL -ER - BE RIGHT WITH YOU!
RONNIE LODGE! YOU HAVE A DATE WITH THAT BOY!
W-ELL, I DID SORT OF....
..B-BUT IT'S JUST TO GET MY MIND OFF THE TRAGEDY OF LOSING DEAR ARCHIE! T-TO KEEP ME FROM BREAKING DOWN!
2

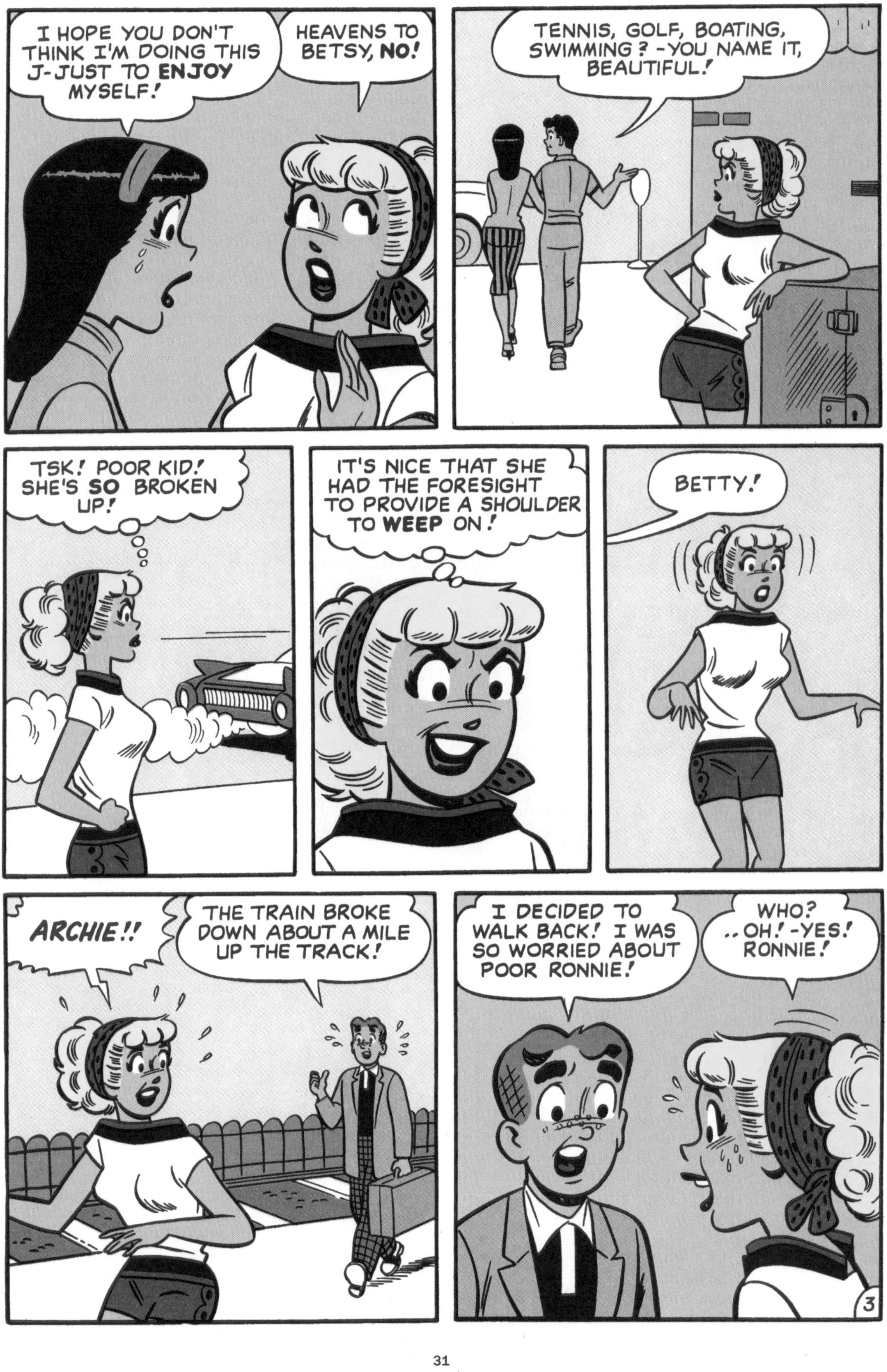
I HOPE YOU DON'T THINK I'M DOING THIS J-JUST TO ENJOY MYSELF!
HEAVENS TO BETSY, NO!
TENNIS, GOLF, BOATING, SWIMMING? -YOU NAME IT, BEAUTIFUL!
TSK! POOR KID! SHE'S SO BROKEN UP!
IT'S NICE THAT SHE HAD THE FORESIGHT TO PROVIDE A SHOULDER TO WEEP ON!
BETTY!
ARCHIE!!
THE TRAIN BROKE DOWN ABOUT A MILE UP THE TRACK!
I DECIDED TO WALK BACK! I WAS SO WORRIED ABOUT POOR RONNIE!
WHO? ..OH! -YES! RONNIE!
3

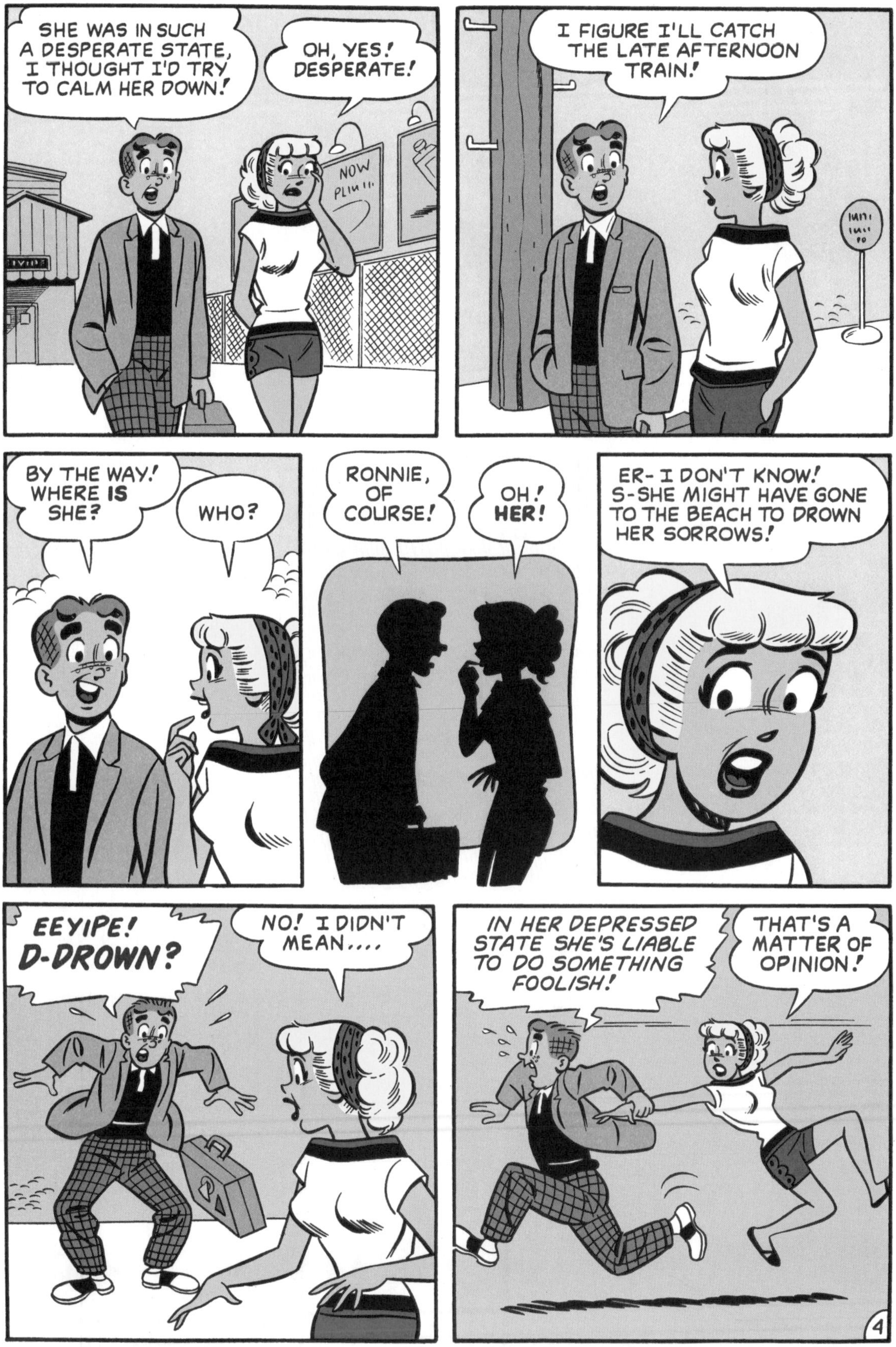
SHE WAS IN SUCH A DESPERATE STATE, I THOUGHT I'D TRY TO CALM HER DOWN!
OH, YES! DESPERATE!
NOW
I FIGURE I'LL CATCH THE LATE AFTERNOON TRAIN!
BY THE WAY! WHERE **IS** SHE?
WHO?
RONNIE, OF COURSE!
OH! **HER!**
ER- I DON'T KNOW! S-SHE MIGHT HAVE GONE TO THE BEACH TO DROWN HER SORROWS!
EEYIPE! D-DROWN?
NO! I DIDN'T MEAN....
IN HER DEPRESSED STATE SHE'S LIABLE TO DO SOMETHING FOOLISH!
THAT'S A MATTER OF OPINION!
4

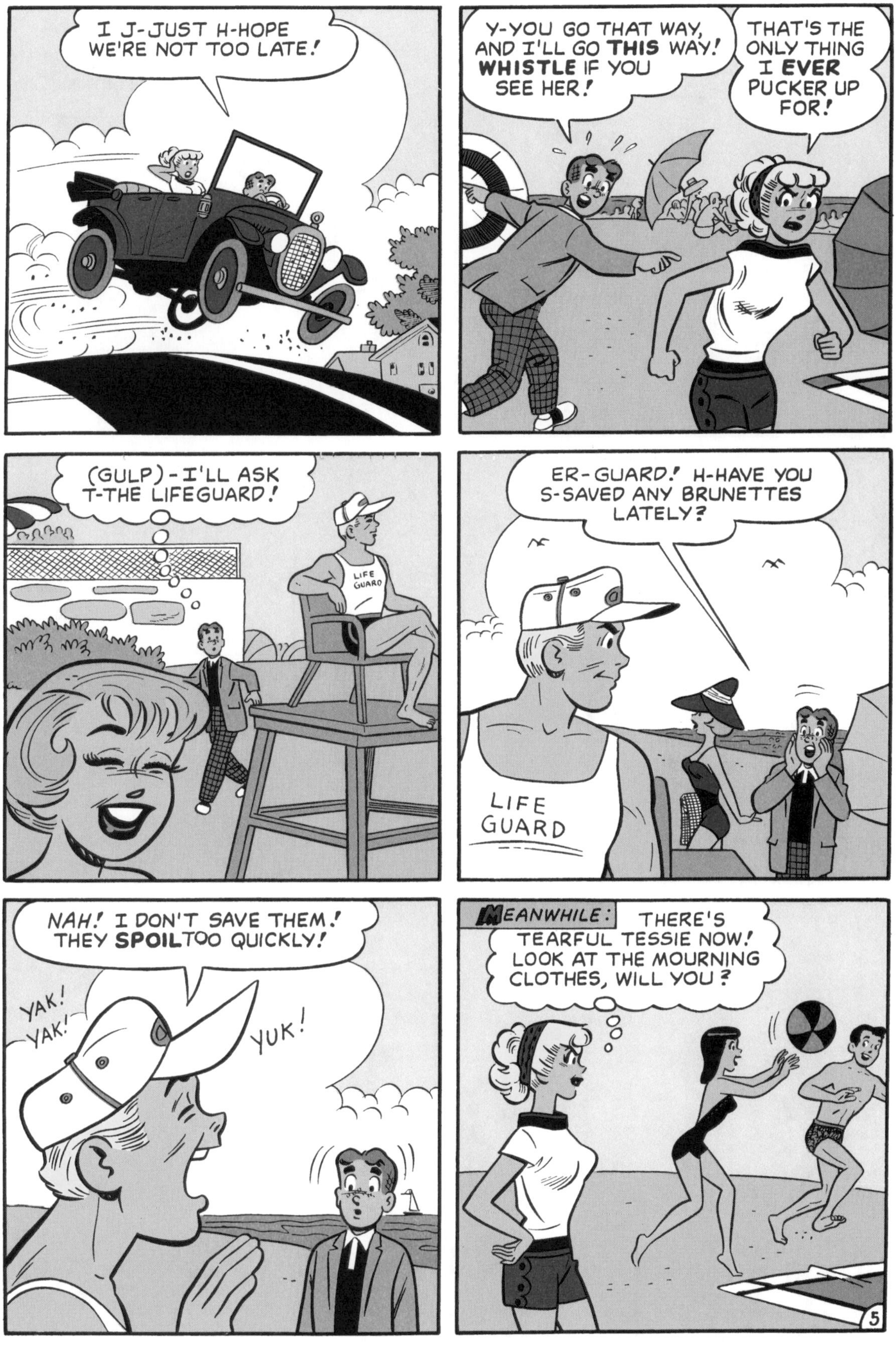
I J-JUST H-HOPE WE'RE NOT TOO LATE!
Y-YOU GO THAT WAY, AND I'LL GO **THIS** WAY! **WHISTLE** IF YOU SEE HER!
THAT'S THE ONLY THING I **EVER** PUCKER UP FOR!
(GULP)-I'LL ASK T-THE LIFEGUARD!
LIFE GUARD
ER-GUARD! H-HAVE YOU S-SAVED ANY BRUNETTES LATELY?
LIFE GUARD
NAH! I DON'T SAVE THEM! THEY **SPOIL** TOO QUICKLY!
YAK! YAK!
YUK!
MEANWHILE:
THERE'S TEARFUL TESSIE NOW! LOOK AT THE MOURNING CLOTHES, WILL YOU?
5

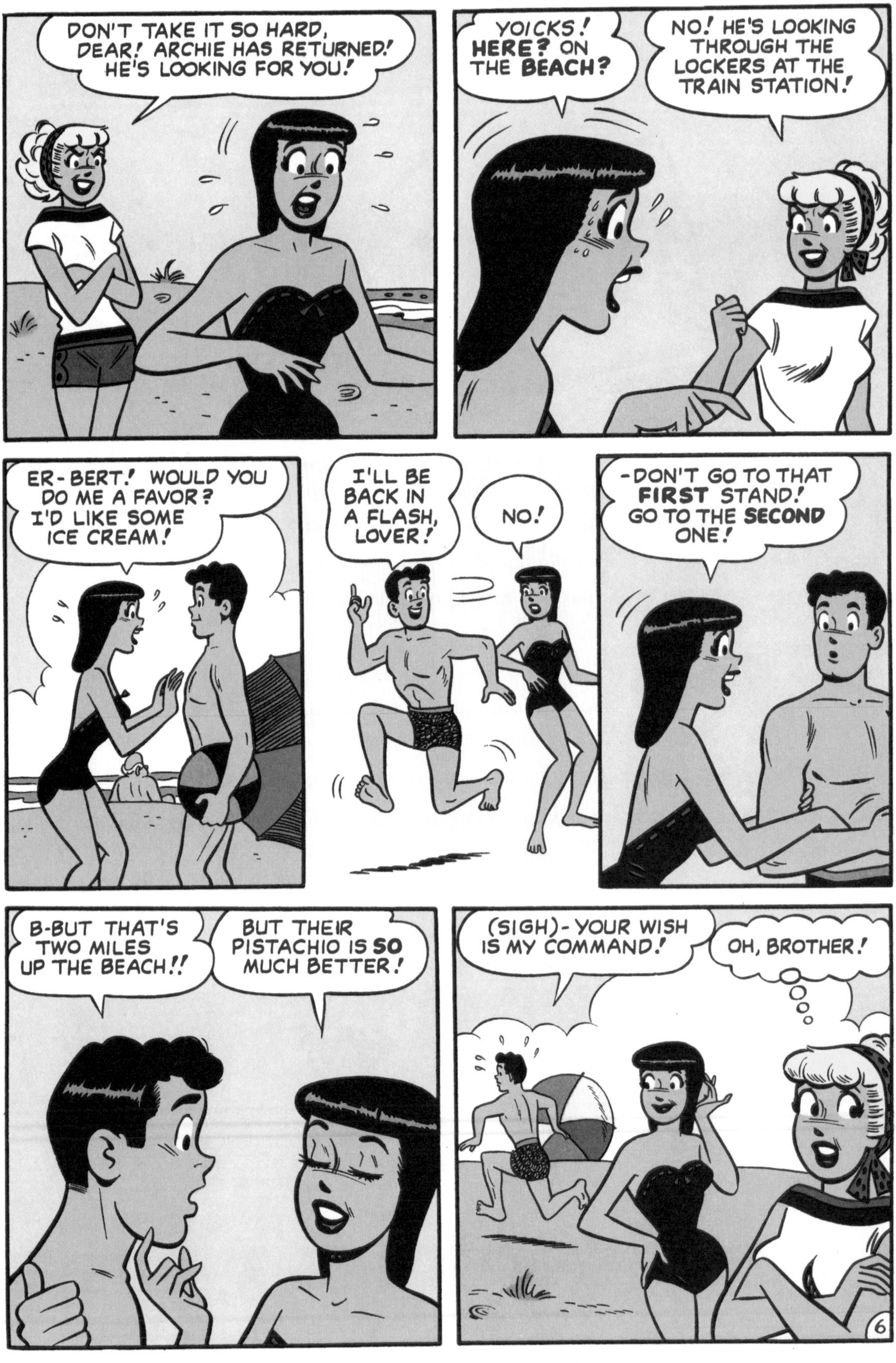
DON'T TAKE IT SO HARD, DEAR! ARCHIE HAS RETURNED! HE'S LOOKING FOR YOU!
YOICKS! HERE? ON THE BEACH?
NO! HE'S LOOKING THROUGH THE LOCKERS AT THE TRAIN STATION!
ER-BERT! WOULD YOU DO ME A FAVOR? I'D LIKE SOME ICE CREAM!
I'LL BE BACK IN A FLASH, LOVER!
NO!
-DON'T GO TO THAT FIRST STAND! GO TO THE SECOND ONE!
B-BUT THAT'S TWO MILES UP THE BEACH!!
BUT THEIR PISTACHIO IS SO MUCH BETTER!
(SIGH)- YOUR WISH IS MY COMMAND!
OH, BROTHER!
6

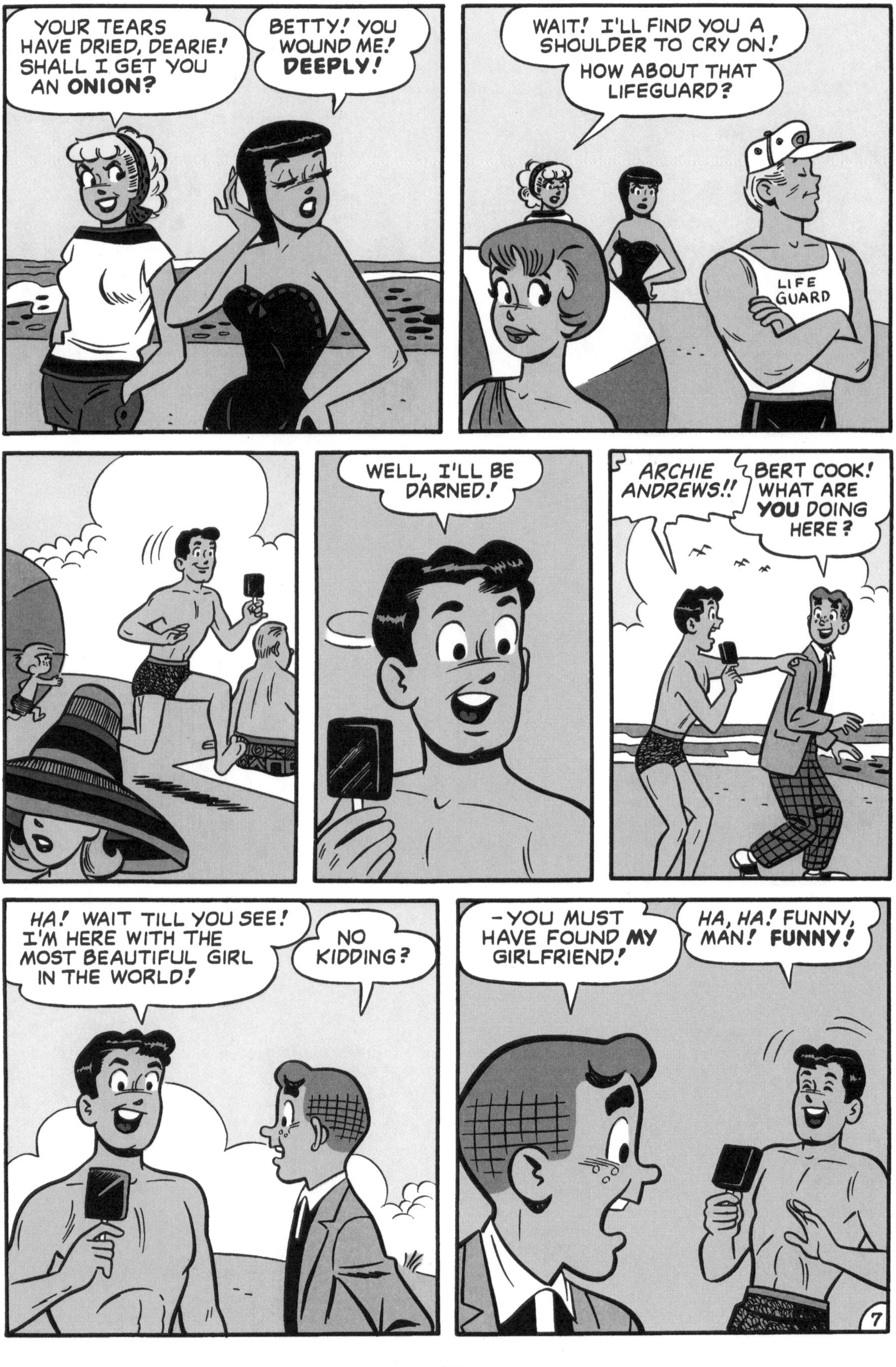
YOUR TEARS HAVE DRIED, DEARIE! SHALL I GET YOU AN ONION?
BETTY! YOU WOUND ME! DEEPLY!
WAIT! I'LL FIND YOU A SHOULDER TO CRY ON!
HOW ABOUT THAT LIFEGUARD?
LIFE GUARD
WELL, I'LL BE DARNED!
ARCHIE ANDREWS!!
BERT COOK! WHAT ARE YOU DOING HERE?
HA! WAIT TILL YOU SEE! I'M HERE WITH THE MOST BEAUTIFUL GIRL IN THE WORLD!
NO KIDDING?
-YOU MUST HAVE FOUND MY GIRLFRIEND!
HA, HA! FUNNY, MAN! FUNNY!
7

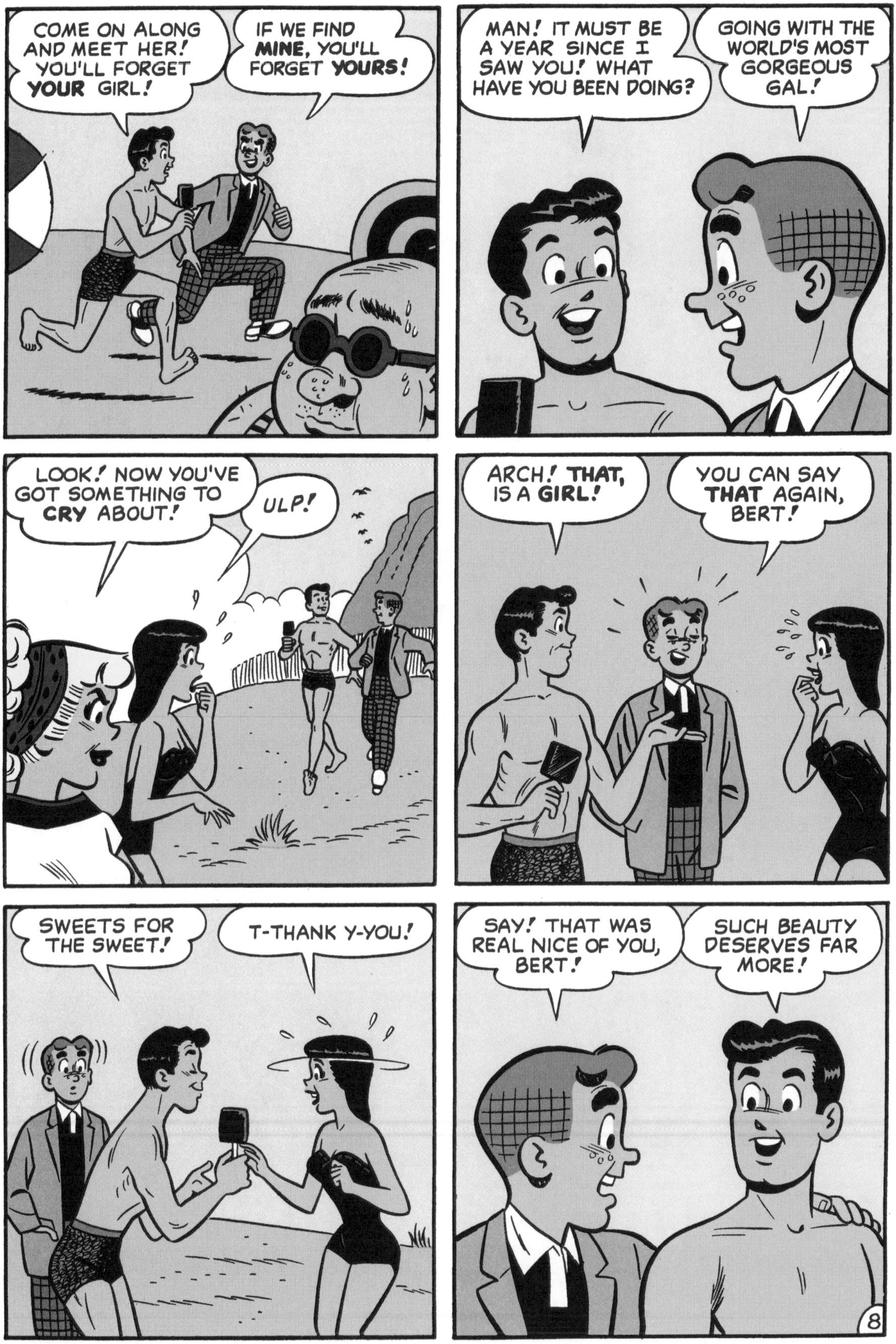
COME ON ALONG AND MEET HER! YOU'LL FORGET **YOUR** GIRL!
IF WE FIND **MINE**, YOU'LL FORGET **YOURS!**
MAN! IT MUST BE A YEAR SINCE I SAW YOU! WHAT HAVE YOU BEEN DOING?
GOING WITH THE WORLD'S MOST GORGEOUS GAL!
LOOK! NOW YOU'VE GOT SOMETHING TO **CRY** ABOUT!
ULP!
ARCH! **THAT**, IS A **GIRL!**
YOU CAN SAY **THAT** AGAIN, BERT!
SWEETS FOR THE SWEET!
T-THANK Y-YOU!
SAY! THAT WAS REAL NICE OF YOU, BERT!
SUCH BEAUTY DESERVES FAR MORE!
8

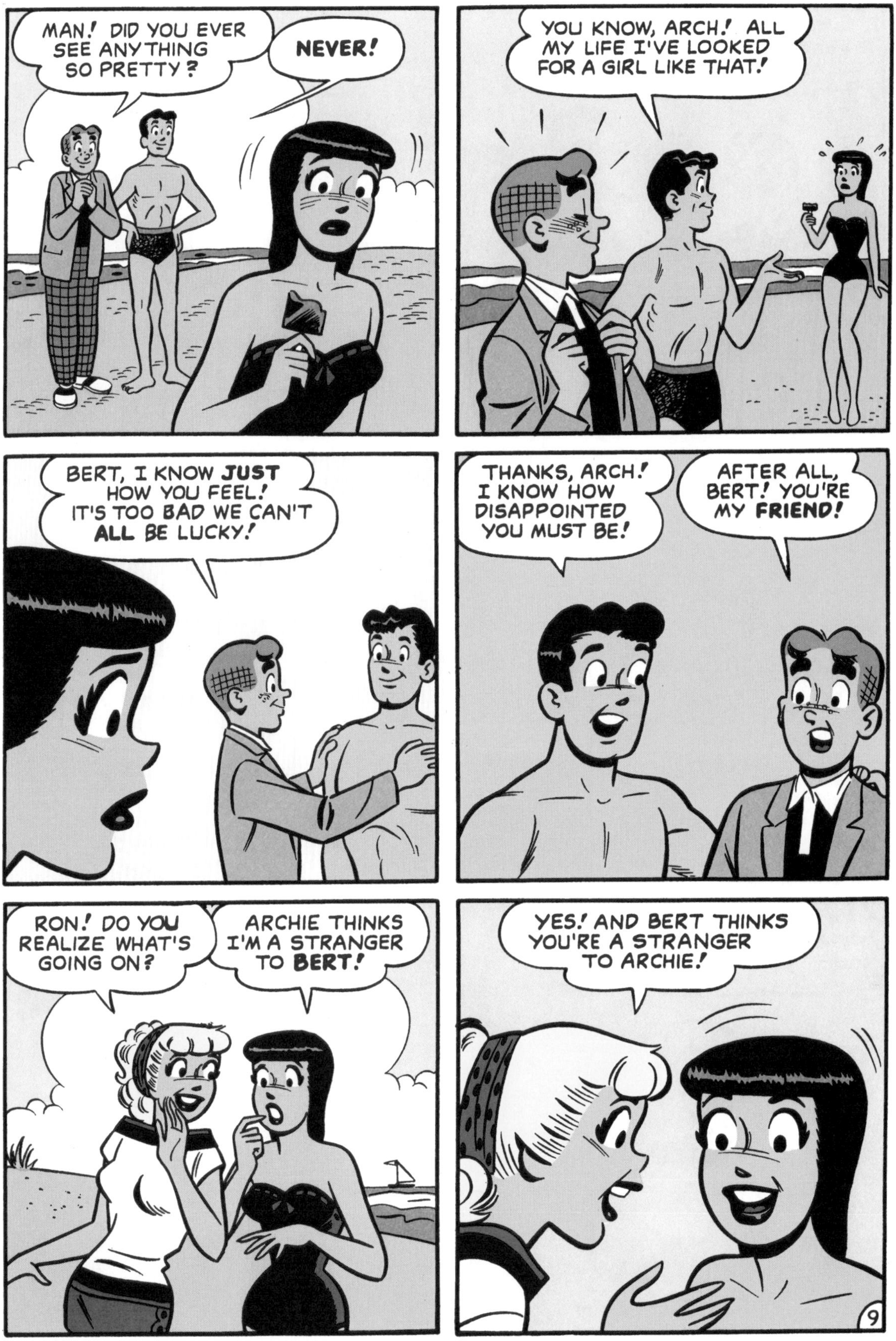
MAN! DID YOU EVER SEE ANYTHING SO PRETTY?
NEVER!
YOU KNOW, ARCH! ALL MY LIFE I'VE LOOKED FOR A GIRL LIKE THAT!
BERT, I KNOW JUST HOW YOU FEEL! IT'S TOO BAD WE CAN'T ALL BE LUCKY!
THANKS, ARCH! I KNOW HOW DISAPPOINTED YOU MUST BE!
AFTER ALL, BERT! YOU'RE MY FRIEND!
RON! DO YOU REALIZE WHAT'S GOING ON?
ARCHIE THINKS I'M A STRANGER TO BERT!
YES! AND BERT THINKS YOU'RE A STRANGER TO ARCHIE!
9

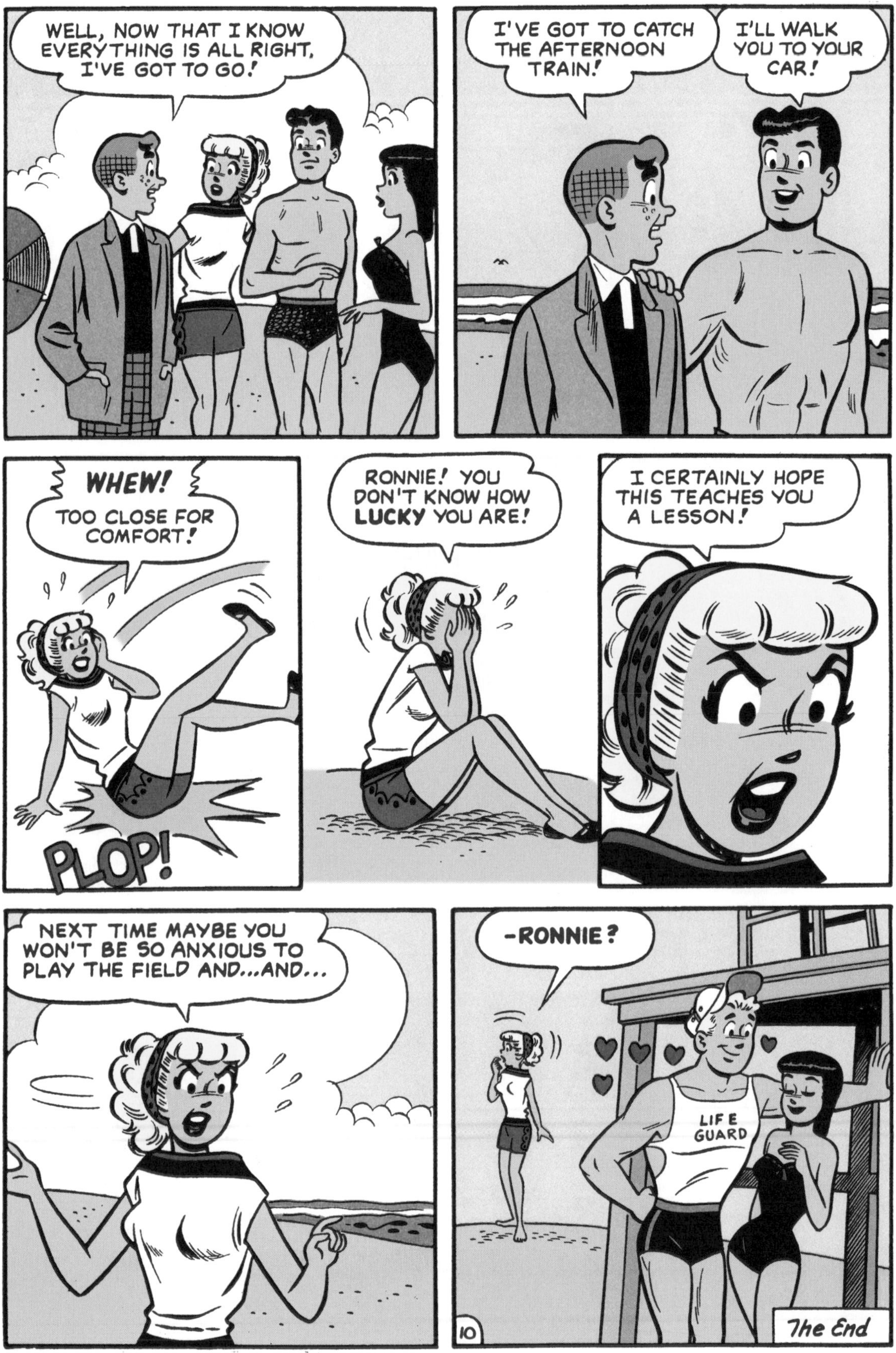
WELL, NOW THAT I KNOW EVERYTHING IS ALL RIGHT, I'VE GOT TO GO!
I'VE GOT TO CATCH THE AFTERNOON TRAIN!
I'LL WALK YOU TO YOUR CAR!
WHEW!
TOO CLOSE FOR COMFORT!
PLOP!
RONNIE! YOU DON'T KNOW HOW LUCKY YOU ARE!
I CERTAINLY HOPE THIS TEACHES YOU A LESSON!
NEXT TIME MAYBE YOU WON'T BE SO ANXIOUS TO PLAY THE FIELD AND...AND...
-RONNIE?
LIFE GUARD
10
The End

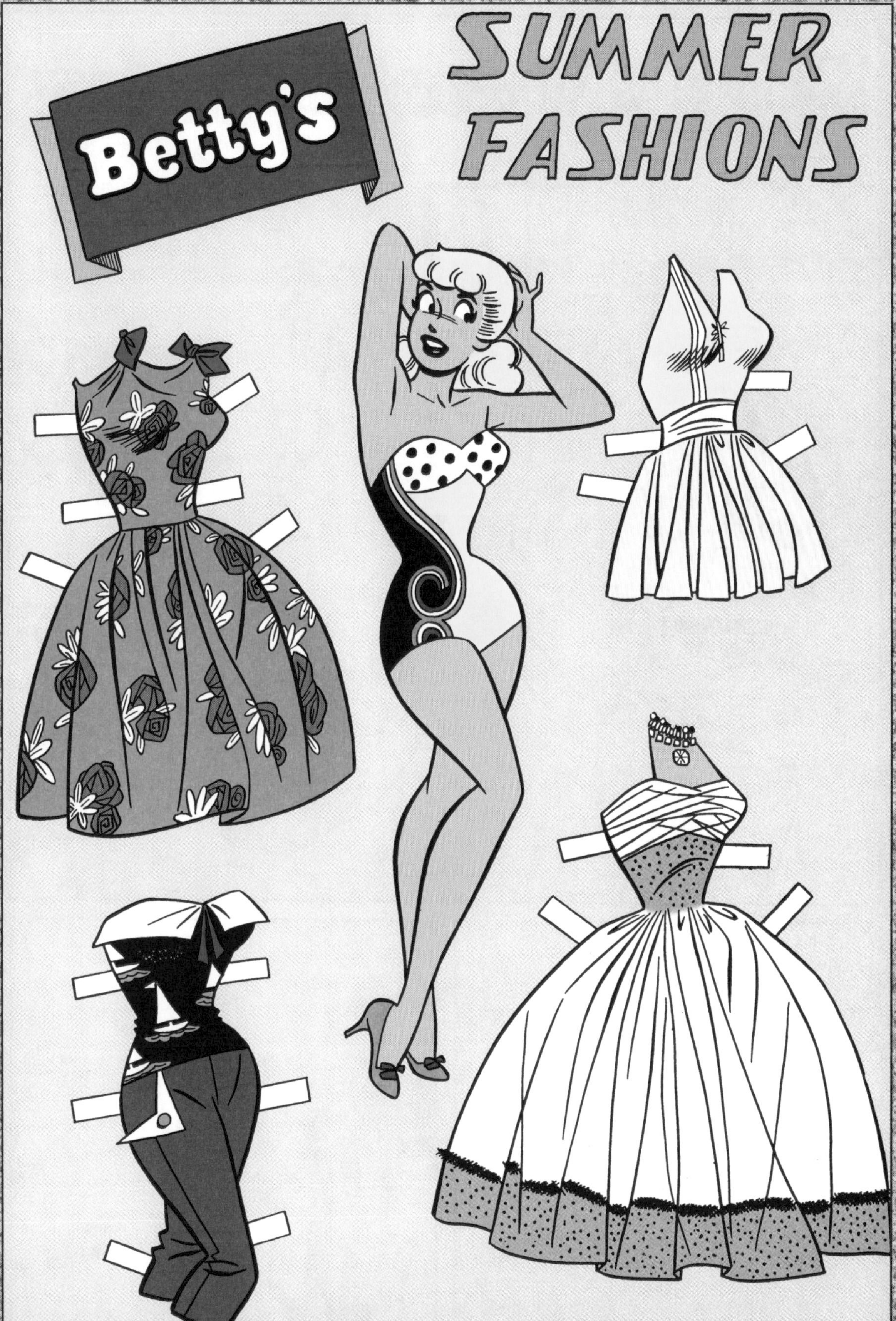
Betty's
SUMMER FASHIONS

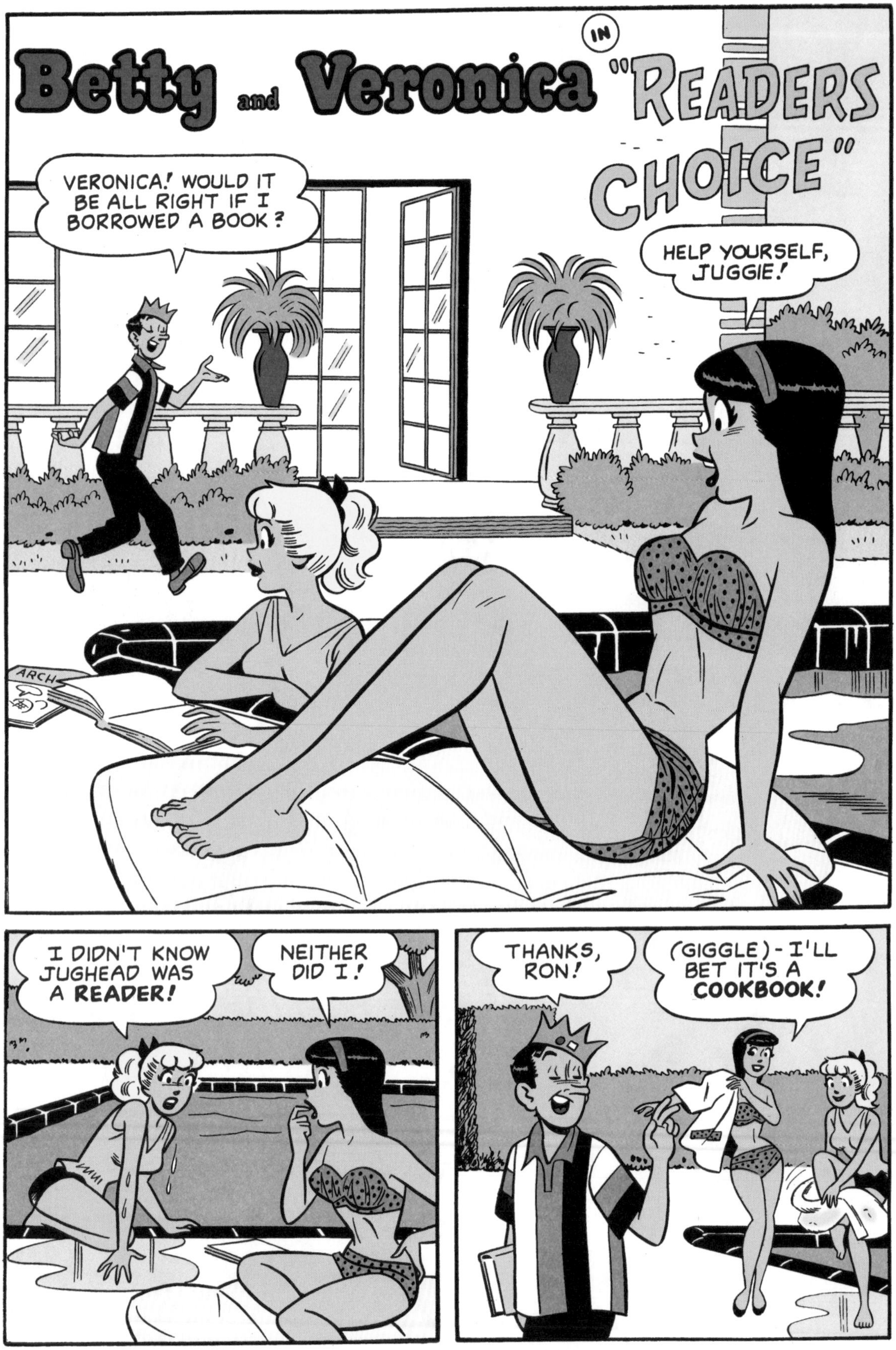
Betty and Veronica IN "READERS CHOICE"
VERONICA! WOULD IT BE ALL RIGHT IF I BORROWED A BOOK?
HELP YOURSELF, JUGGIE!
ARCH
I DIDN'T KNOW JUGHEAD WAS A READER!
NEITHER DID I!
THANKS, RON!
(GIGGLE)- I'LL BET IT'S A COOKBOOK!

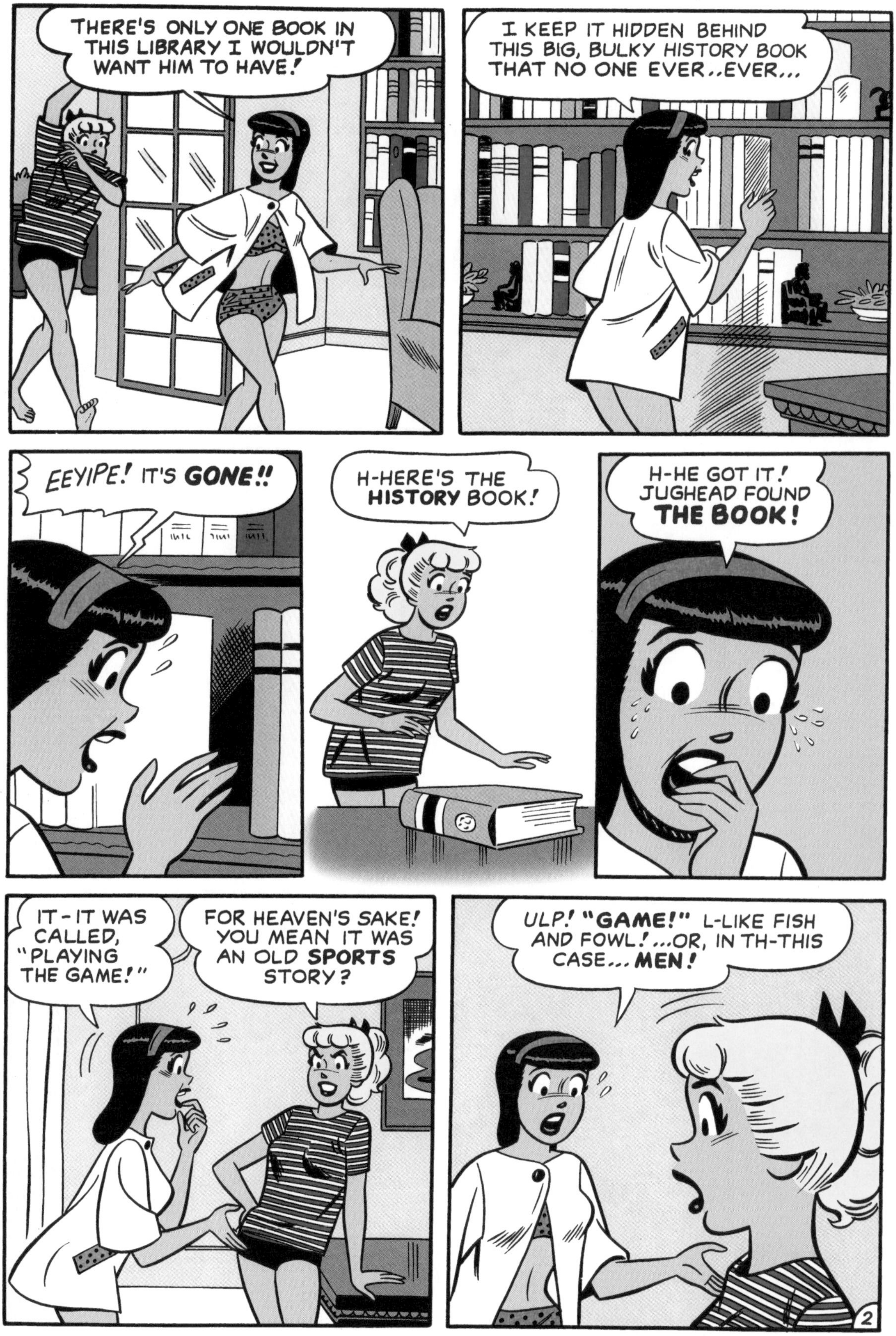
THERE'S ONLY ONE BOOK IN THIS LIBRARY I WOULDN'T WANT HIM TO HAVE!
I KEEP IT HIDDEN BEHIND THIS BIG, BULKY HISTORY BOOK THAT NO ONE EVER..EVER...
EEYIPE! IT'S GONE!!
H-HERE'S THE HISTORY BOOK!
H-HE GOT IT! JUGHEAD FOUND THE BOOK!
IT-IT WAS CALLED, "PLAYING THE GAME!"
FOR HEAVEN'S SAKE! YOU MEAN IT WAS AN OLD SPORTS STORY?
ULP! "GAME!" L-LIKE FISH AND FOWL!...OR, IN TH-THIS CASE...MEN!
2

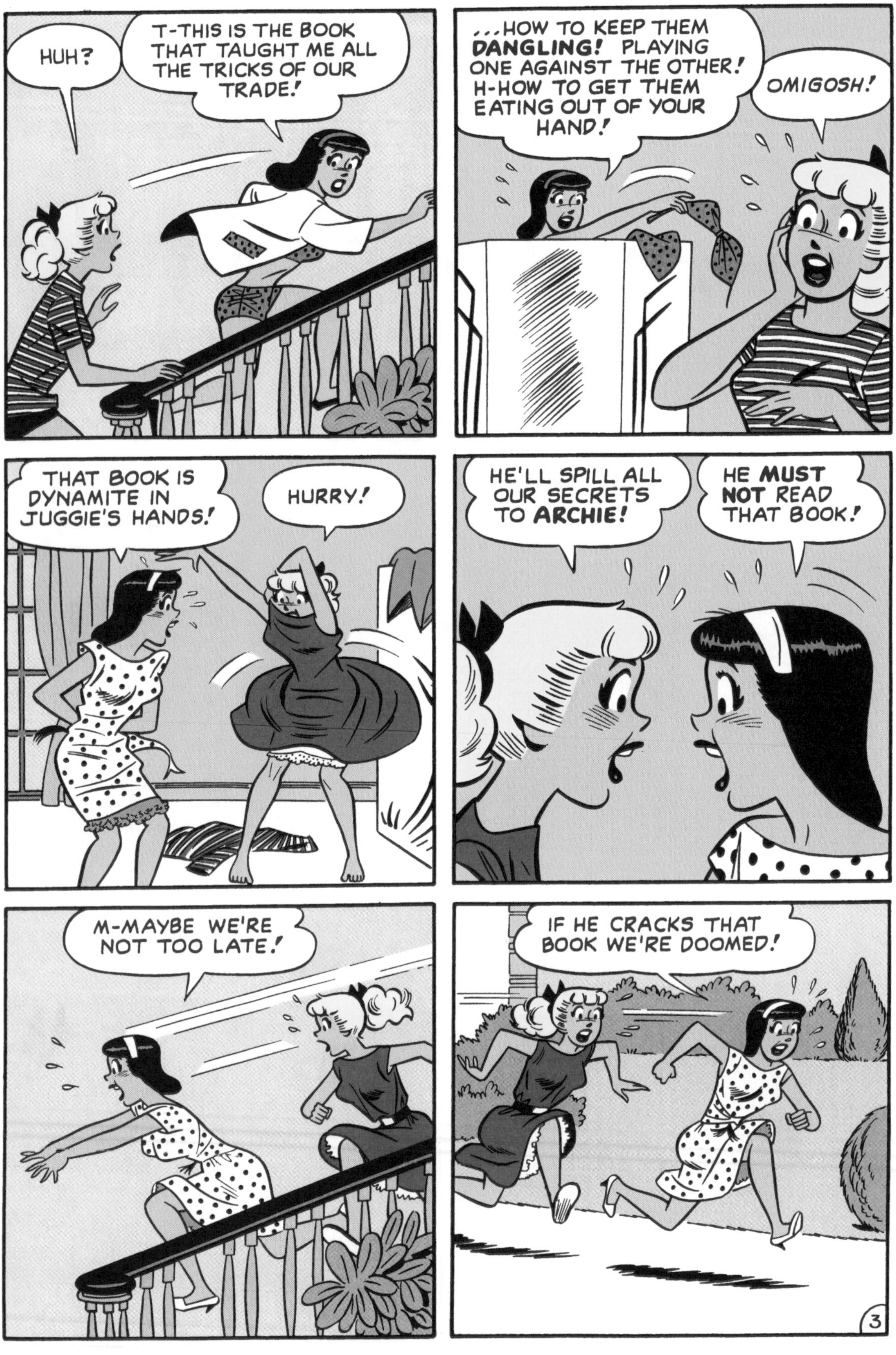
HUH?
T-THIS IS THE BOOK THAT TAUGHT ME ALL THE TRICKS OF OUR TRADE!
...HOW TO KEEP THEM DANGLING! PLAYING ONE AGAINST THE OTHER! H-HOW TO GET THEM EATING OUT OF YOUR HAND!
OMIGOSH!
THAT BOOK IS DYNAMITE IN JUGGIE'S HANDS!
HURRY!
HE'LL SPILL ALL OUR SECRETS TO ARCHIE!
HE MUST NOT READ THAT BOOK!
M-MAYBE WE'RE NOT TOO LATE!
IF HE CRACKS THAT BOOK WE'RE DOOMED!
3

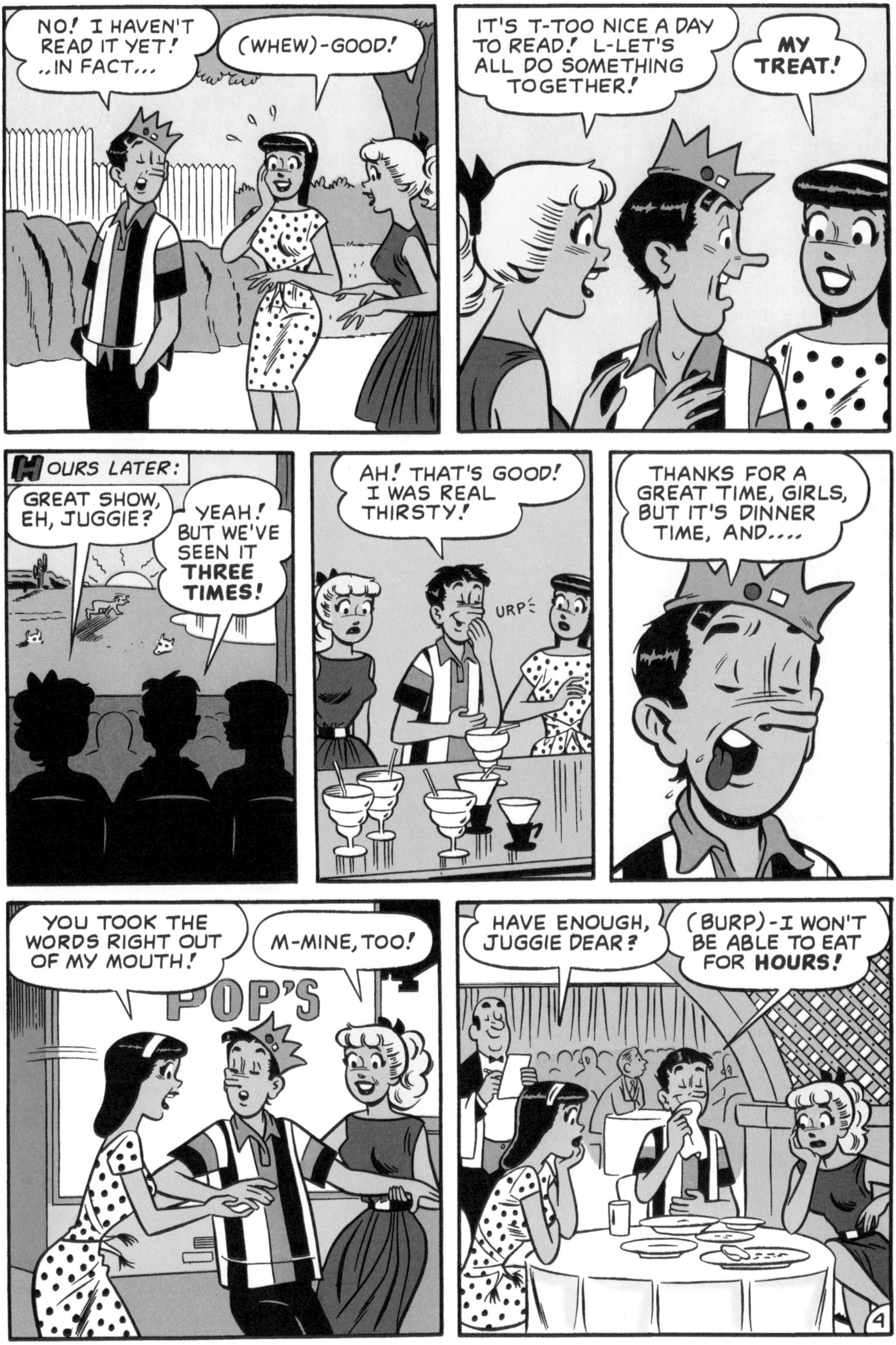
NO! I HAVEN'T READ IT YET! ..IN FACT...
(WHEW)-GOOD!
IT'S T-TOO NICE A DAY TO READ! L-LET'S ALL DO SOMETHING TOGETHER!
MY TREAT!
HOURS LATER:
GREAT SHOW, EH, JUGGIE?
YEAH! BUT WE'VE SEEN IT THREE TIMES!
AH! THAT'S GOOD! I WAS REAL THIRSTY!
URP
THANKS FOR A GREAT TIME, GIRLS, BUT IT'S DINNER TIME, AND....
YOU TOOK THE WORDS RIGHT OUT OF MY MOUTH!
M-MINE, TOO!
POP'S
HAVE ENOUGH, JUGGIE DEAR?
(BURP)-I WON'T BE ABLE TO EAT FOR HOURS!
4

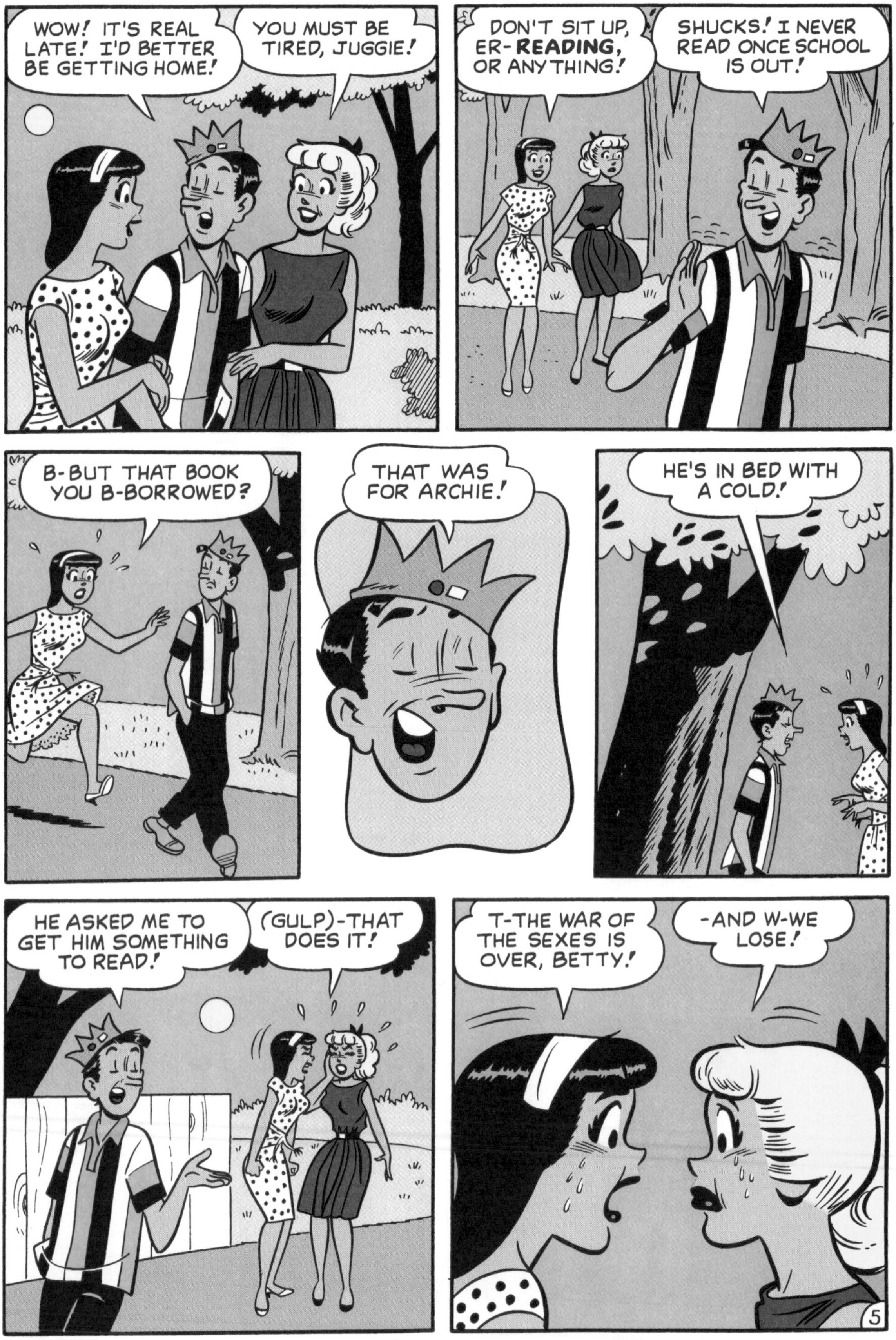
WOW! IT'S REAL LATE! I'D BETTER BE GETTING HOME!
YOU MUST BE TIRED, JUGGIE!
DON'T SIT UP, ER-**READING**, OR ANYTHING!
SHUCKS! I NEVER READ ONCE SCHOOL IS OUT!
B-BUT THAT BOOK YOU B-BORROWED?
THAT WAS FOR ARCHIE!
HE'S IN BED WITH A COLD!
HE ASKED ME TO GET HIM SOMETHING TO READ!
(GULP)-THAT DOES IT!
T-THE WAR OF THE SEXES IS OVER, BETTY!
-AND W-WE LOSE!
5

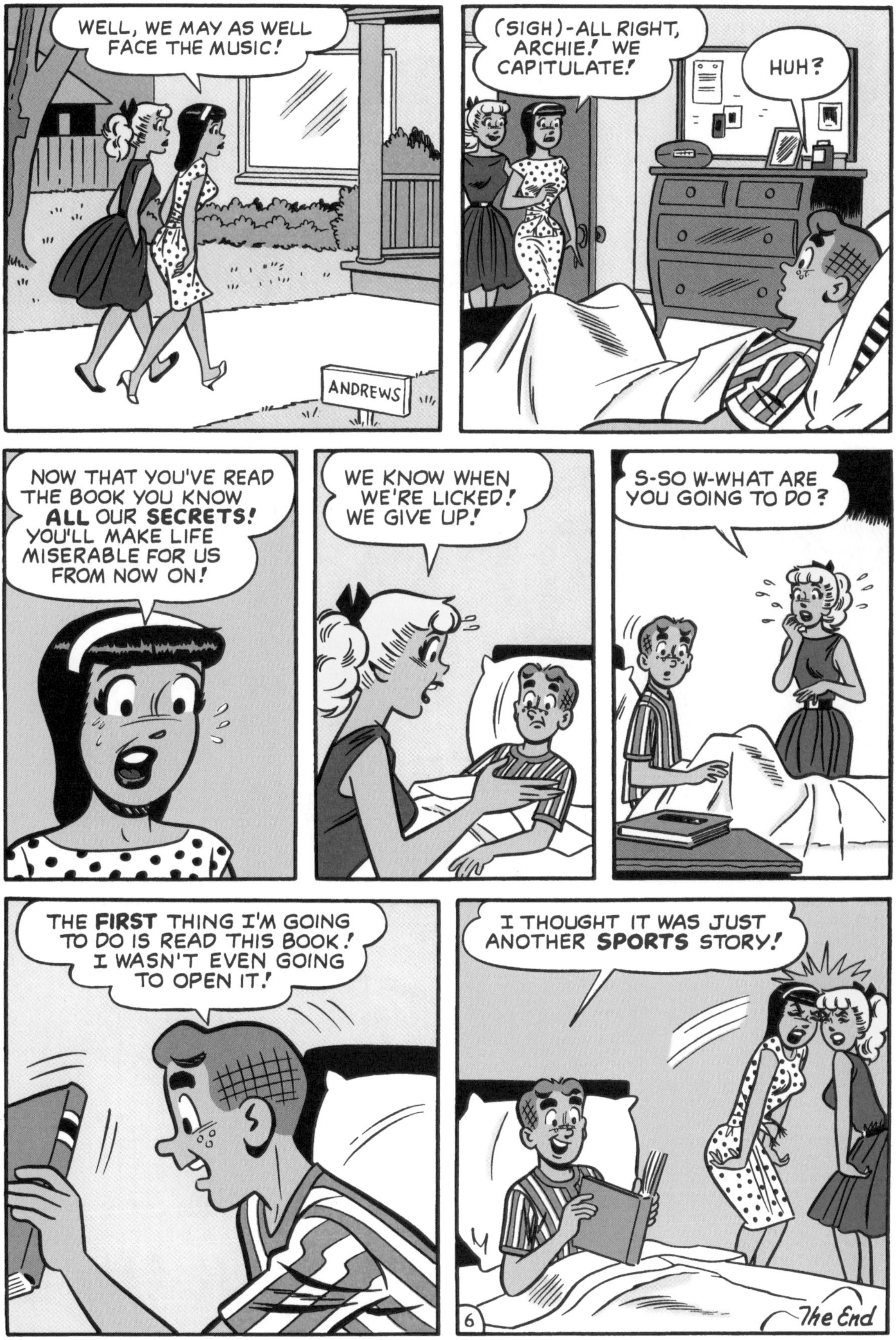
WELL, WE MAY AS WELL FACE THE MUSIC!
ANDREWS
(SIGH)-ALL RIGHT, ARCHIE! WE CAPITULATE!
HUH?
NOW THAT YOU'VE READ THE BOOK YOU KNOW ALL OUR SECRETS! YOU'LL MAKE LIFE MISERABLE FOR US FROM NOW ON!
WE KNOW WHEN WE'RE LICKED! WE GIVE UP!
S-SO W-WHAT ARE YOU GOING TO DO?
THE FIRST THING I'M GOING TO DO IS READ THIS BOOK! I WASN'T EVEN GOING TO OPEN IT!
I THOUGHT IT WAS JUST ANOTHER SPORTS STORY!
6
The End

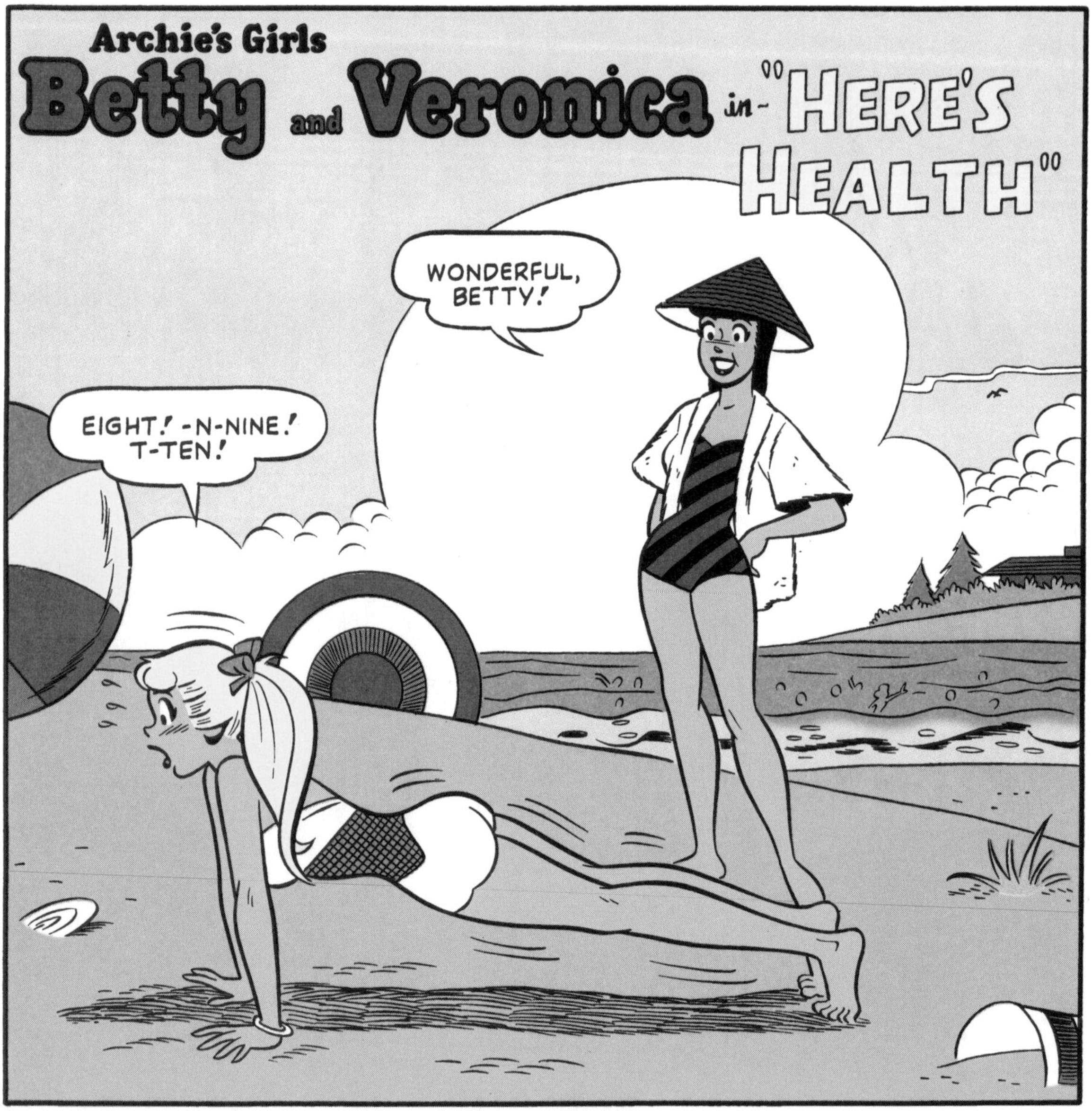
Archie's Girls
Betty and Veronica in- "HERE'S HEALTH"
EIGHT! -N-NINE! T-TEN!
WONDERFUL, BETTY!

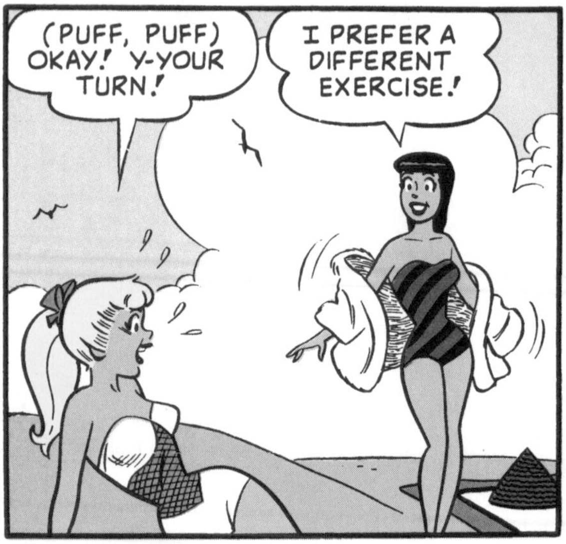
(PUFF, PUFF) OKAY! Y-YOUR TURN!
I PREFER A DIFFERENT EXERCISE!

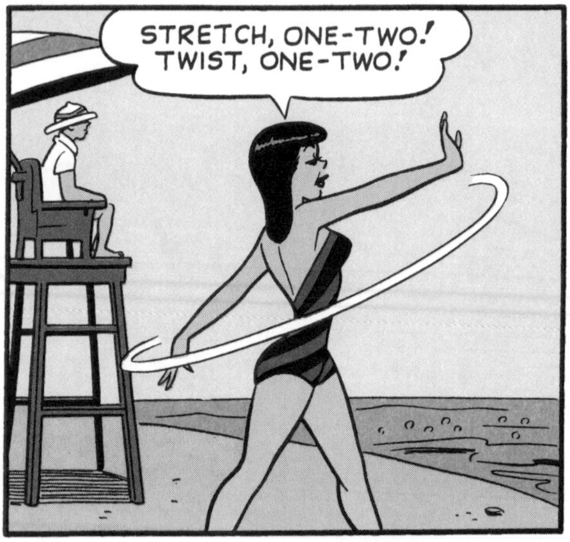
STRETCH, ONE-TWO! TWIST, ONE-TWO!

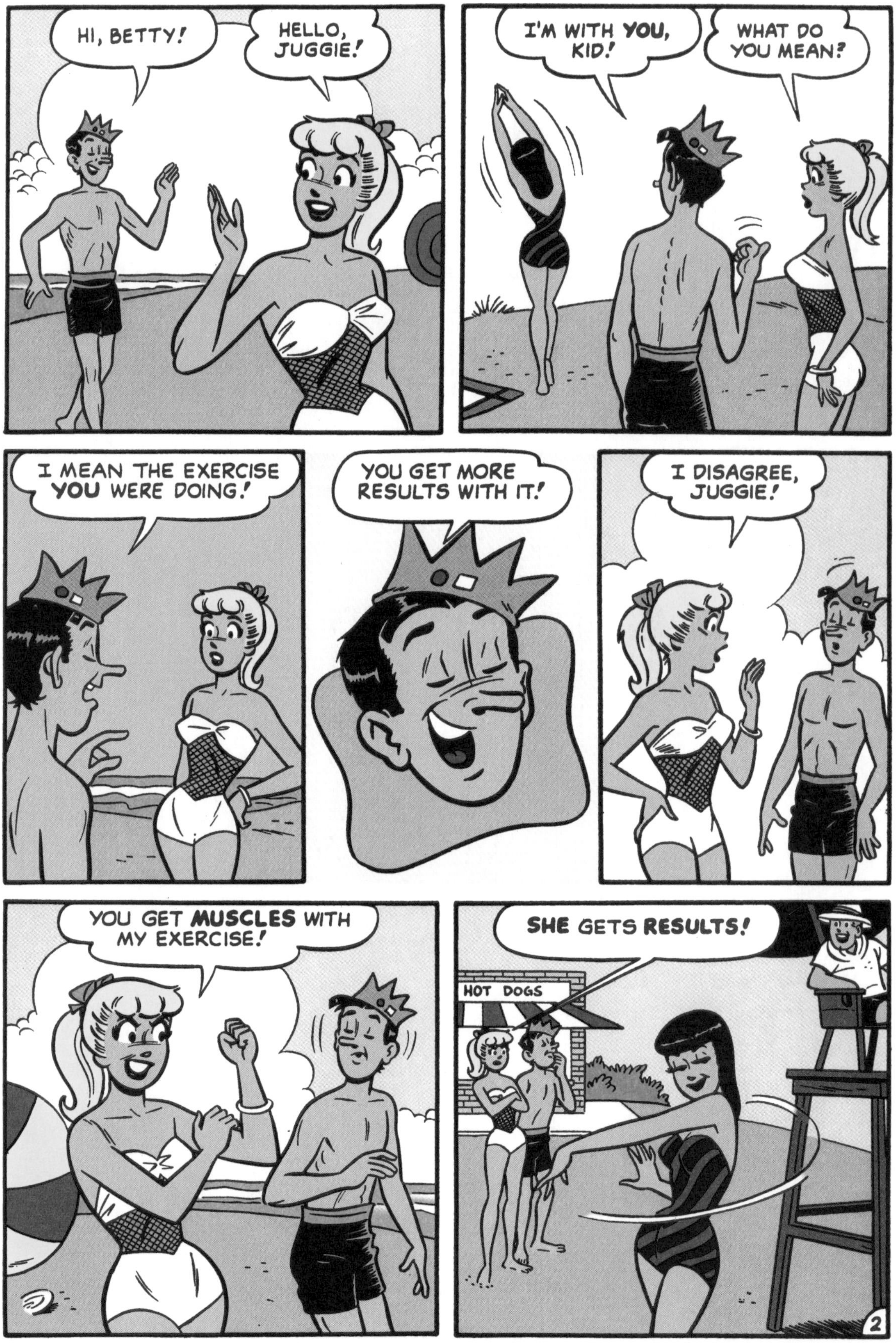
HI, BETTY!
HELLO, JUGGIE!
I'M WITH YOU, KID!
WHAT DO YOU MEAN?
I MEAN THE EXERCISE YOU WERE DOING!
YOU GET MORE RESULTS WITH IT!
I DISAGREE, JUGGIE!
YOU GET MUSCLES WITH MY EXERCISE!
SHE GETS RESULTS!
HOT DOGS
2

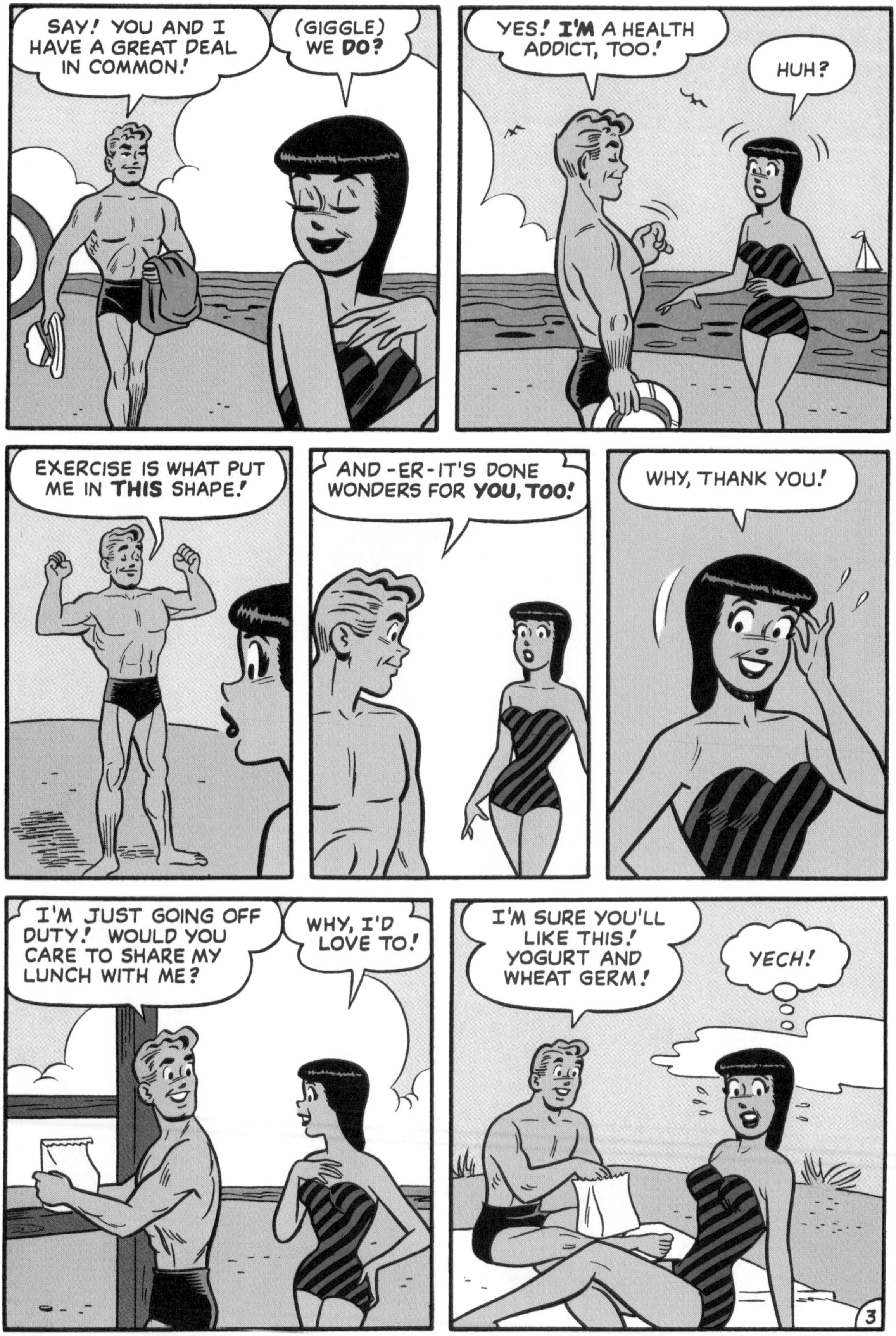
SAY! YOU AND I HAVE A GREAT DEAL IN COMMON!
(GIGGLE) WE DO?
YES! I'M A HEALTH ADDICT, TOO!
HUH?
EXERCISE IS WHAT PUT ME IN THIS SHAPE!
AND-ER-IT'S DONE WONDERS FOR YOU, TOO!
WHY, THANK YOU!
I'M JUST GOING OFF DUTY! WOULD YOU CARE TO SHARE MY LUNCH WITH ME?
WHY, I'D LOVE TO!
I'M SURE YOU'LL LIKE THIS! YOGURT AND WHEAT GERM!
YECH!
3

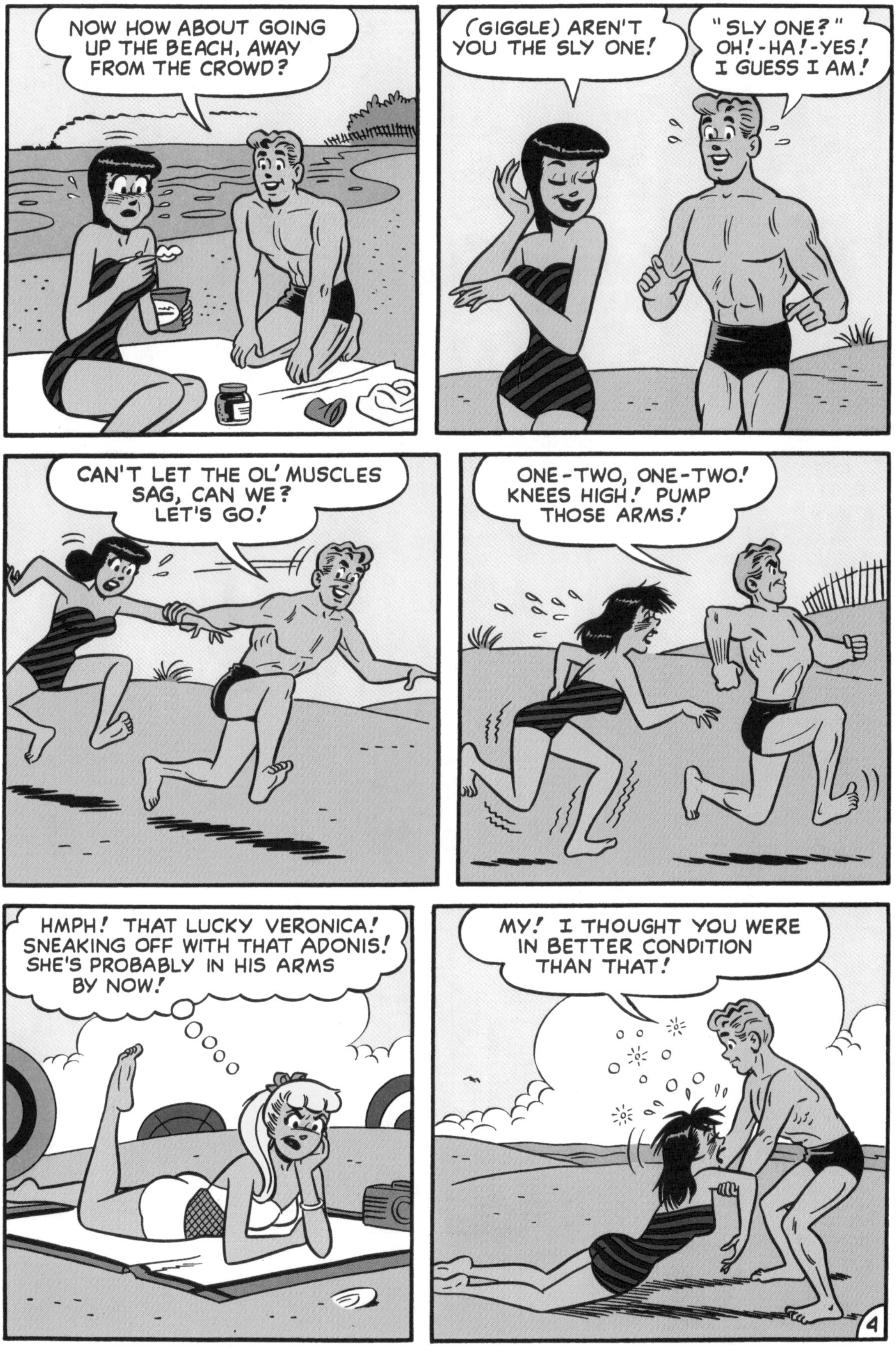
NOW HOW ABOUT GOING UP THE BEACH, AWAY FROM THE CROWD?
(GIGGLE) AREN'T YOU THE SLY ONE!
"SLY ONE?" OH! -HA! -YES! I GUESS I AM!
CAN'T LET THE OL' MUSCLES SAG, CAN WE? LET'S GO!
ONE-TWO, ONE-TWO! KNEES HIGH! PUMP THOSE ARMS!
HMPH! THAT LUCKY VERONICA! SNEAKING OFF WITH THAT ADONIS! SHE'S PROBABLY IN HIS ARMS BY NOW!
MY! I THOUGHT YOU WERE IN BETTER CONDITION THAN THAT!
4

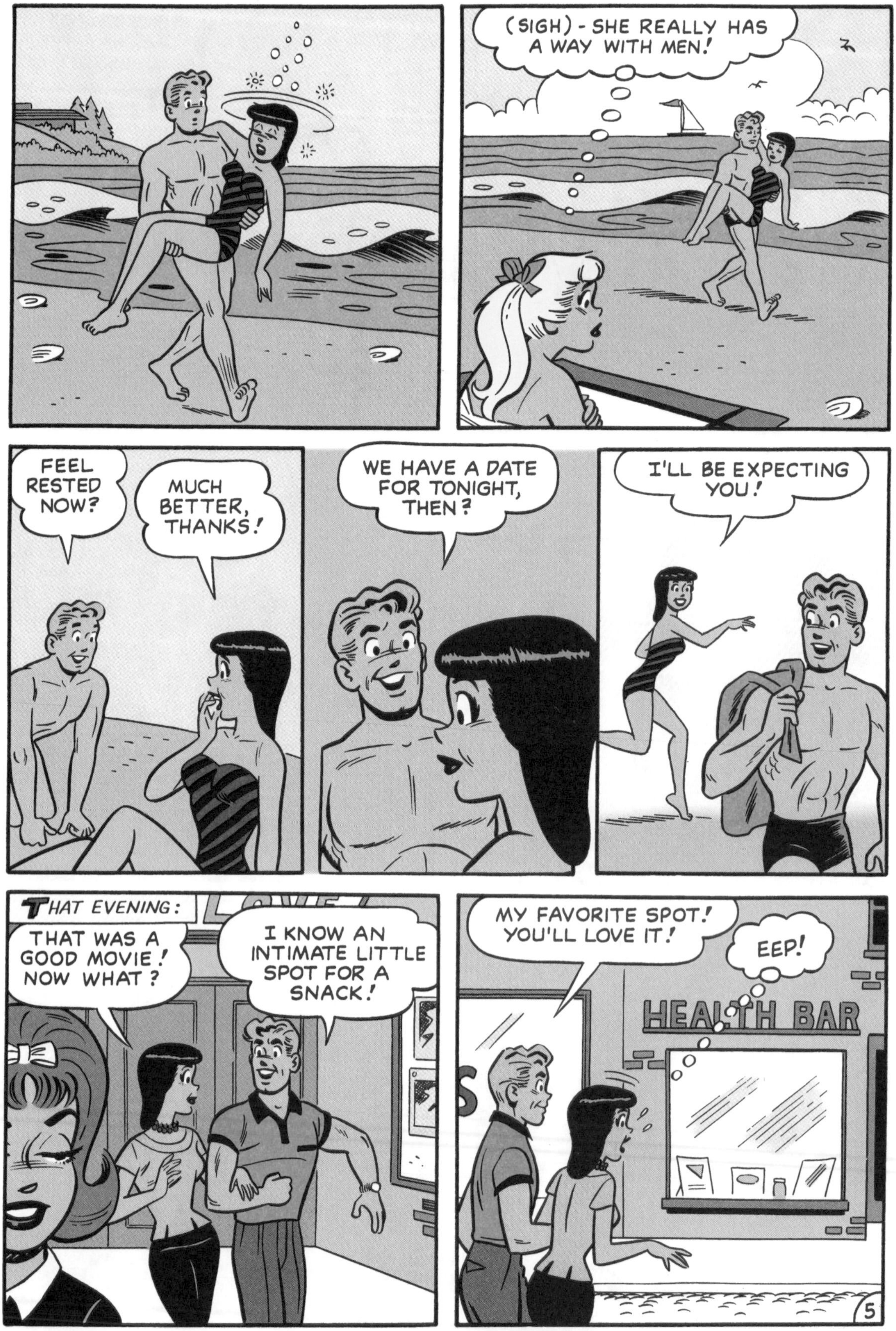
(SIGH) - SHE REALLY HAS A WAY WITH MEN!
FEEL RESTED NOW?
MUCH BETTER, THANKS!
WE HAVE A DATE FOR TONIGHT, THEN?
I'LL BE EXPECTING YOU!
THAT EVENING:
THAT WAS A GOOD MOVIE! NOW WHAT?
I KNOW AN INTIMATE LITTLE SPOT FOR A SNACK!
MY FAVORITE SPOT! YOU'LL LOVE IT!
EEP!
HEALTH BAR
5

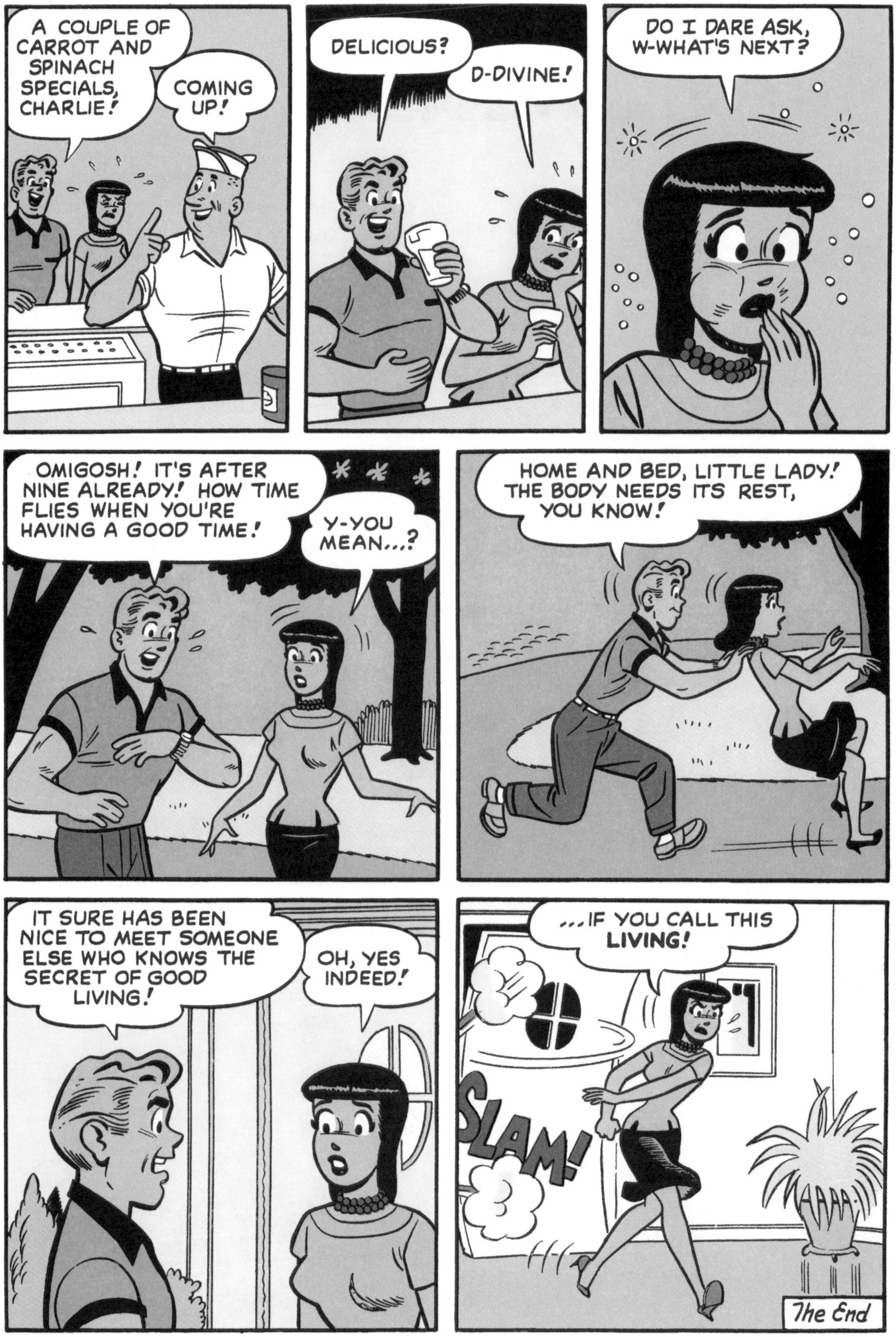
A COUPLE OF CARROT AND SPINACH SPECIALS, CHARLIE!
COMING UP!
DELICIOUS?
D-DIVINE!
DO I DARE ASK, W-WHAT'S NEXT?
OMIGOSH! IT'S AFTER NINE ALREADY! HOW TIME FLIES WHEN YOU'RE HAVING A GOOD TIME!
Y-YOU MEAN...?
HOME AND BED, LITTLE LADY! THE BODY NEEDS ITS REST, YOU KNOW!
IT SURE HAS BEEN NICE TO MEET SOMEONE ELSE WHO KNOWS THE SECRET OF GOOD LIVING!
OH, YES INDEED!
...IF YOU CALL THIS **LIVING!**
SLAM!
The End

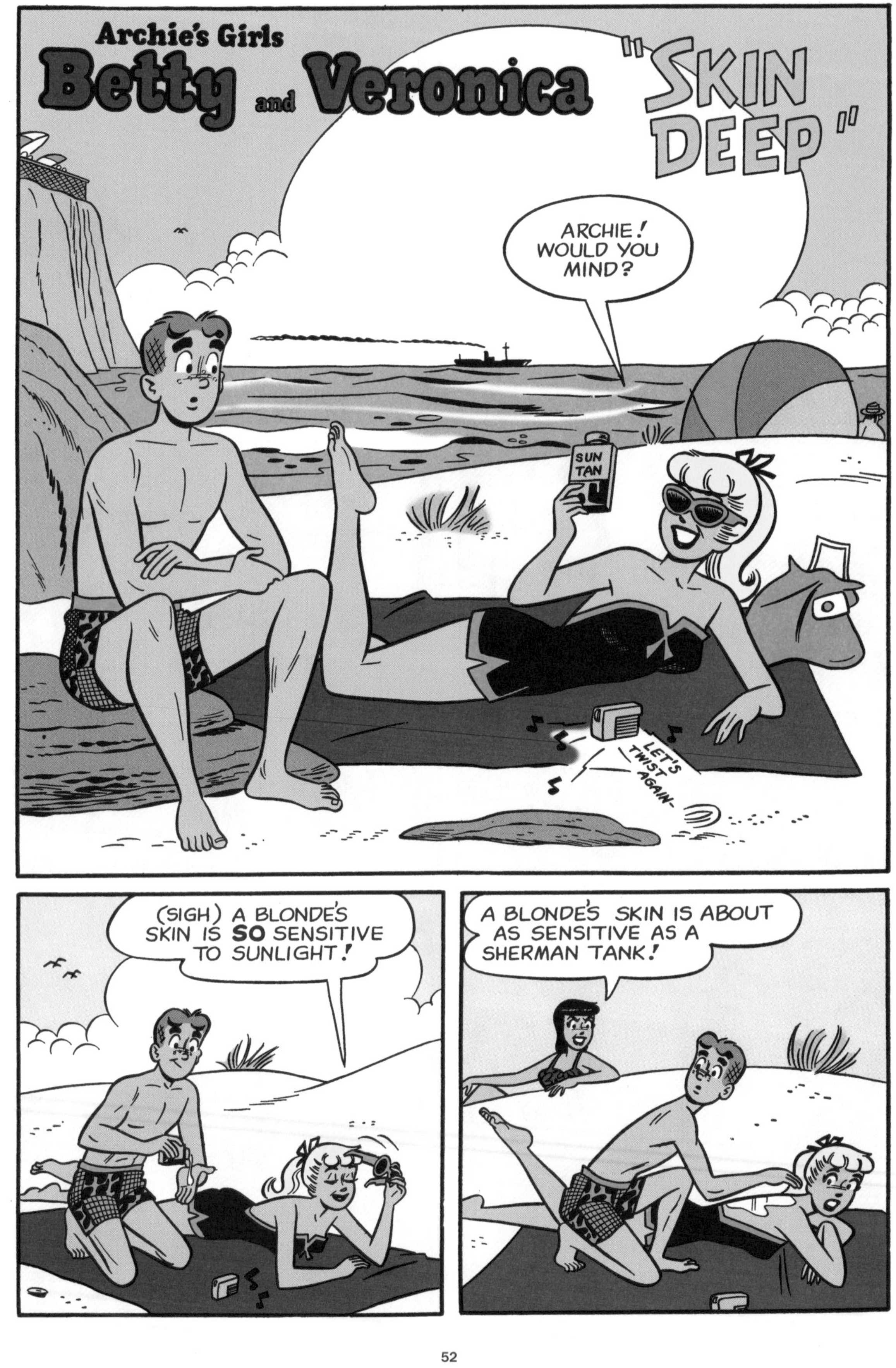
Archie's Girls
Betty and Veronica
"SKIN DEEP"
ARCHIE! WOULD YOU MIND?
SUN TAN
LET'S TWIST AGAIN-
(SIGH) A BLONDE'S SKIN IS **SO** SENSITIVE TO SUNLIGHT!
A BLONDE'S SKIN IS ABOUT AS SENSITIVE AS A SHERMAN TANK!

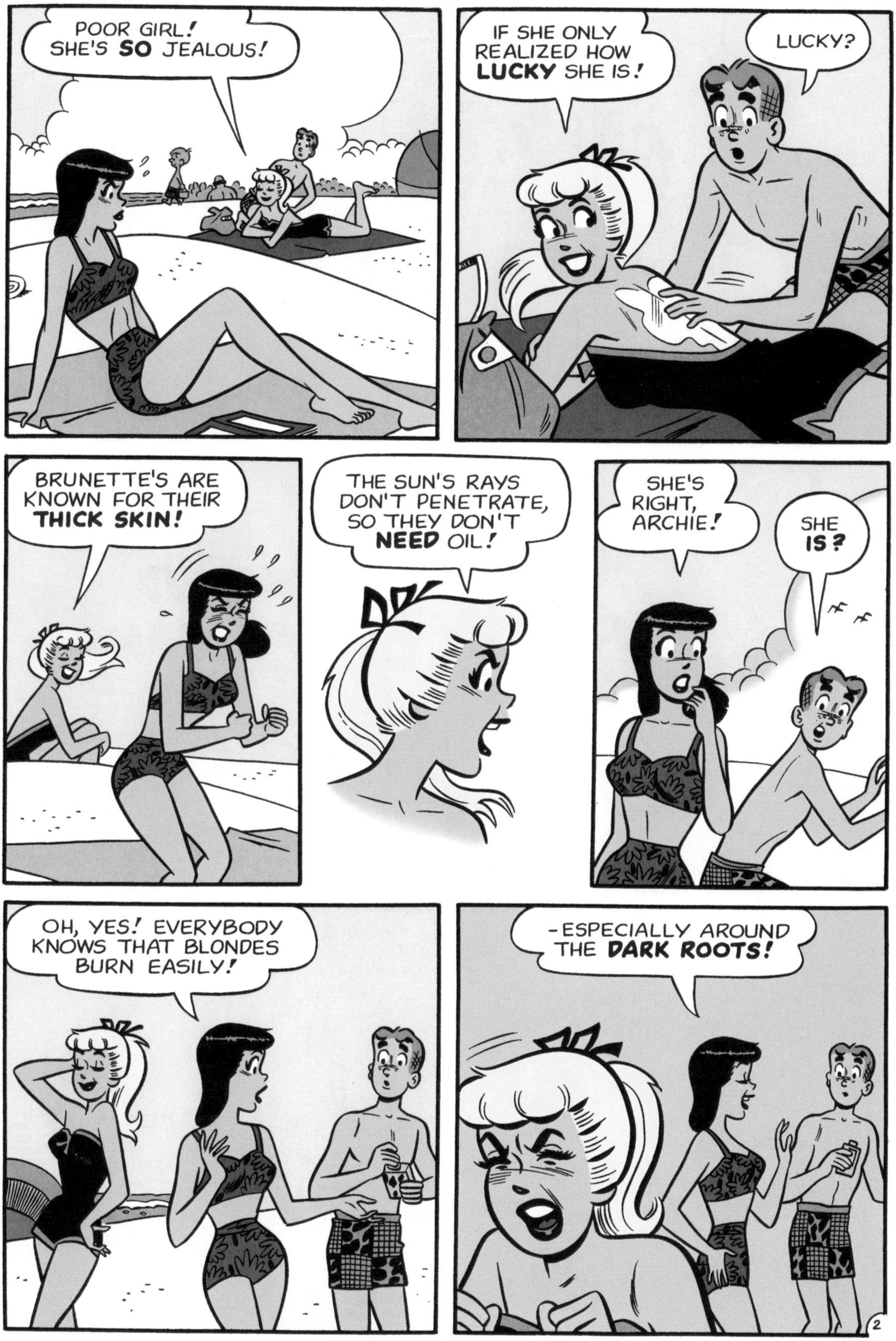
POOR GIRL! SHE'S SO JEALOUS!
IF SHE ONLY REALIZED HOW LUCKY SHE IS!
LUCKY?
BRUNETTE'S ARE KNOWN FOR THEIR THICK SKIN!
THE SUN'S RAYS DON'T PENETRATE, SO THEY DON'T NEED OIL!
SHE'S RIGHT, ARCHIE!
SHE IS?
OH, YES! EVERYBODY KNOWS THAT BLONDES BURN EASILY!
-ESPECIALLY AROUND THE DARK ROOTS!
2

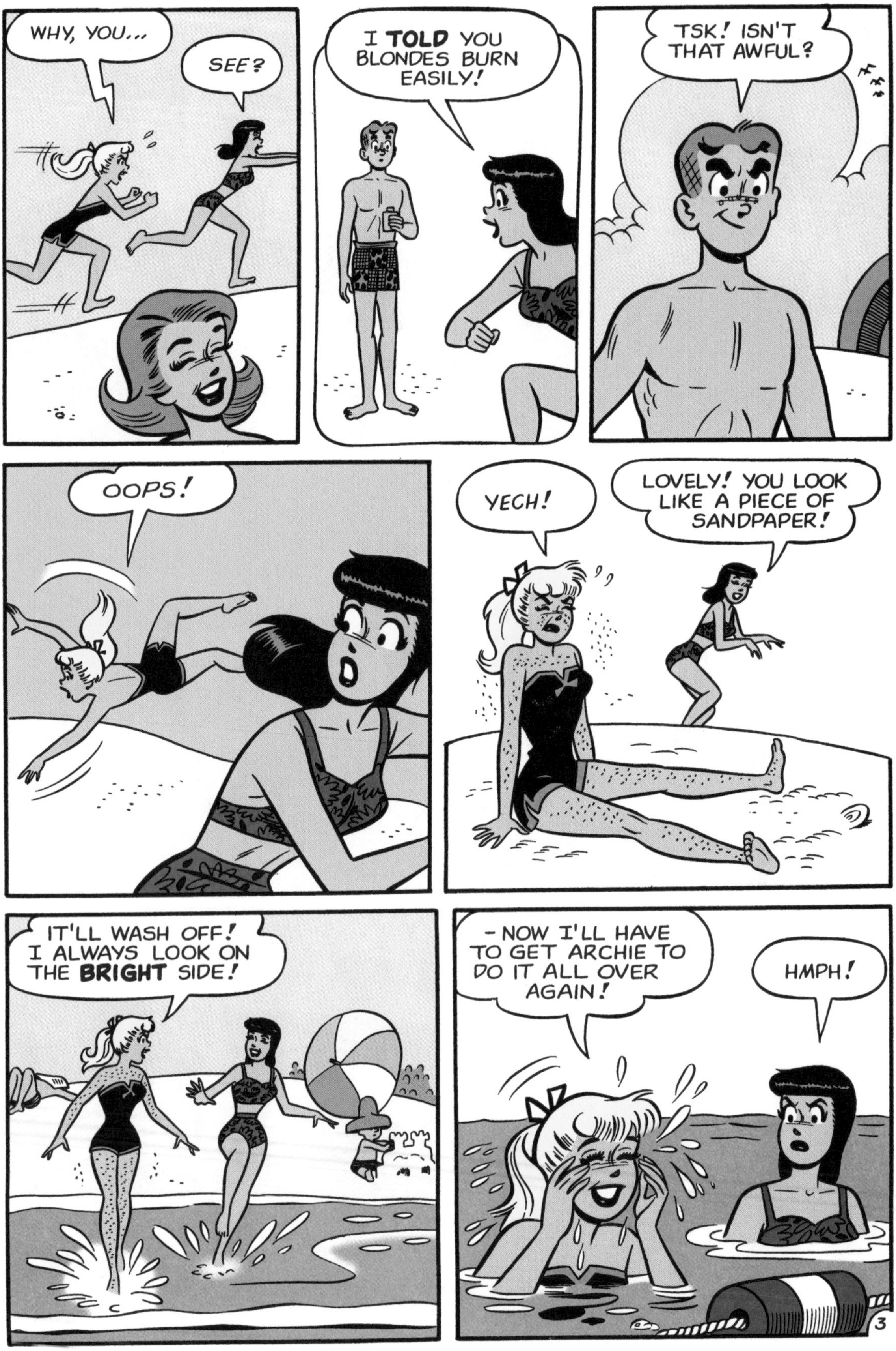
WHY, YOU...
SEE?
I TOLD YOU BLONDES BURN EASILY!
TSK! ISN'T THAT AWFUL?
OOPS!
YECH!
LOVELY! YOU LOOK LIKE A PIECE OF SANDPAPER!
IT'LL WASH OFF! I ALWAYS LOOK ON THE BRIGHT SIDE!
-NOW I'LL HAVE TO GET ARCHIE TO DO IT ALL OVER AGAIN!
HMPH!
3

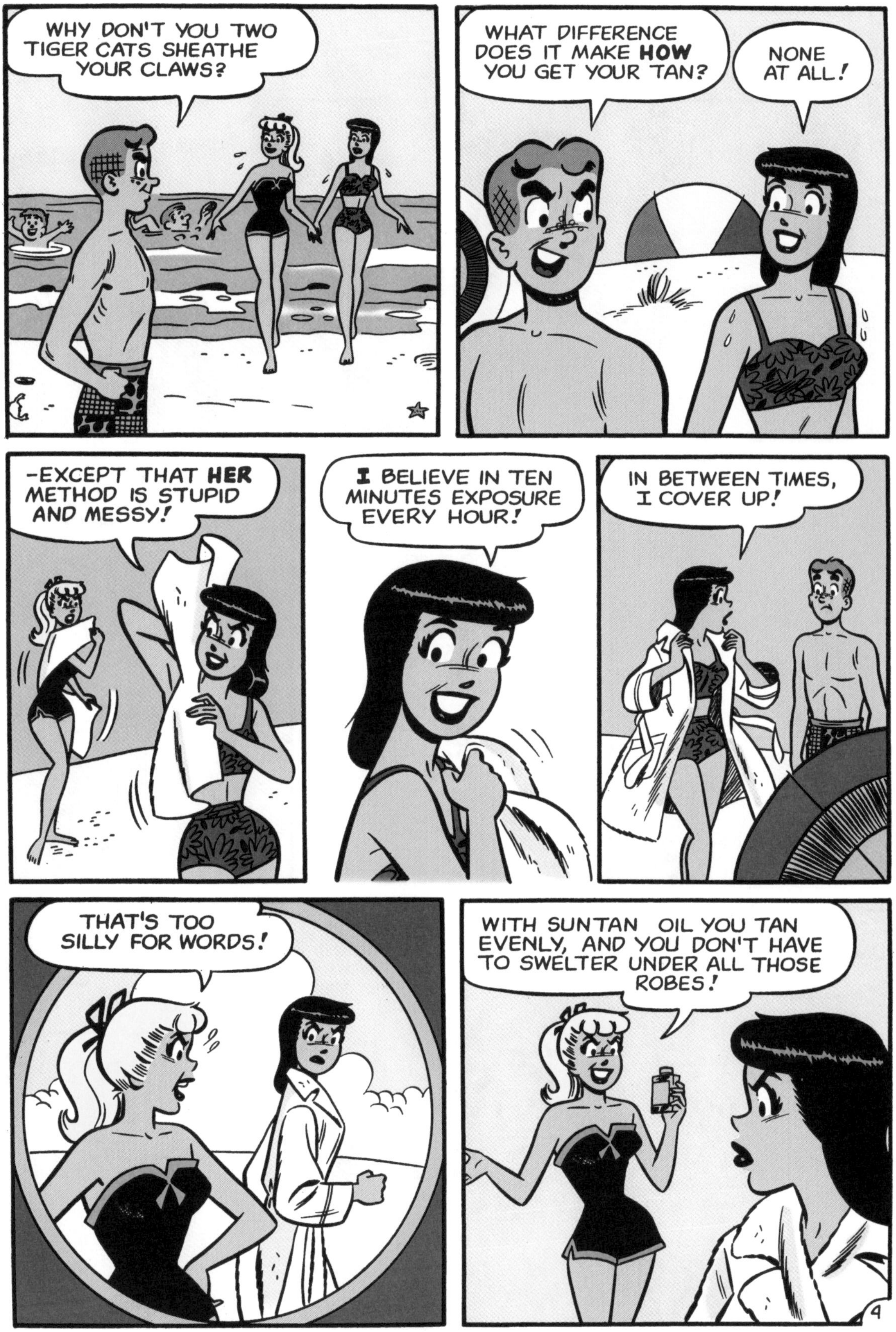
WHY DON'T YOU TWO TIGER CATS SHEATHE YOUR CLAWS?
WHAT DIFFERENCE DOES IT MAKE HOW YOU GET YOUR TAN?
NONE AT ALL!
-EXCEPT THAT HER METHOD IS STUPID AND MESSY!
I BELIEVE IN TEN MINUTES EXPOSURE EVERY HOUR!
IN BETWEEN TIMES, I COVER UP!
THAT'S TOO SILLY FOR WORDS!
WITH SUNTAN OIL YOU TAN EVENLY, AND YOU DON'T HAVE TO SWELTER UNDER ALL THOSE ROBES!
4

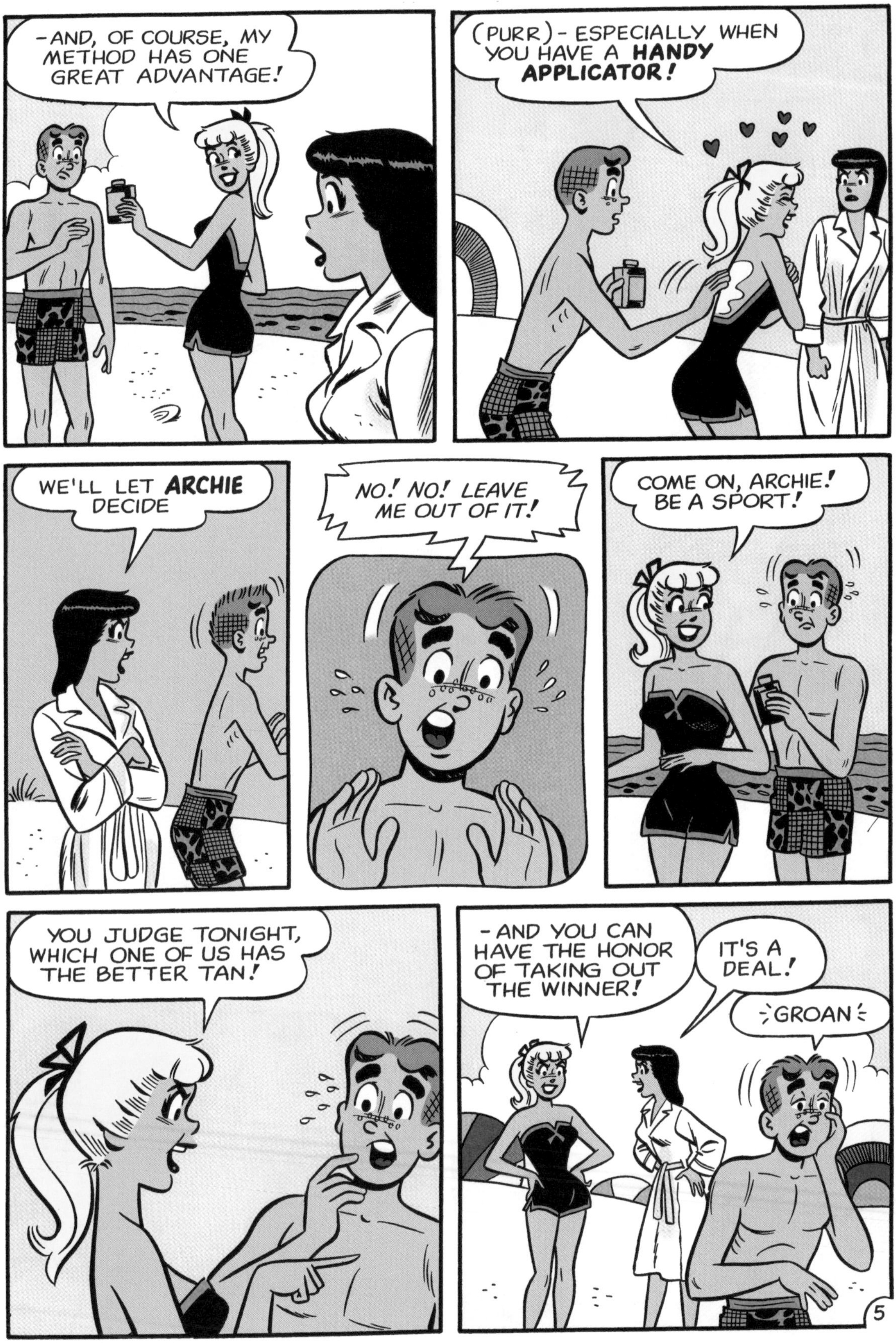
-AND, OF COURSE, MY METHOD HAS ONE GREAT ADVANTAGE!
(PURR)- ESPECIALLY WHEN YOU HAVE A **HANDY APPLICATOR**!
WE'LL LET **ARCHIE** DECIDE
NO! NO! LEAVE ME OUT OF IT!
COME ON, ARCHIE! BE A SPORT!
YOU JUDGE TONIGHT, WHICH ONE OF US HAS THE BETTER TAN!
-AND YOU CAN HAVE THE HONOR OF TAKING OUT THE WINNER!
IT'S A DEAL!
GROAN
5

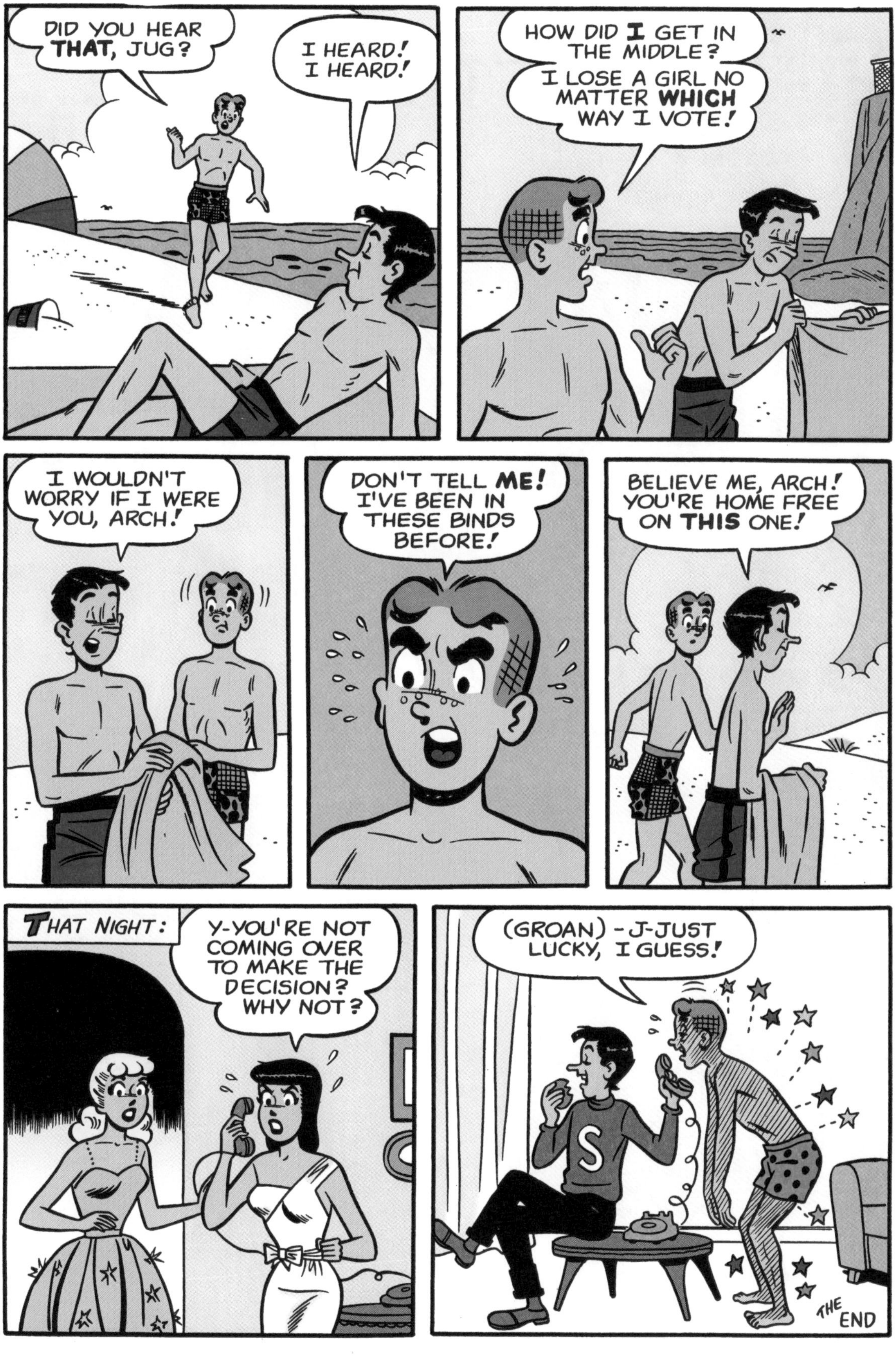
DID YOU HEAR **THAT**, JUG?
I HEARD! I HEARD!
HOW DID **I** GET IN THE MIDDLE?
I LOSE A GIRL NO MATTER **WHICH** WAY I VOTE!
I WOULDN'T WORRY IF I WERE YOU, ARCH!
DON'T TELL **ME**! I'VE BEEN IN THESE BINDS BEFORE!
BELIEVE ME, ARCH! YOU'RE HOME FREE ON **THIS** ONE!
THAT NIGHT:
Y-YOU'RE NOT COMING OVER TO MAKE THE DECISION? WHY NOT?
(GROAN) - J-JUST LUCKY, I GUESS!
THE END

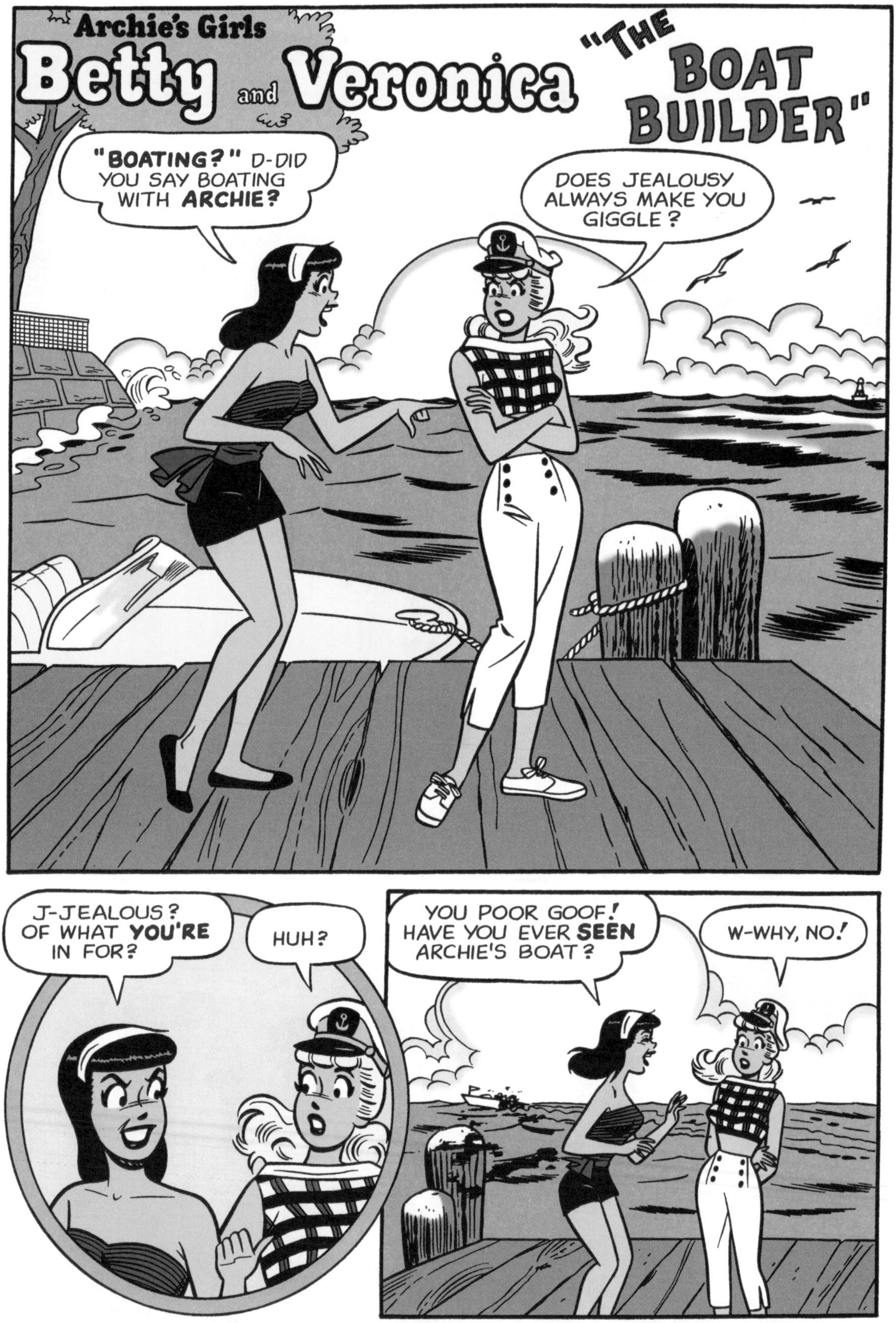
Archie's Girls
Betty and Veronica
"THE BOAT BUILDER"
"BOATING?" D-DID YOU SAY BOATING WITH ARCHIE?
DOES JEALOUSY ALWAYS MAKE YOU GIGGLE?
J-JEALOUS? OF WHAT YOU'RE IN FOR?
HUH?
YOU POOR GOOF! HAVE YOU EVER SEEN ARCHIE'S BOAT?
W-WHY, NO!

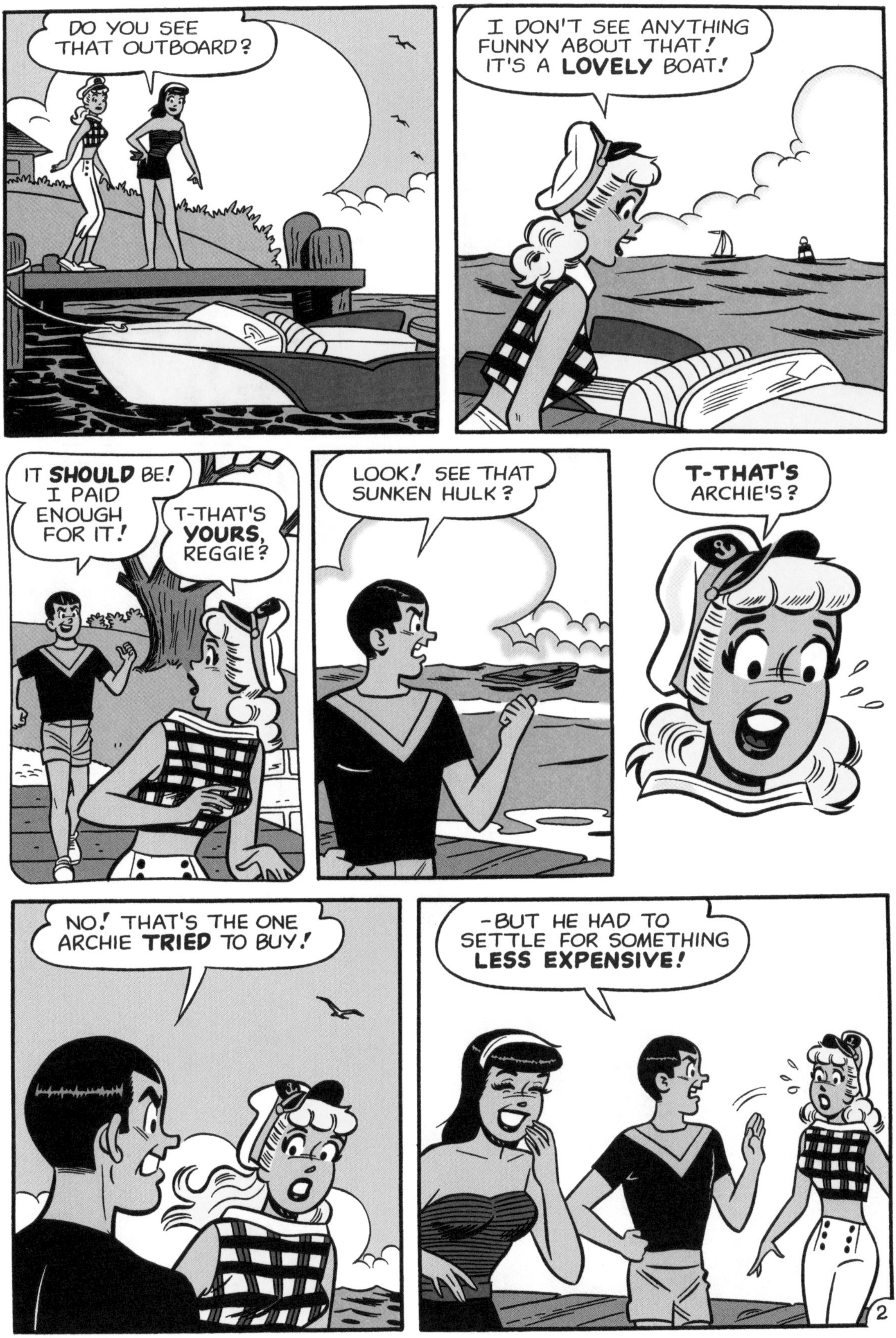
DO YOU SEE THAT OUTBOARD?
I DON'T SEE ANYTHING FUNNY ABOUT THAT! IT'S A LOVELY BOAT!
IT SHOULD BE! I PAID ENOUGH FOR IT!
T-THAT'S YOURS, REGGIE?
LOOK! SEE THAT SUNKEN HULK?
T-THAT'S ARCHIE'S?
NO! THAT'S THE ONE ARCHIE TRIED TO BUY!
-BUT HE HAD TO SETTLE FOR SOMETHING LESS EXPENSIVE!
2

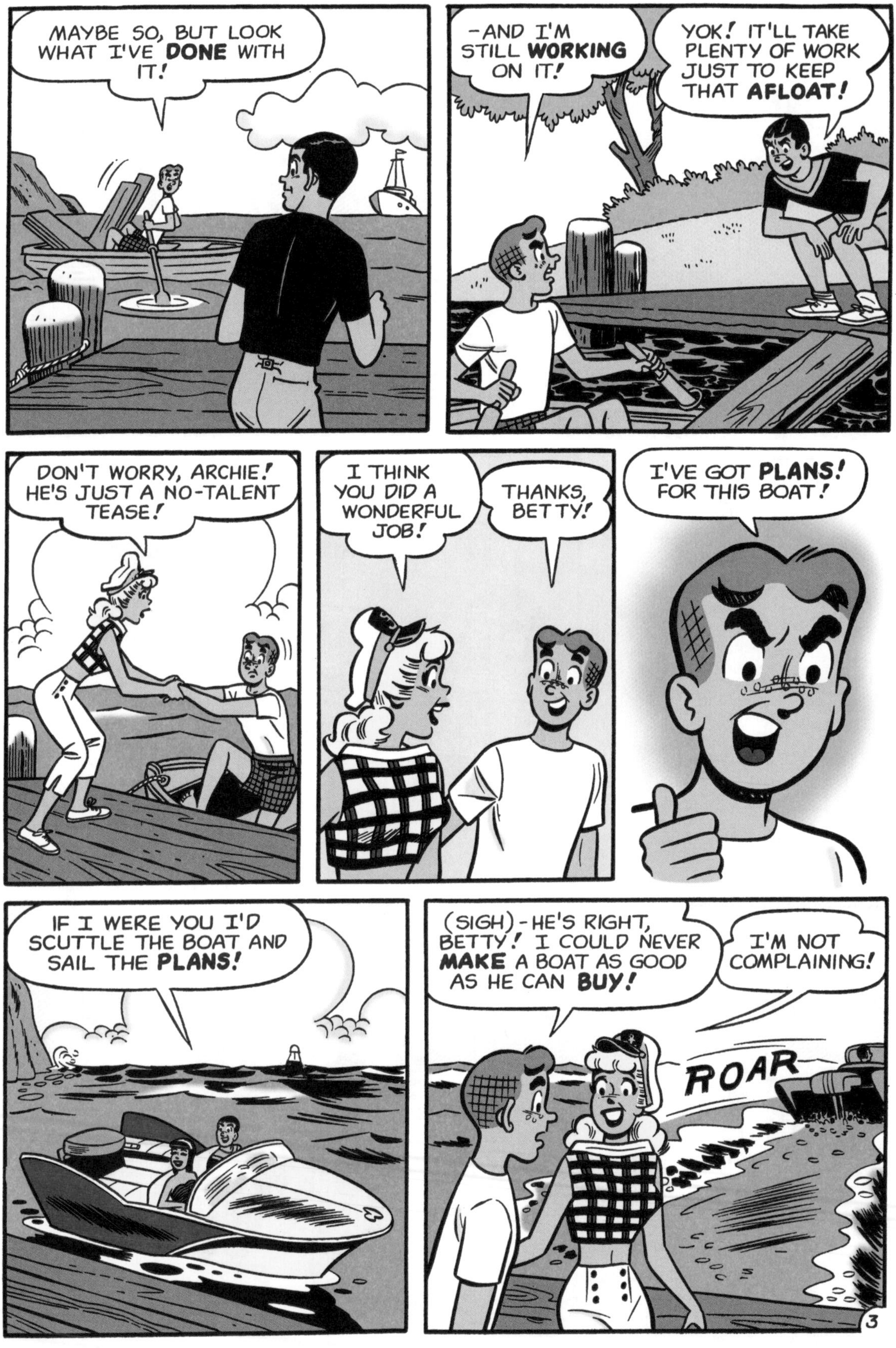
MAYBE SO, BUT LOOK WHAT I'VE **DONE** WITH IT!
-AND I'M STILL **WORKING** ON IT!
YOK! IT'LL TAKE PLENTY OF WORK JUST TO KEEP THAT **AFLOAT**!
DON'T WORRY, ARCHIE! HE'S JUST A NO-TALENT TEASE!
I THINK YOU DID A WONDERFUL JOB!
THANKS, BETTY!
I'VE GOT **PLANS**! FOR THIS BOAT!
IF I WERE YOU I'D SCUTTLE THE BOAT AND SAIL THE **PLANS**!
(SIGH)-HE'S RIGHT, BETTY! I COULD NEVER **MAKE** A BOAT AS GOOD AS HE CAN **BUY**!
I'M NOT COMPLAINING!
ROAR
3

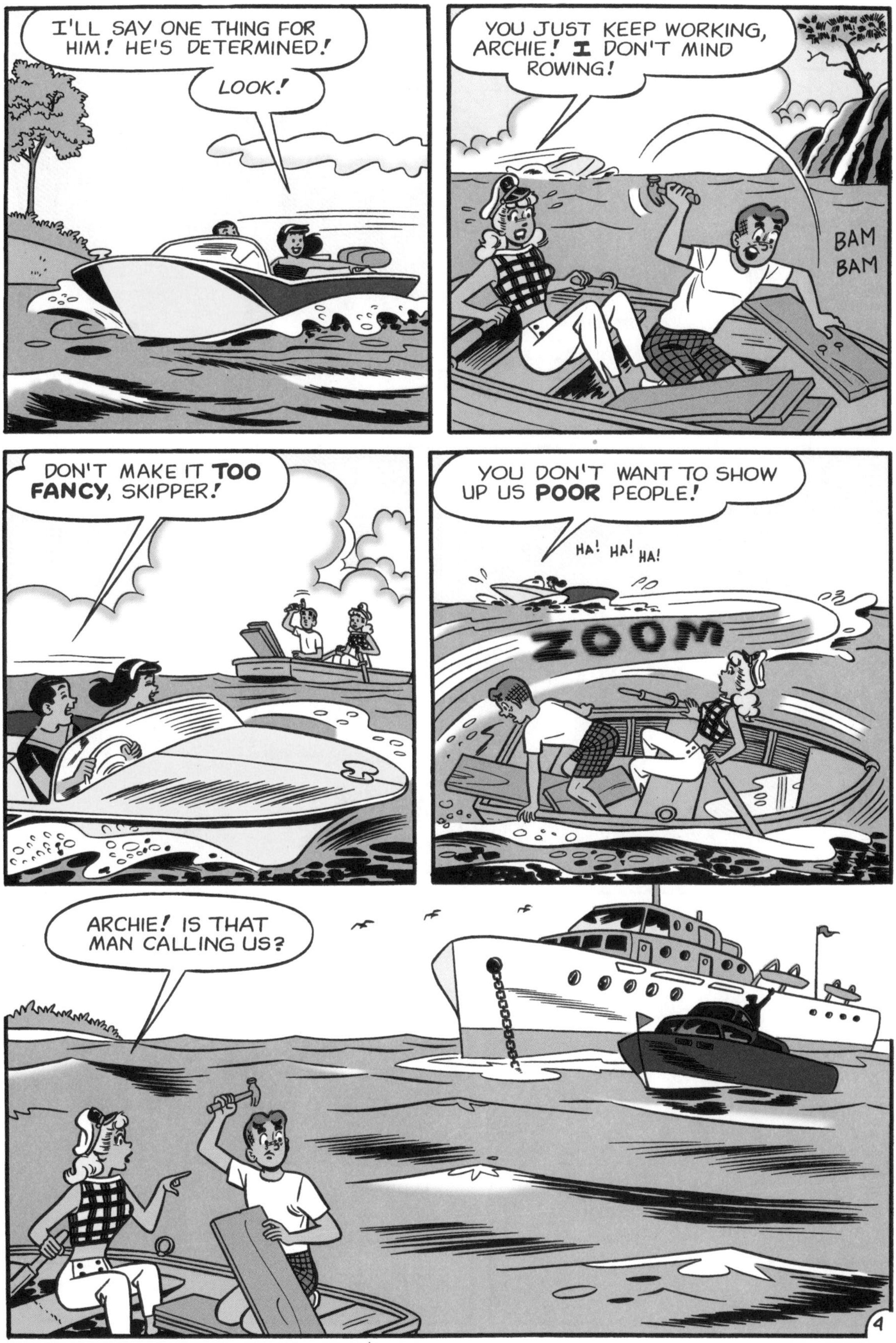
I'LL SAY ONE THING FOR HIM! HE'S DETERMINED!
LOOK!
YOU JUST KEEP WORKING, ARCHIE! I DON'T MIND ROWING!
BAM BAM
DON'T MAKE IT TOO FANCY, SKIPPER!
YOU DON'T WANT TO SHOW UP US POOR PEOPLE!
HA! HA! HA!
ZOOM
ARCHIE! IS THAT MAN CALLING US?
4

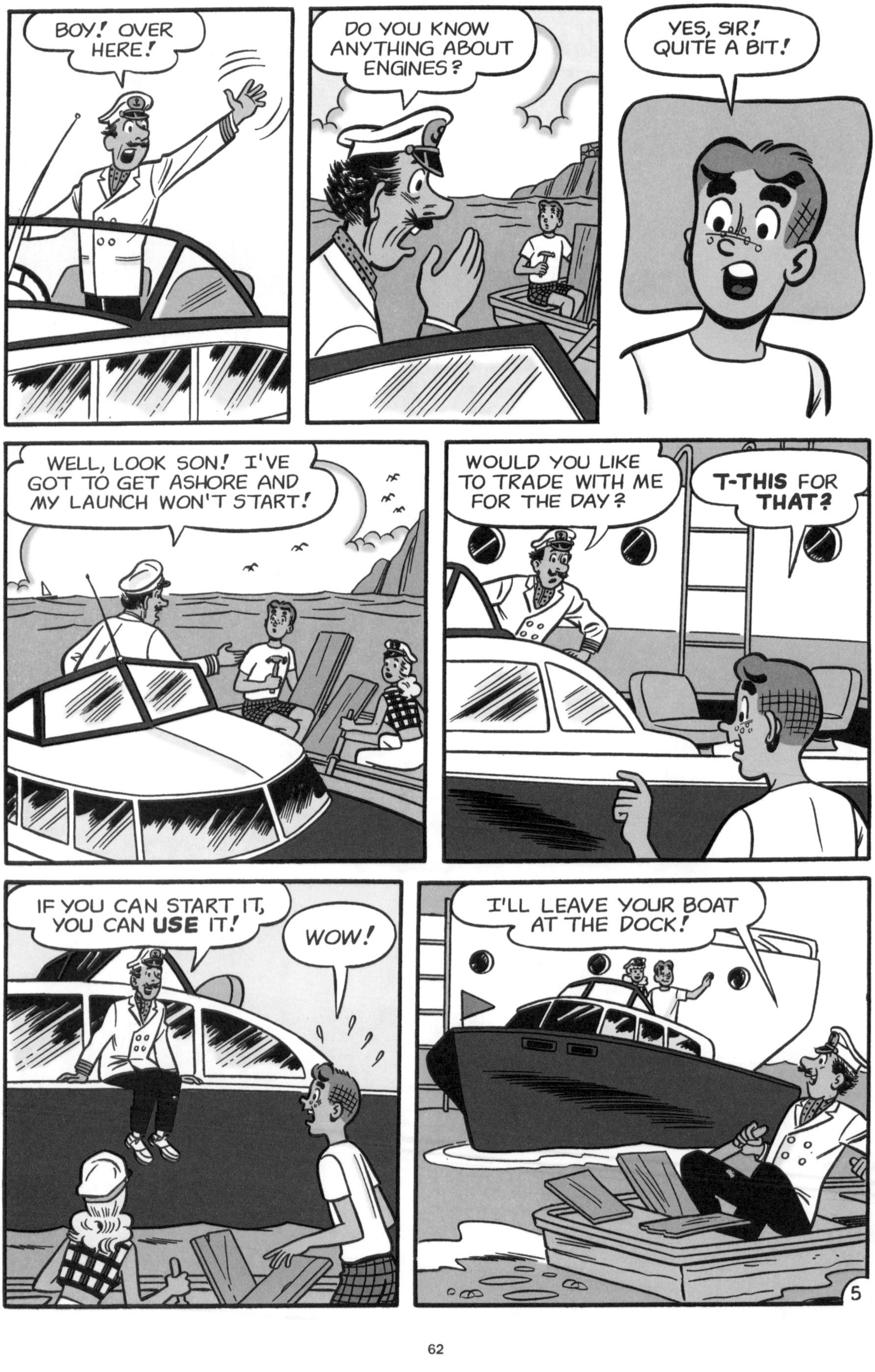
BOY! OVER HERE!
DO YOU KNOW ANYTHING ABOUT ENGINES?
YES, SIR! QUITE A BIT!
WELL, LOOK SON! I'VE GOT TO GET ASHORE AND MY LAUNCH WON'T START!
WOULD YOU LIKE TO TRADE WITH ME FOR THE DAY?
T-THIS FOR THAT?
IF YOU CAN START IT, YOU CAN USE IT!
WOW!
I'LL LEAVE YOUR BOAT AT THE DOCK!
5

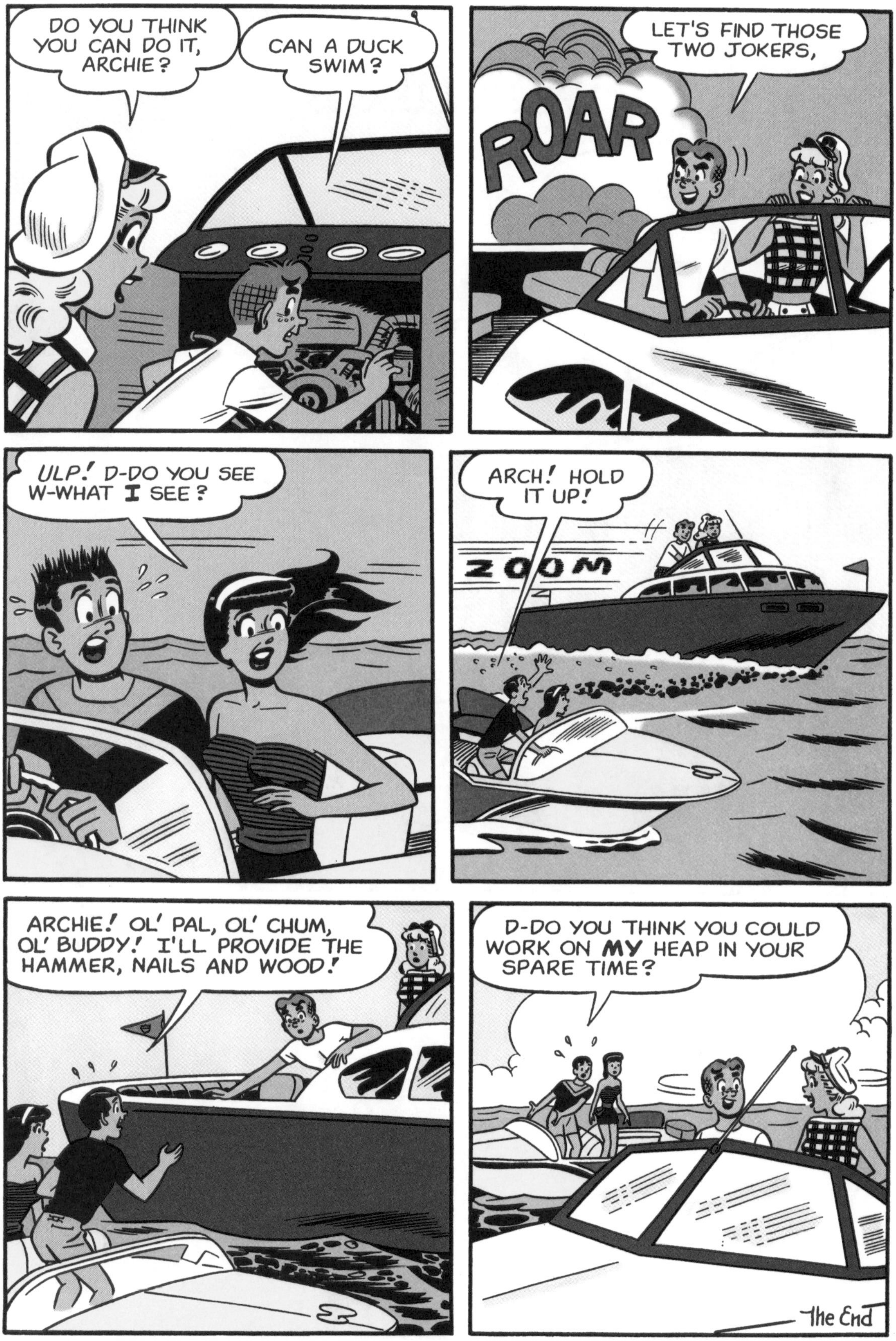
DO YOU THINK YOU CAN DO IT, ARCHIE?
CAN A DUCK SWIM?
LET'S FIND THOSE TWO JOKERS,
ROAR
ULP! D-DO YOU SEE W-WHAT I SEE?
ARCH! HOLD IT UP!
ZOOM
ARCHIE! OL' PAL, OL' CHUM, OL' BUDDY! I'LL PROVIDE THE HAMMER, NAILS AND WOOD!
D-DO YOU THINK YOU COULD WORK ON MY HEAP IN YOUR SPARE TIME?
The End

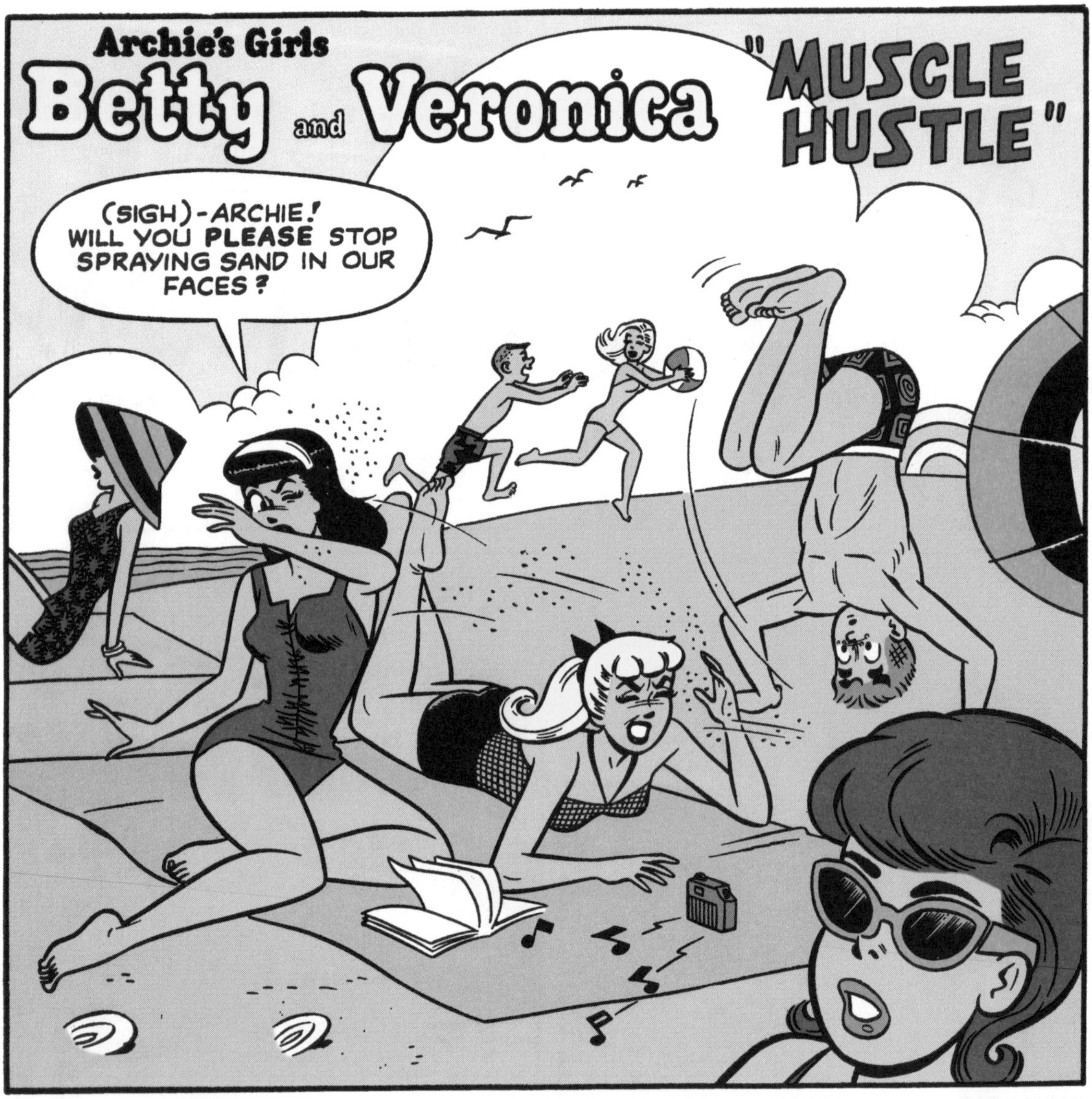
Archie's Girls
Betty and Veronica
"MUSCLE HUSTLE"
(SIGH)-ARCHIE! WILL YOU PLEASE STOP SPRAYING SAND IN OUR FACES?

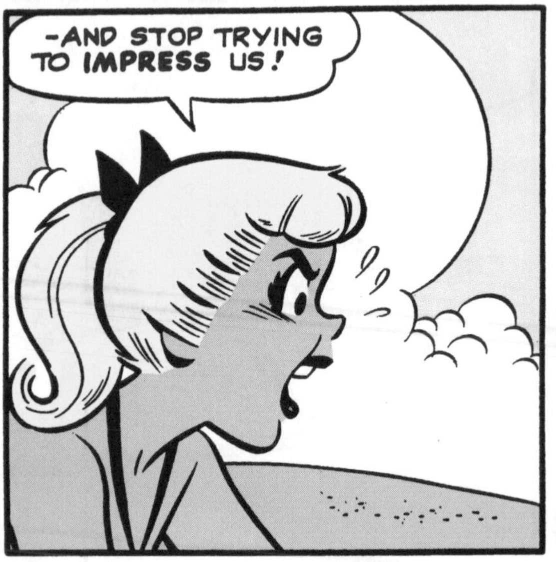
-AND STOP TRYING TO IMPRESS US!

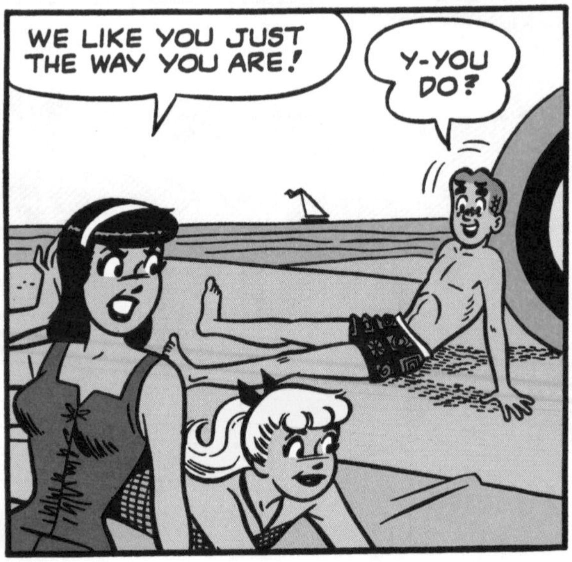
WE LIKE YOU JUST THE WAY YOU ARE!
Y-YOU DO?

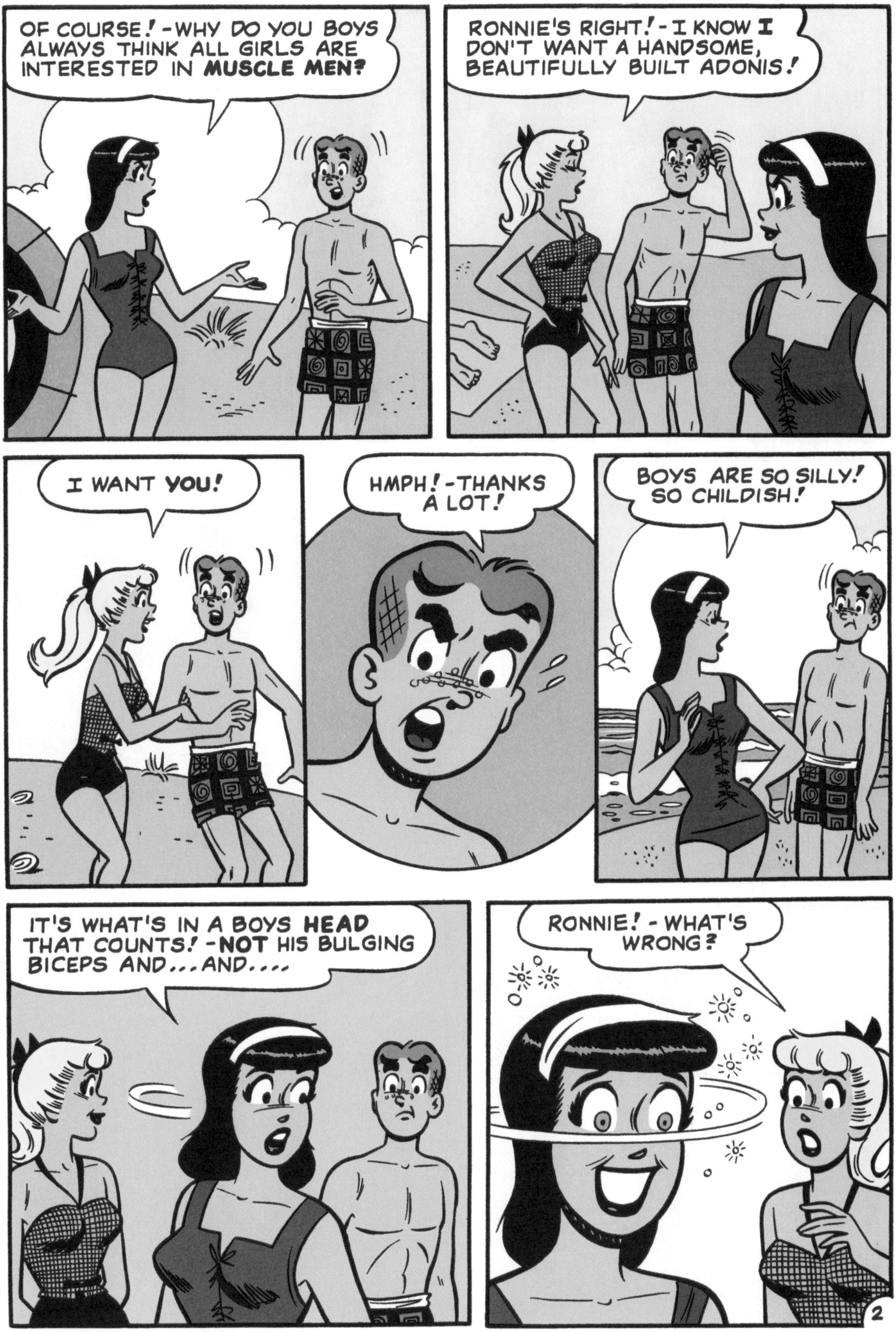
OF COURSE! -WHY DO YOU BOYS ALWAYS THINK ALL GIRLS ARE INTERESTED IN **MUSCLE MEN**?
RONNIE'S RIGHT! -I KNOW **I** DON'T WANT A HANDSOME, BEAUTIFULLY BUILT ADONIS!
I WANT **YOU**!
HMPH! -THANKS A LOT!
BOYS ARE SO SILLY! SO CHILDISH!
IT'S WHAT'S IN A BOYS **HEAD** THAT COUNTS! -**NOT** HIS BULGING BICEPS AND...AND....
RONNIE! -WHAT'S WRONG?
2

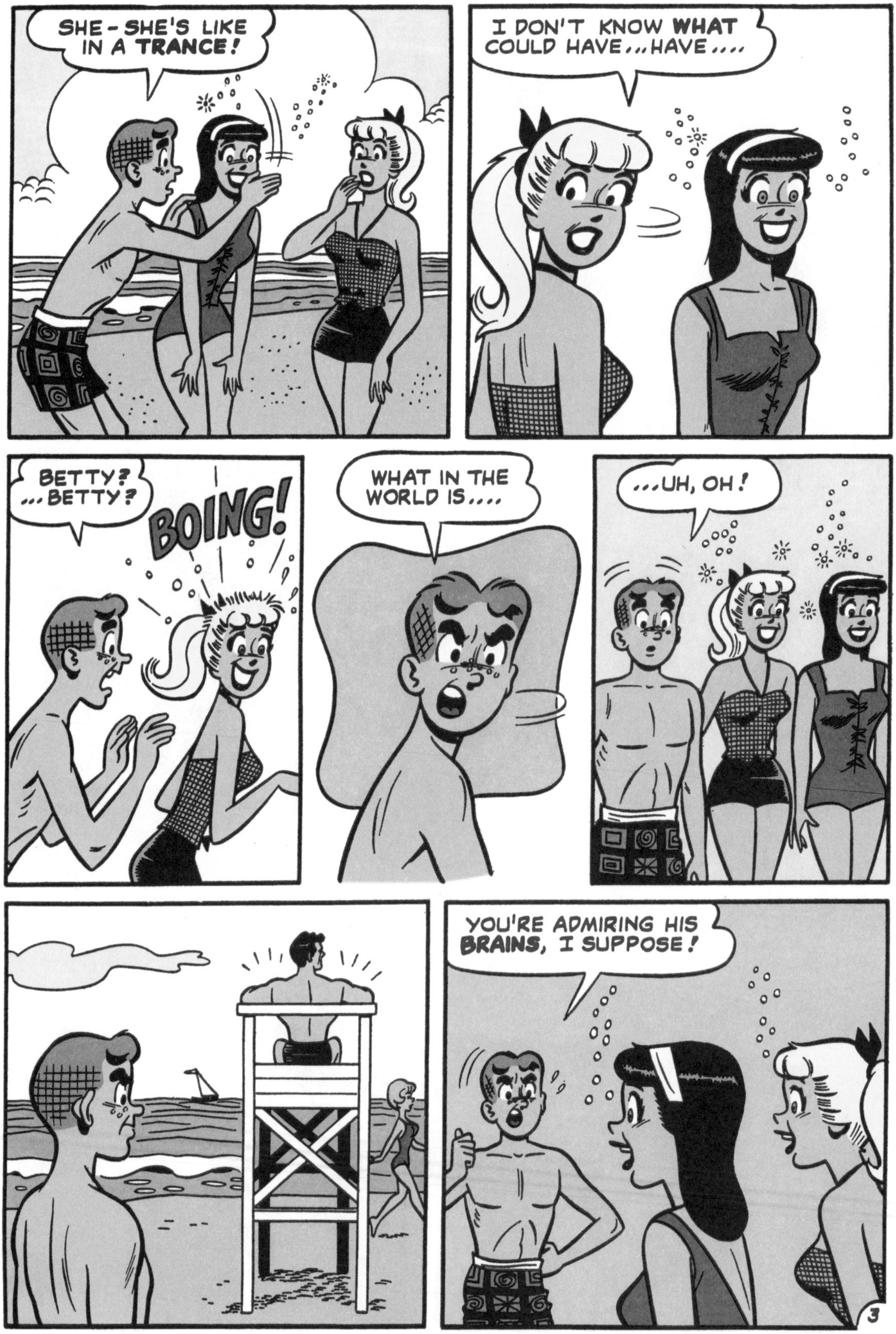
SHE - SHE'S LIKE IN A **TRANCE**!
I DON'T KNOW **WHAT** COULD HAVE... HAVE....
BETTY? ...BETTY?
BOING!
WHAT IN THE WORLD IS....
...UH, OH!
YOU'RE ADMIRING HIS **BRAINS**, I SUPPOSE!
3

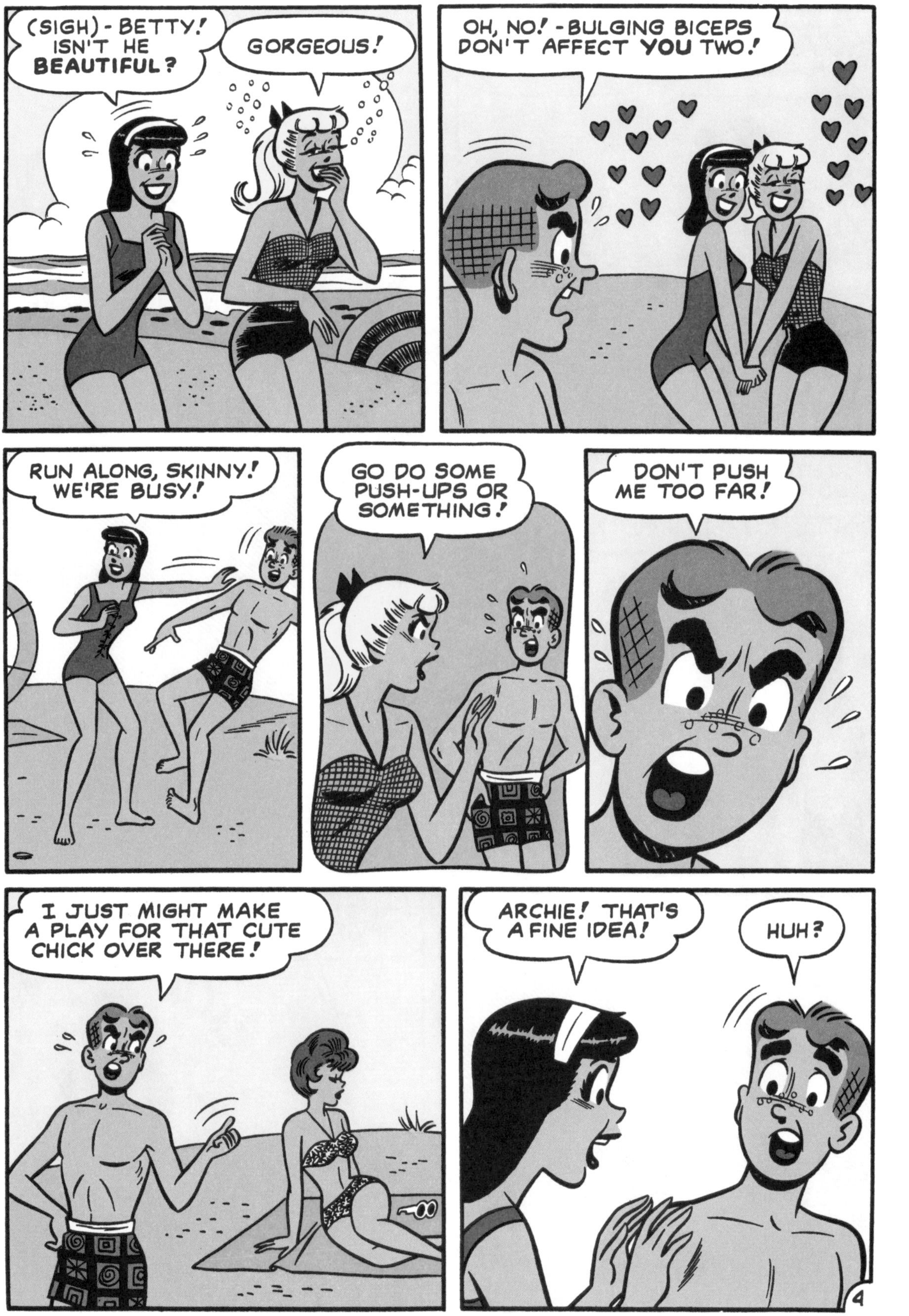
(SIGH) - BETTY! ISN'T HE BEAUTIFUL?
GORGEOUS!
OH, NO! - BULGING BICEPS DON'T AFFECT YOU TWO!
RUN ALONG, SKINNY! WE'RE BUSY!
GO DO SOME PUSH-UPS OR SOMETHING!
DON'T PUSH ME TOO FAR!
I JUST MIGHT MAKE A PLAY FOR THAT CUTE CHICK OVER THERE!
ARCHIE! THAT'S A FINE IDEA!
HUH?
4

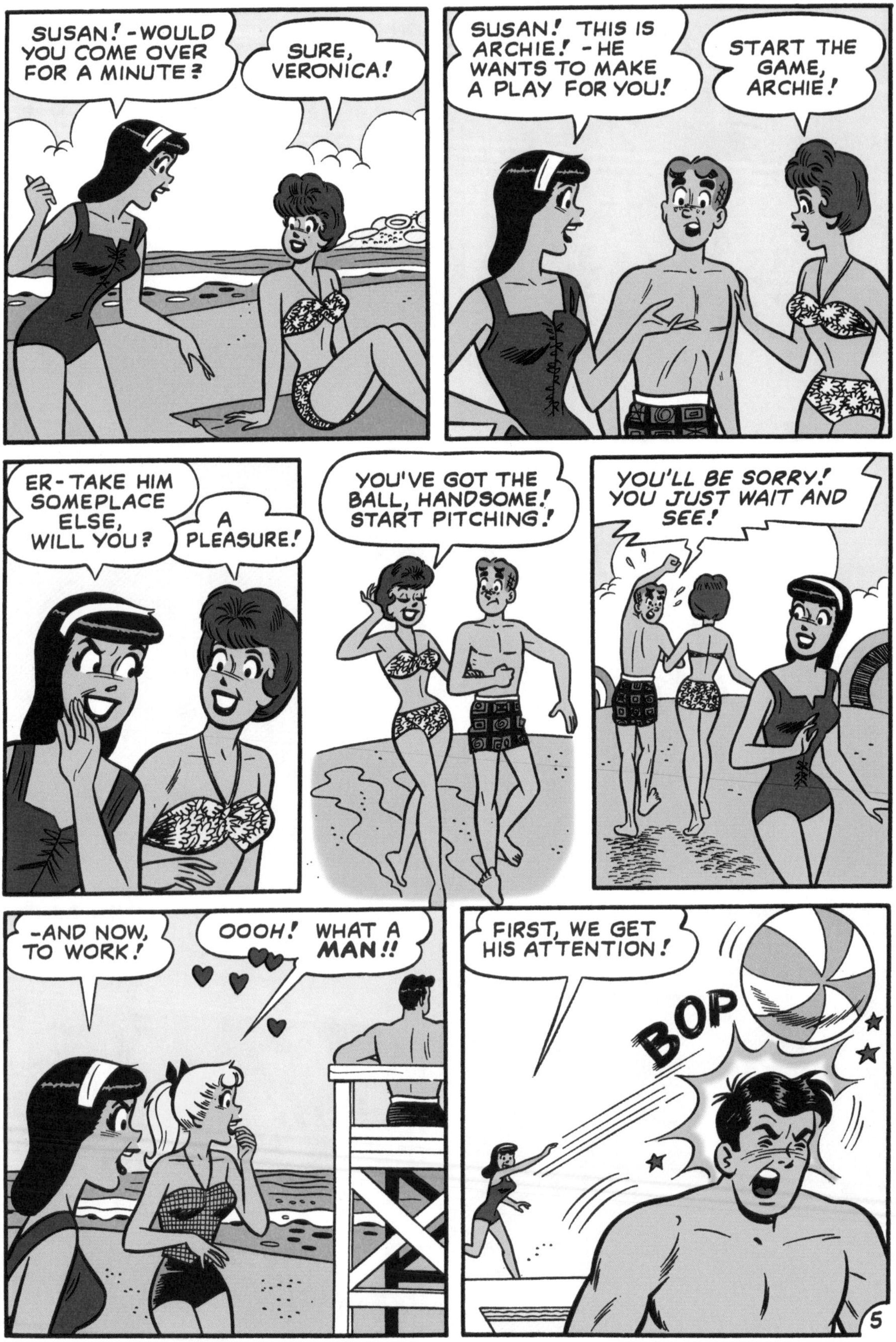
SUSAN! -WOULD YOU COME OVER FOR A MINUTE?
SURE, VERONICA!
SUSAN! THIS IS ARCHIE! -HE WANTS TO MAKE A PLAY FOR YOU!
START THE GAME, ARCHIE!
ER-TAKE HIM SOMEPLACE ELSE, WILL YOU?
A PLEASURE!
YOU'VE GOT THE BALL, HANDSOME! START PITCHING!
YOU'LL BE SORRY! YOU JUST WAIT AND SEE!
-AND NOW, TO WORK!
OOOH! WHAT A MAN!!
FIRST, WE GET HIS ATTENTION!
BOP
5

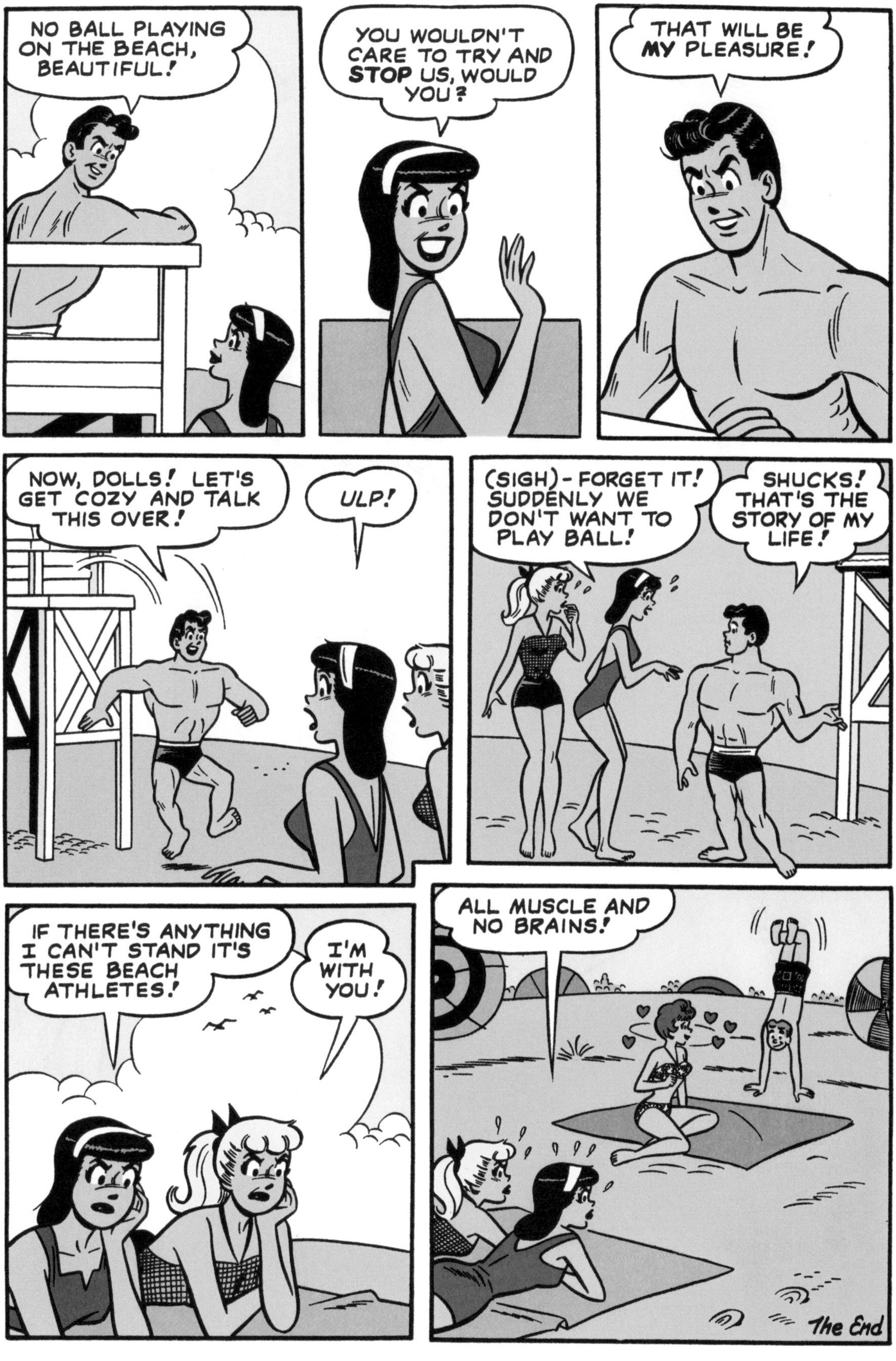
NO BALL PLAYING ON THE BEACH, BEAUTIFUL!
YOU WOULDN'T CARE TO TRY AND STOP US, WOULD YOU?
THAT WILL BE MY PLEASURE!
NOW, DOLLS! LET'S GET COZY AND TALK THIS OVER!
ULP!
(SIGH) - FORGET IT! SUDDENLY WE DON'T WANT TO PLAY BALL!
SHUCKS! THAT'S THE STORY OF MY LIFE!
IF THERE'S ANYTHING I CAN'T STAND IT'S THESE BEACH ATHLETES!
I'M WITH YOU!
ALL MUSCLE AND NO BRAINS!
The End

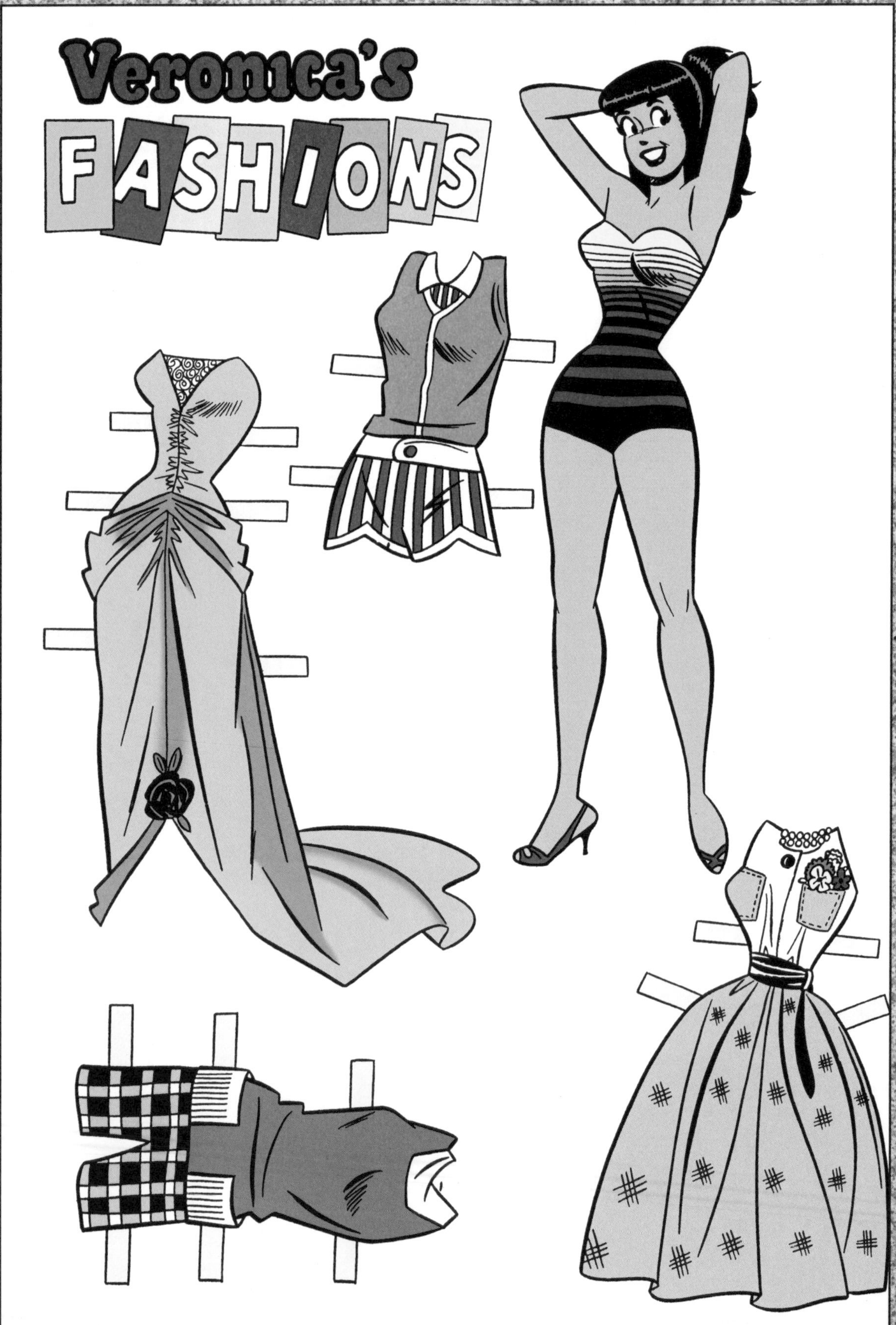
Veronica's
FASHIONS

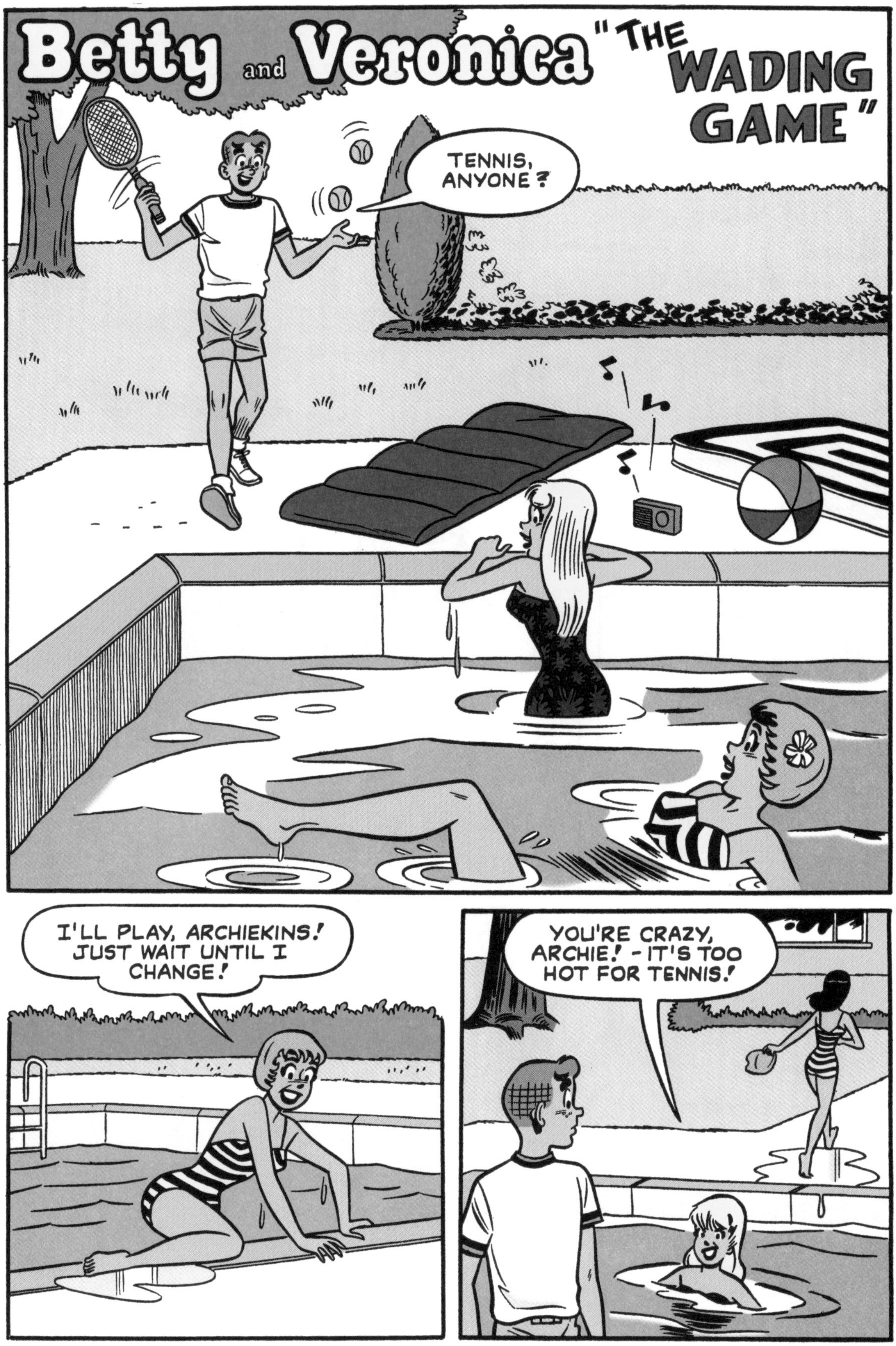

Betty and Veronica "THE WADING GAME"
TENNIS, ANYONE?
I'LL PLAY, ARCHIEKINS! JUST WAIT UNTIL I CHANGE!
YOU'RE CRAZY, ARCHIE! - IT'S TOO HOT FOR TENNIS!

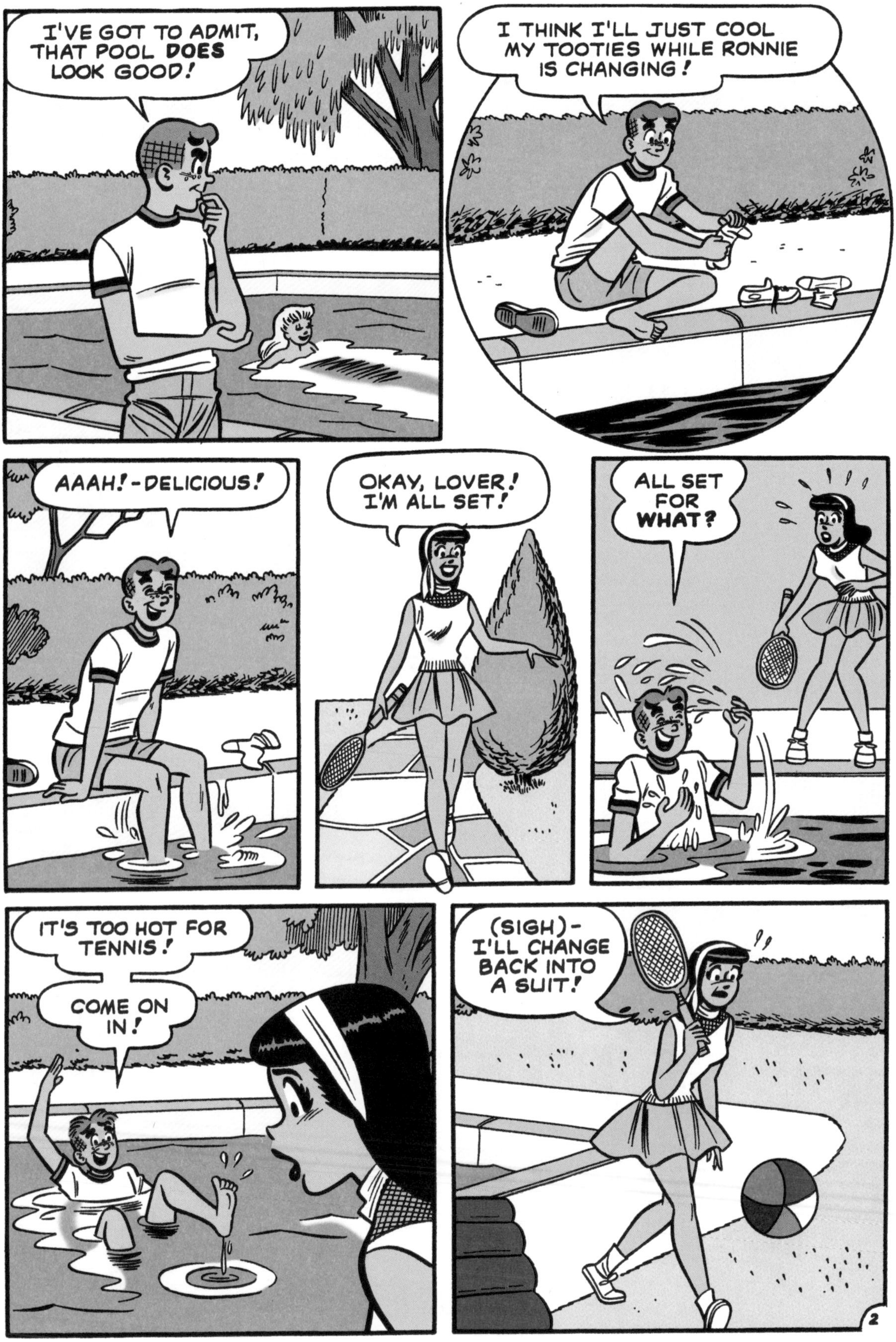
I'VE GOT TO ADMIT, THAT POOL **DOES** LOOK GOOD!
I THINK I'LL JUST COOL MY TOOTIES WHILE RONNIE IS CHANGING!
AAAH!-DELICIOUS!
OKAY, LOVER! I'M ALL SET!
ALL SET FOR **WHAT?**
IT'S TOO HOT FOR TENNIS!
COME ON IN!
(SIGH)- I'LL CHANGE BACK INTO A SUIT!
2

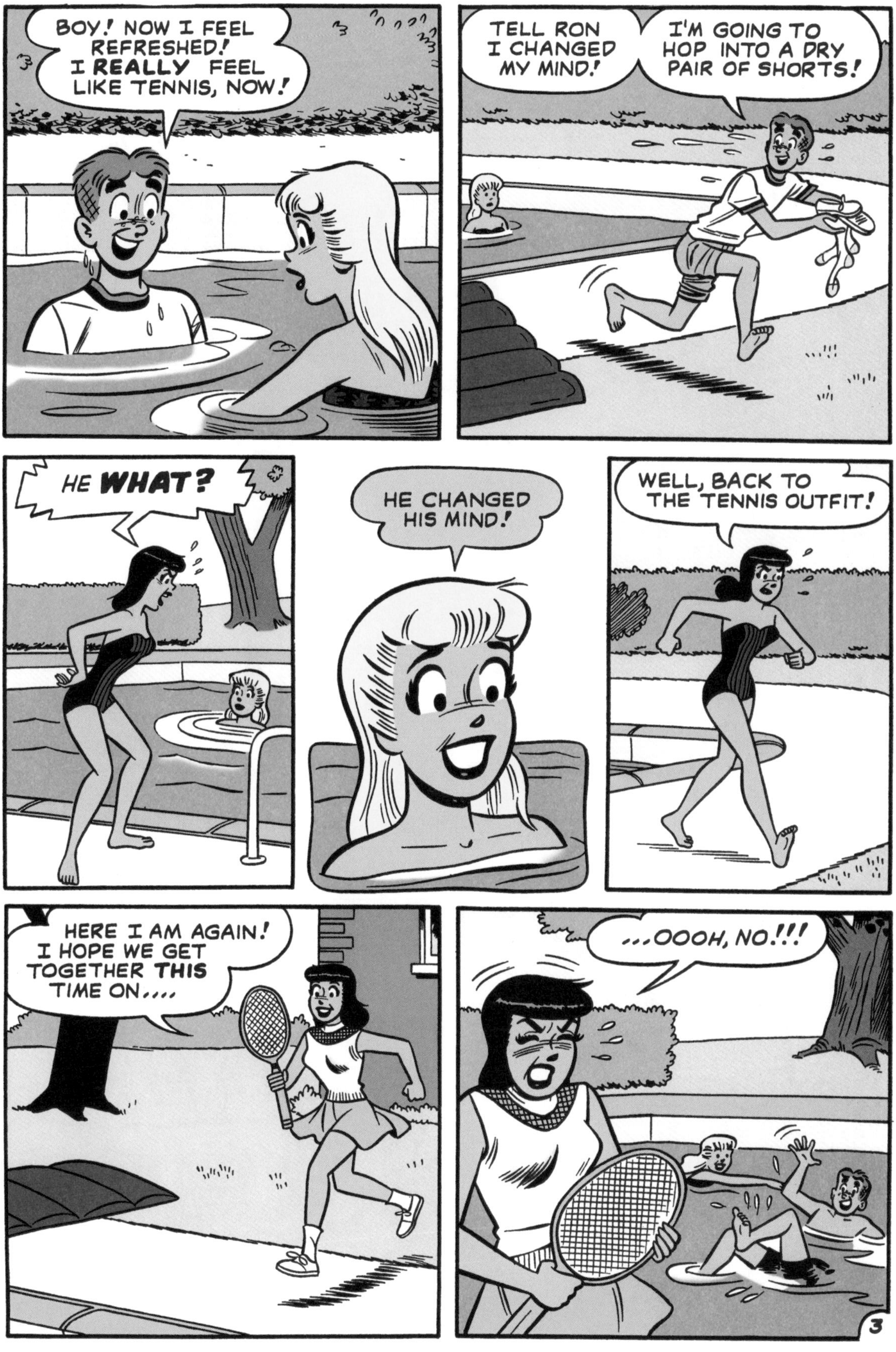
BOY! NOW I FEEL REFRESHED! I REALLY FEEL LIKE TENNIS, NOW!
TELL RON I CHANGED MY MIND!
I'M GOING TO HOP INTO A DRY PAIR OF SHORTS!
HE WHAT?
HE CHANGED HIS MIND!
WELL, BACK TO THE TENNIS OUTFIT!
HERE I AM AGAIN! I HOPE WE GET TOGETHER THIS TIME ON....
...OOOH, NO!!!
3

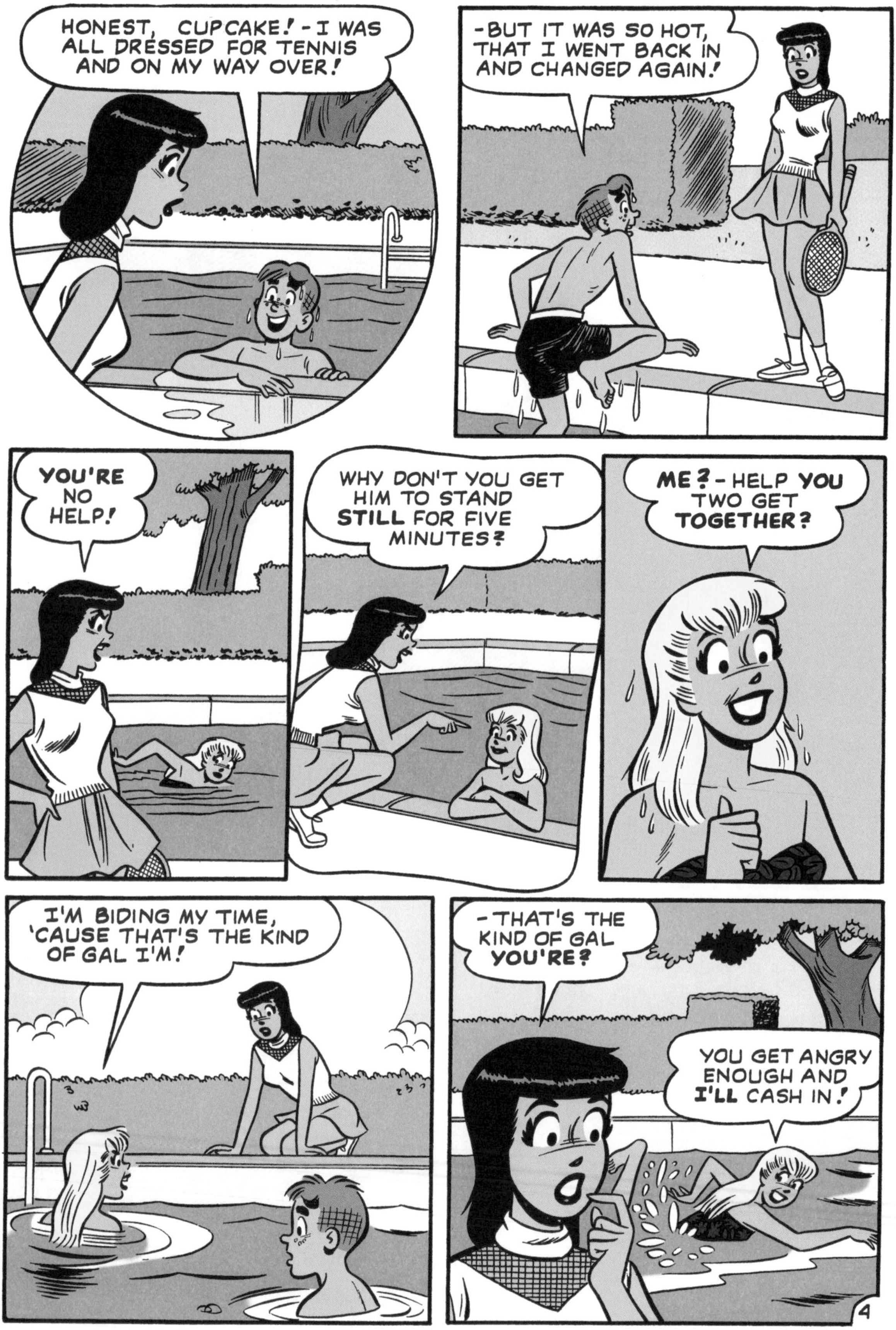
HONEST, CUPCAKE! - I WAS ALL DRESSED FOR TENNIS AND ON MY WAY OVER!
-BUT IT WAS SO HOT, THAT I WENT BACK IN AND CHANGED AGAIN!
YOU'RE NO HELP!
WHY DON'T YOU GET HIM TO STAND STILL FOR FIVE MINUTES?
ME? - HELP YOU TWO GET TOGETHER?
I'M BIDING MY TIME, 'CAUSE THAT'S THE KIND OF GAL I'M!
-THAT'S THE KIND OF GAL YOU'RE?
YOU GET ANGRY ENOUGH AND I'LL CASH IN!
4

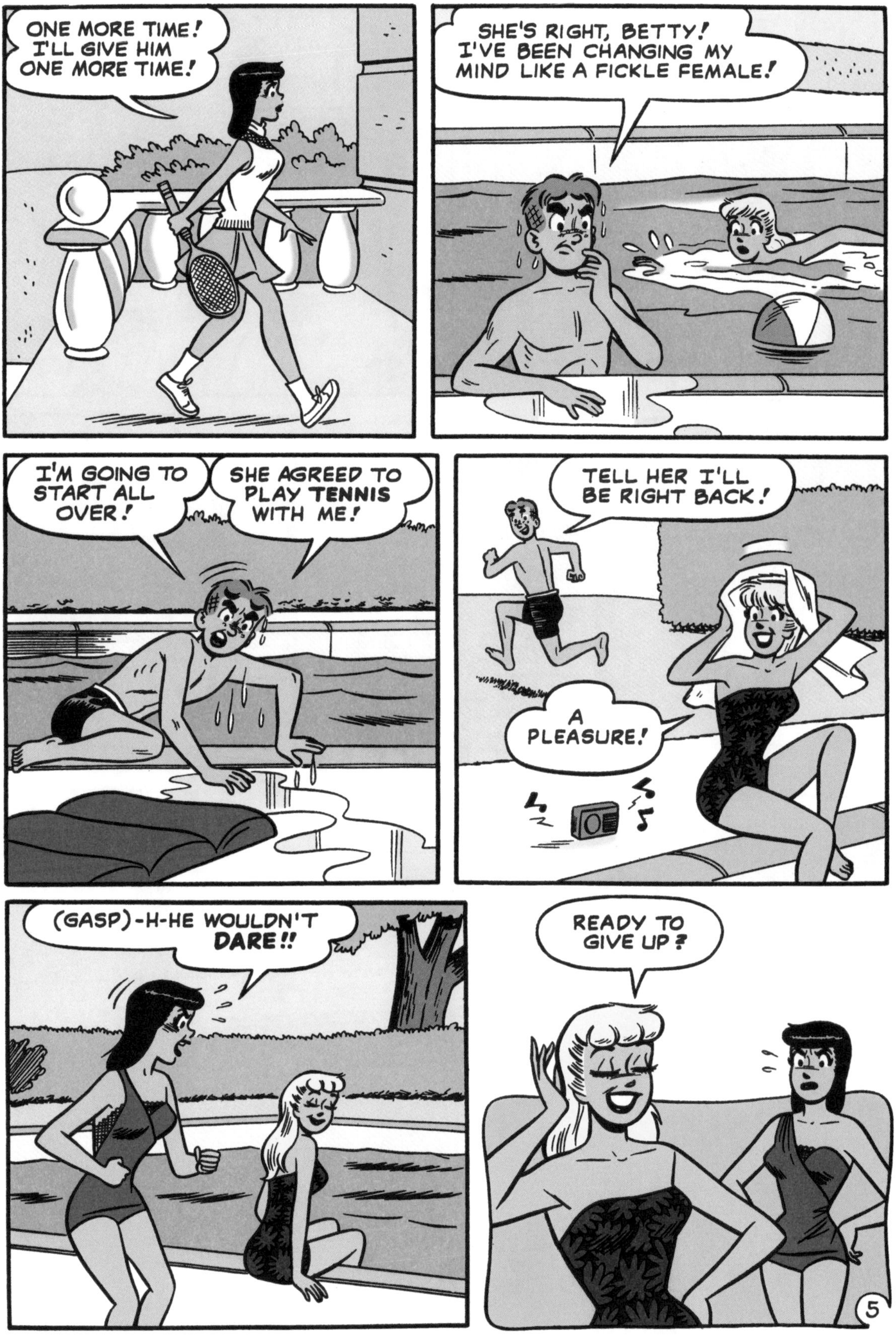
ONE MORE TIME! I'LL GIVE HIM ONE MORE TIME!
SHE'S RIGHT, BETTY! I'VE BEEN CHANGING MY MIND LIKE A FICKLE FEMALE!
I'M GOING TO START ALL OVER!
SHE AGREED TO PLAY TENNIS WITH ME!
TELL HER I'LL BE RIGHT BACK!
A PLEASURE!
(GASP)-H-HE WOULDN'T DARE!!
READY TO GIVE UP?
5

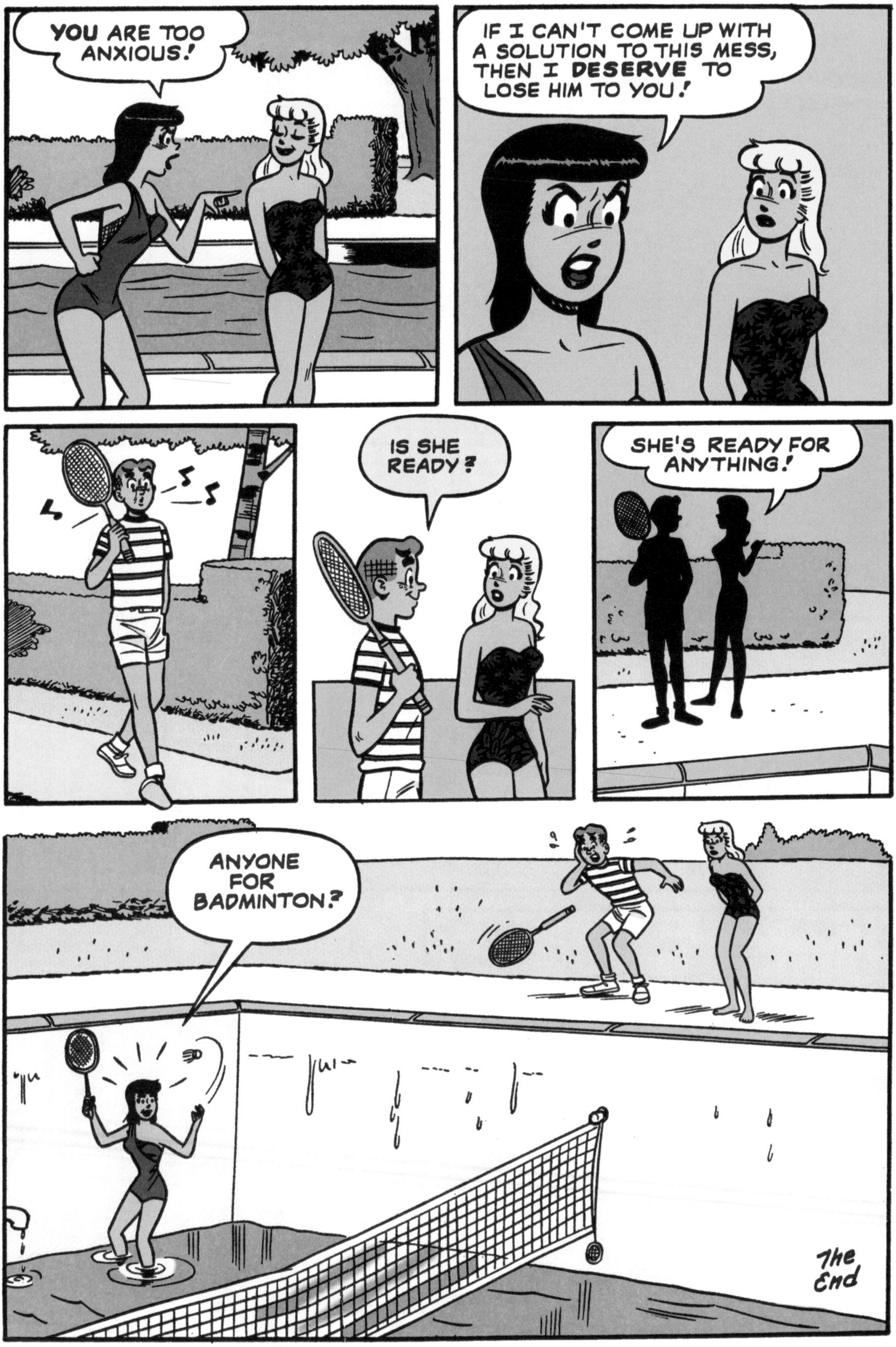
YOU ARE TOO ANXIOUS!
IF I CAN'T COME UP WITH A SOLUTION TO THIS MESS, THEN I DESERVE TO LOSE HIM TO YOU!
IS SHE READY?
SHE'S READY FOR ANYTHING!
ANYONE FOR BADMINTON?
The End

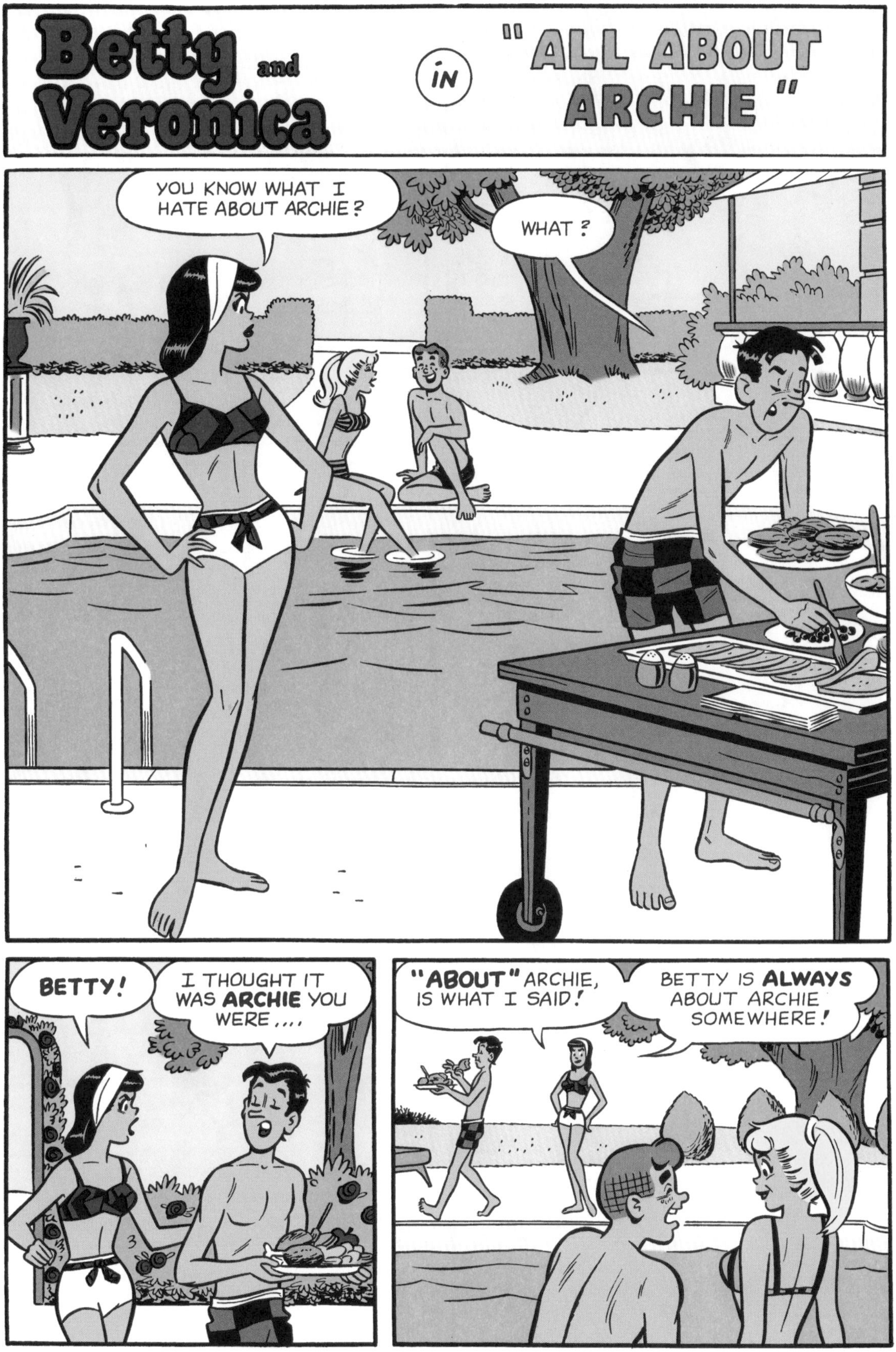
Betty and Veronica
IN
"ALL ABOUT ARCHIE"
YOU KNOW WHAT I HATE ABOUT ARCHIE?
WHAT?
BETTY!
I THOUGHT IT WAS ARCHIE YOU WERE....
"ABOUT" ARCHIE, IS WHAT I SAID!
BETTY IS ALWAYS ABOUT ARCHIE SOMEWHERE!

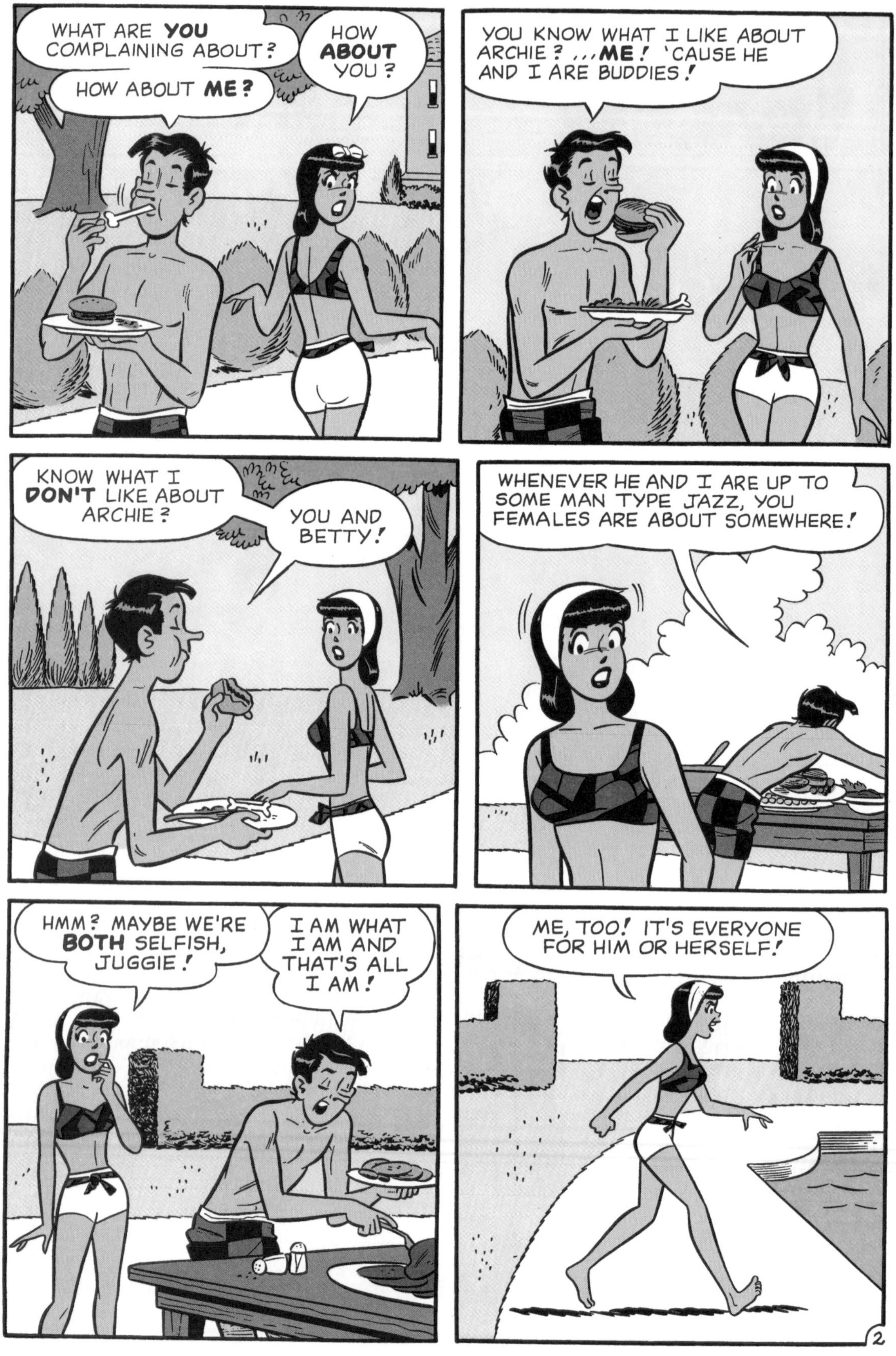
WHAT ARE YOU COMPLAINING ABOUT?
HOW ABOUT ME?
HOW ABOUT YOU?
YOU KNOW WHAT I LIKE ABOUT ARCHIE? ...ME! 'CAUSE HE AND I ARE BUDDIES!
KNOW WHAT I DON'T LIKE ABOUT ARCHIE?
YOU AND BETTY!
WHENEVER HE AND I ARE UP TO SOME MAN TYPE JAZZ, YOU FEMALES ARE ABOUT SOMEWHERE!
HMM? MAYBE WE'RE BOTH SELFISH, JUGGIE!
I AM WHAT I AM AND THAT'S ALL I AM!
ME, TOO! IT'S EVERYONE FOR HIM OR HERSELF!
2

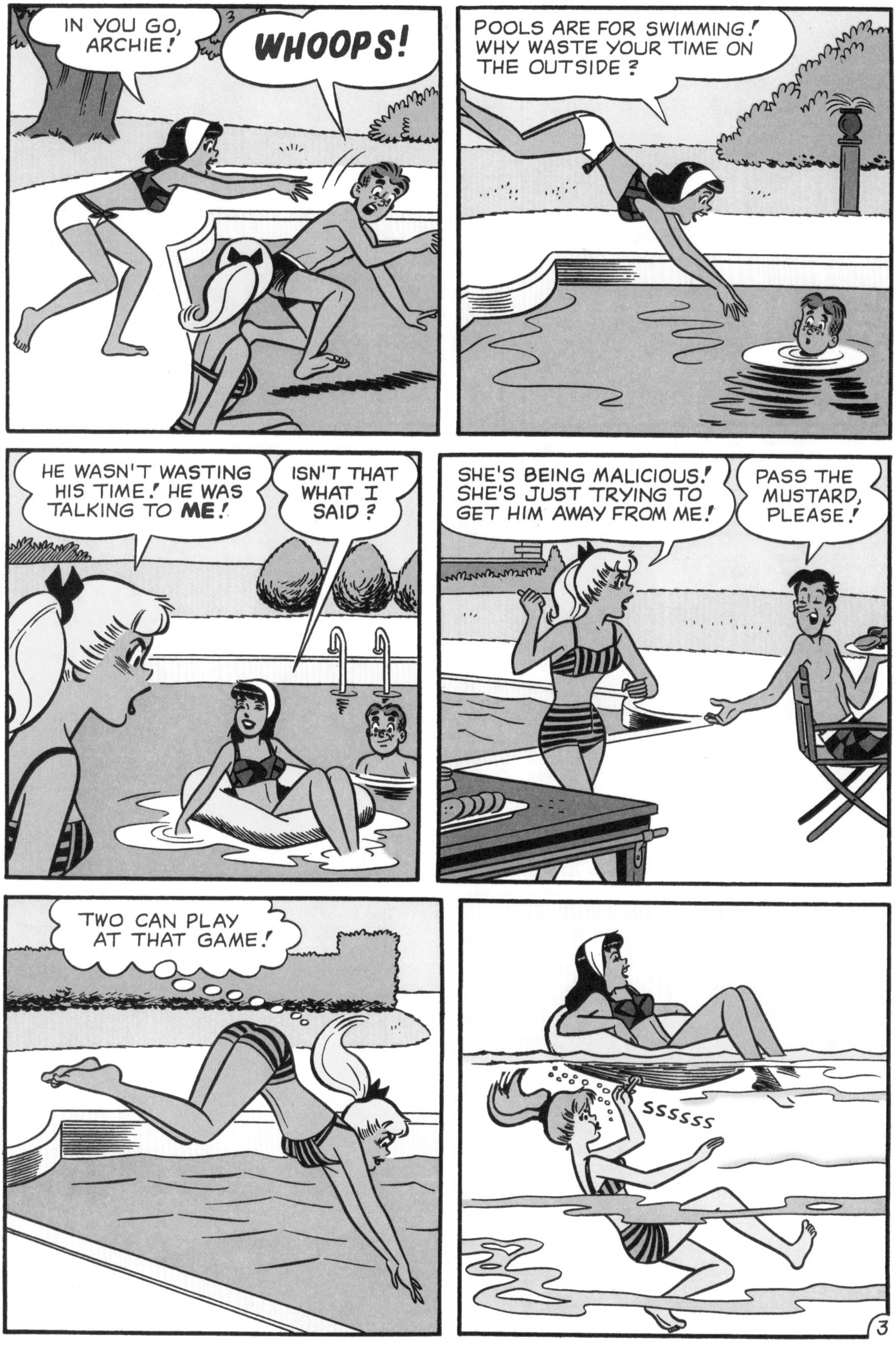
IN YOU GO, ARCHIE!
WHOOPS!
POOLS ARE FOR SWIMMING! WHY WASTE YOUR TIME ON THE OUTSIDE?
HE WASN'T WASTING HIS TIME! HE WAS TALKING TO **ME**!
ISN'T THAT WHAT I SAID?
SHE'S BEING MALICIOUS! SHE'S JUST TRYING TO GET HIM AWAY FROM ME!
PASS THE MUSTARD, PLEASE!
TWO CAN PLAY AT THAT GAME!
SSSSSS
3

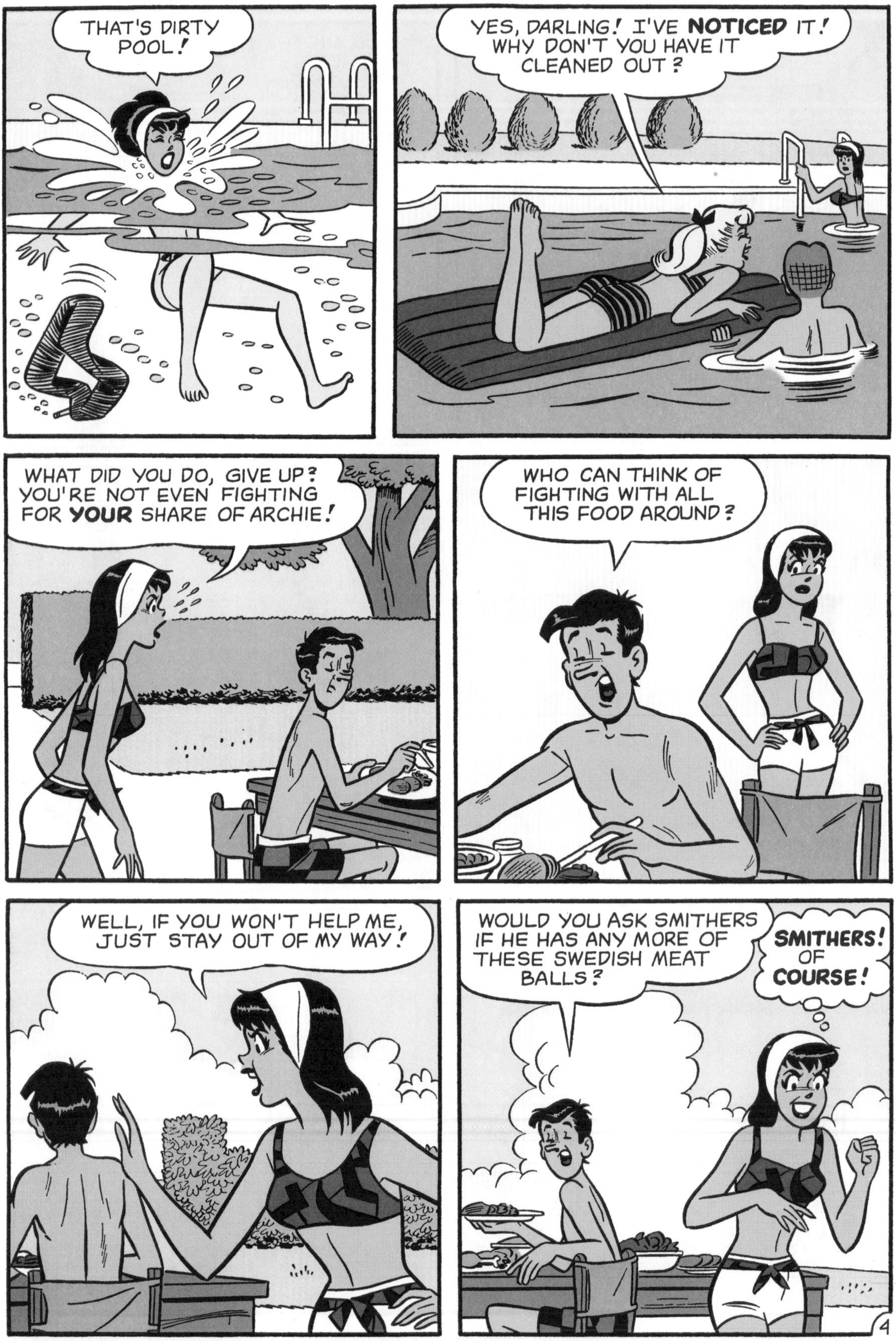
THAT'S DIRTY POOL!
YES, DARLING! I'VE **NOTICED** IT! WHY DON'T YOU HAVE IT CLEANED OUT?
WHAT DID YOU DO, GIVE UP? YOU'RE NOT EVEN FIGHTING FOR **YOUR** SHARE OF ARCHIE!
WHO CAN THINK OF FIGHTING WITH ALL THIS FOOD AROUND?
WELL, IF YOU WON'T HELP ME, JUST STAY OUT OF MY WAY!
WOULD YOU ASK SMITHERS IF HE HAS ANY MORE OF THESE SWEDISH MEAT BALLS?
SMITHERS! OF **COURSE!**
4

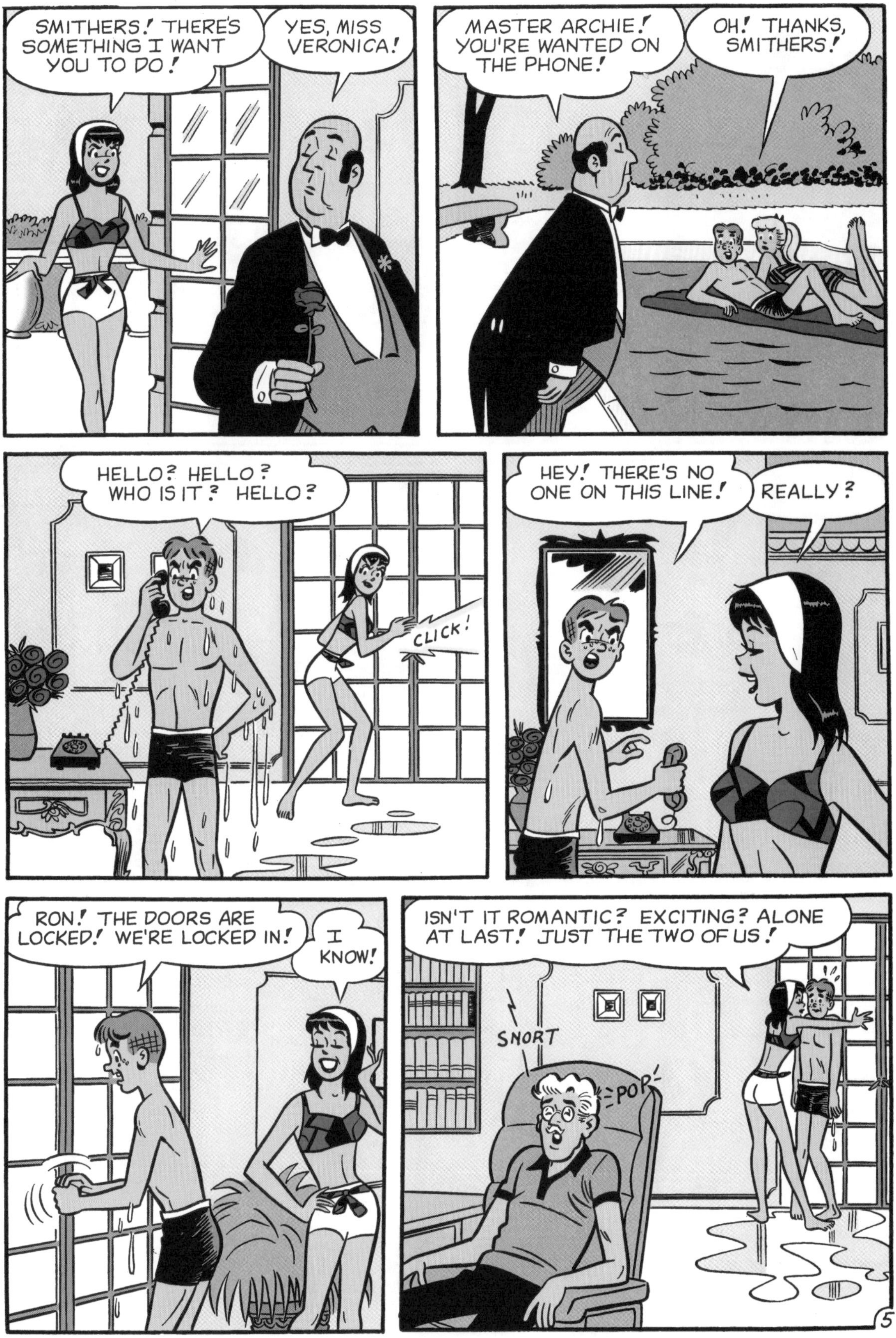
SMITHERS! THERE'S SOMETHING I WANT YOU TO DO!
YES, MISS VERONICA!
MASTER ARCHIE! YOU'RE WANTED ON THE PHONE!
OH! THANKS, SMITHERS!
HELLO? HELLO? WHO IS IT? HELLO?
CLICK!
HEY! THERE'S NO ONE ON THIS LINE!
REALLY?
RON! THE DOORS ARE LOCKED! WE'RE LOCKED IN!
I KNOW!
ISN'T IT ROMANTIC? EXCITING? ALONE AT LAST! JUST THE TWO OF US!
SNORT
POP
5

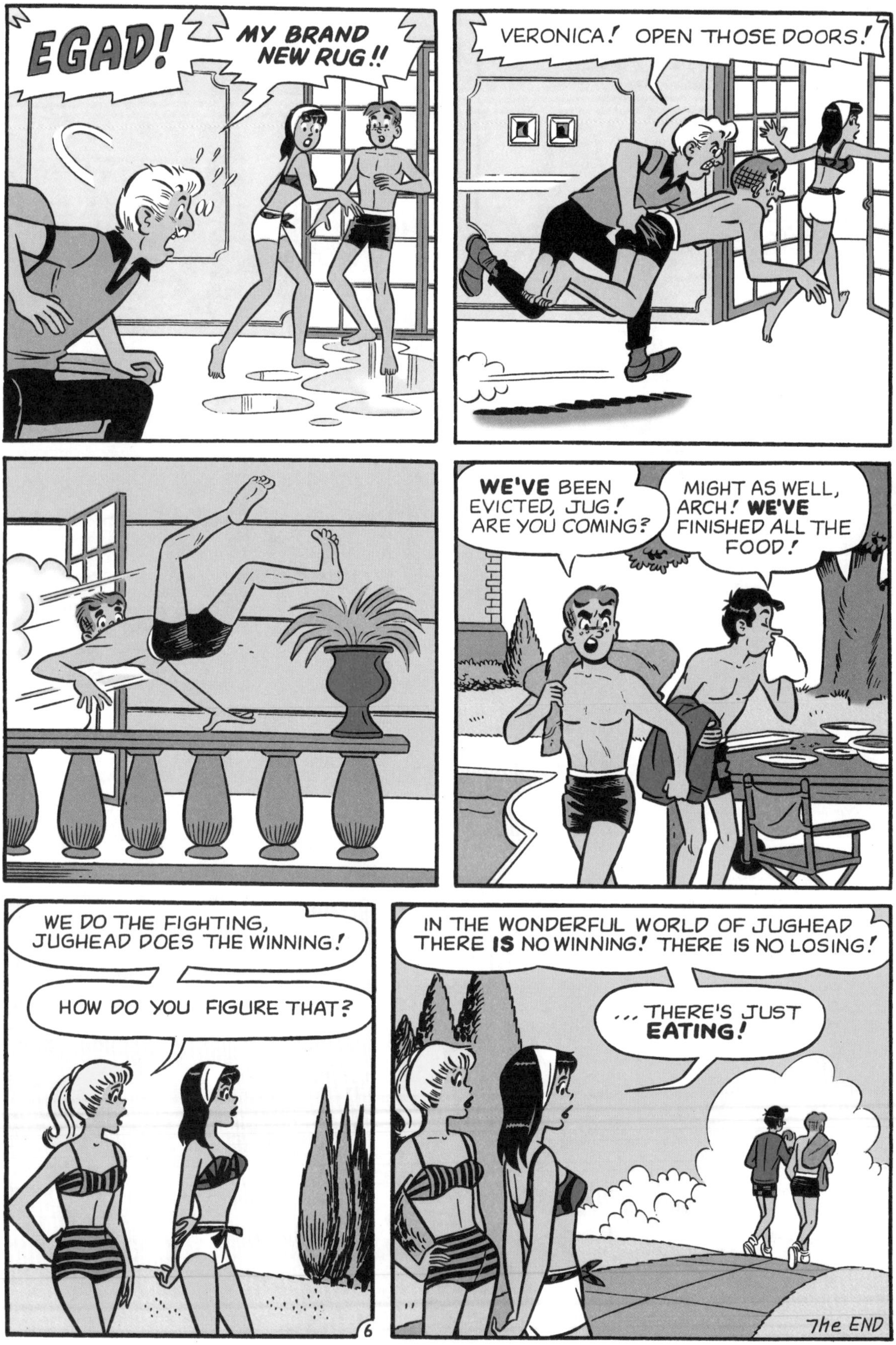
EGAD!
MY BRAND NEW RUG!!
VERONICA! OPEN THOSE DOORS!
WE'VE BEEN EVICTED, JUG! ARE YOU COMING?
MIGHT AS WELL, ARCH! WE'VE FINISHED ALL THE FOOD!
WE DO THE FIGHTING, JUGHEAD DOES THE WINNING!
HOW DO YOU FIGURE THAT?
6
IN THE WONDERFUL WORLD OF JUGHEAD THERE IS NO WINNING! THERE IS NO LOSING!
... THERE'S JUST EATING!
The END

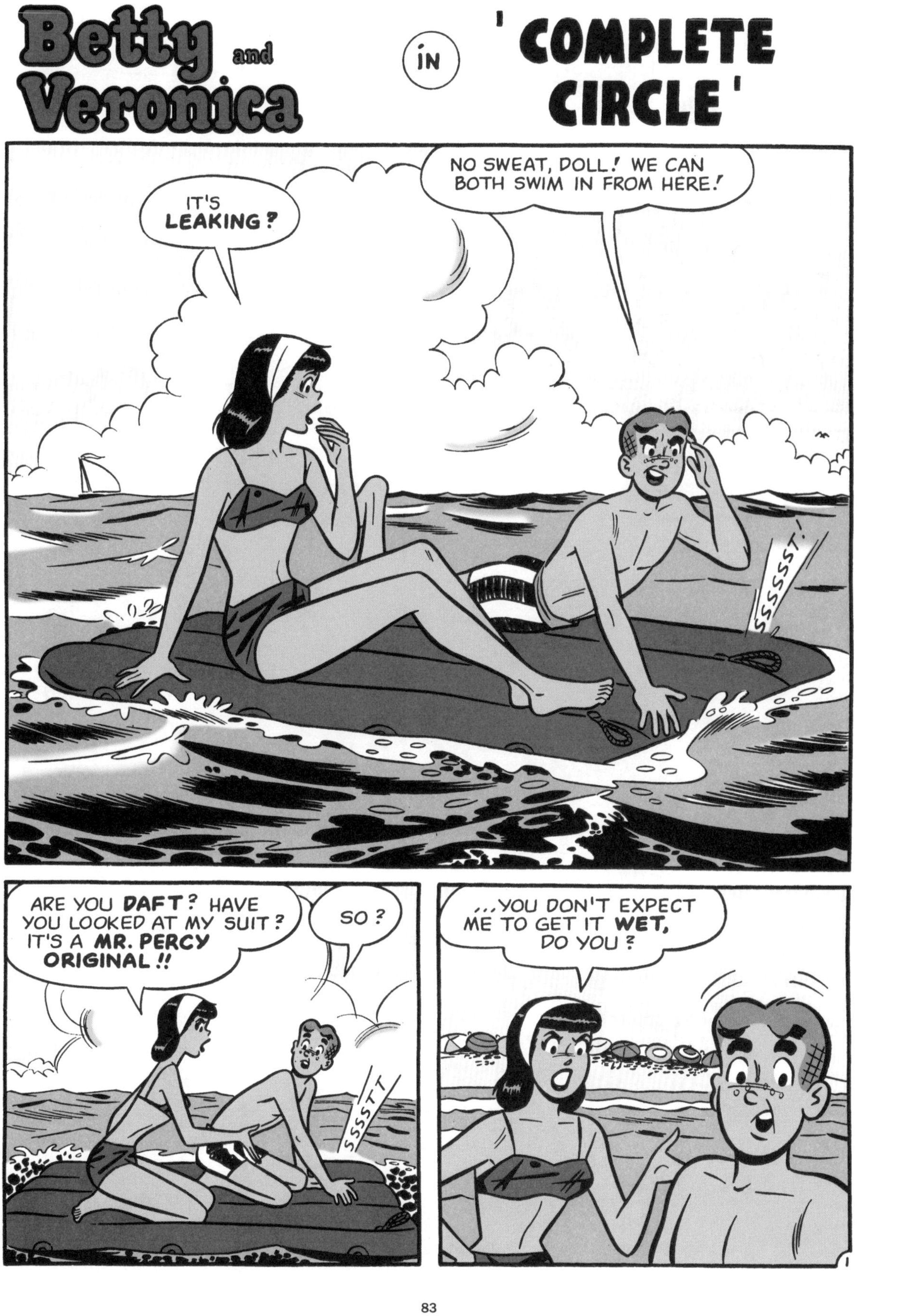
Betty and Veronica
IN
'COMPLETE CIRCLE'
IT'S LEAKING?
NO SWEAT, DOLL! WE CAN BOTH SWIM IN FROM HERE!
SSSSSST!
ARE YOU DAFT? HAVE YOU LOOKED AT MY SUIT? IT'S A MR. PERCY ORIGINAL!!
SO?
SSSSTT
...YOU DON'T EXPECT ME TO GET IT WET, DO YOU?

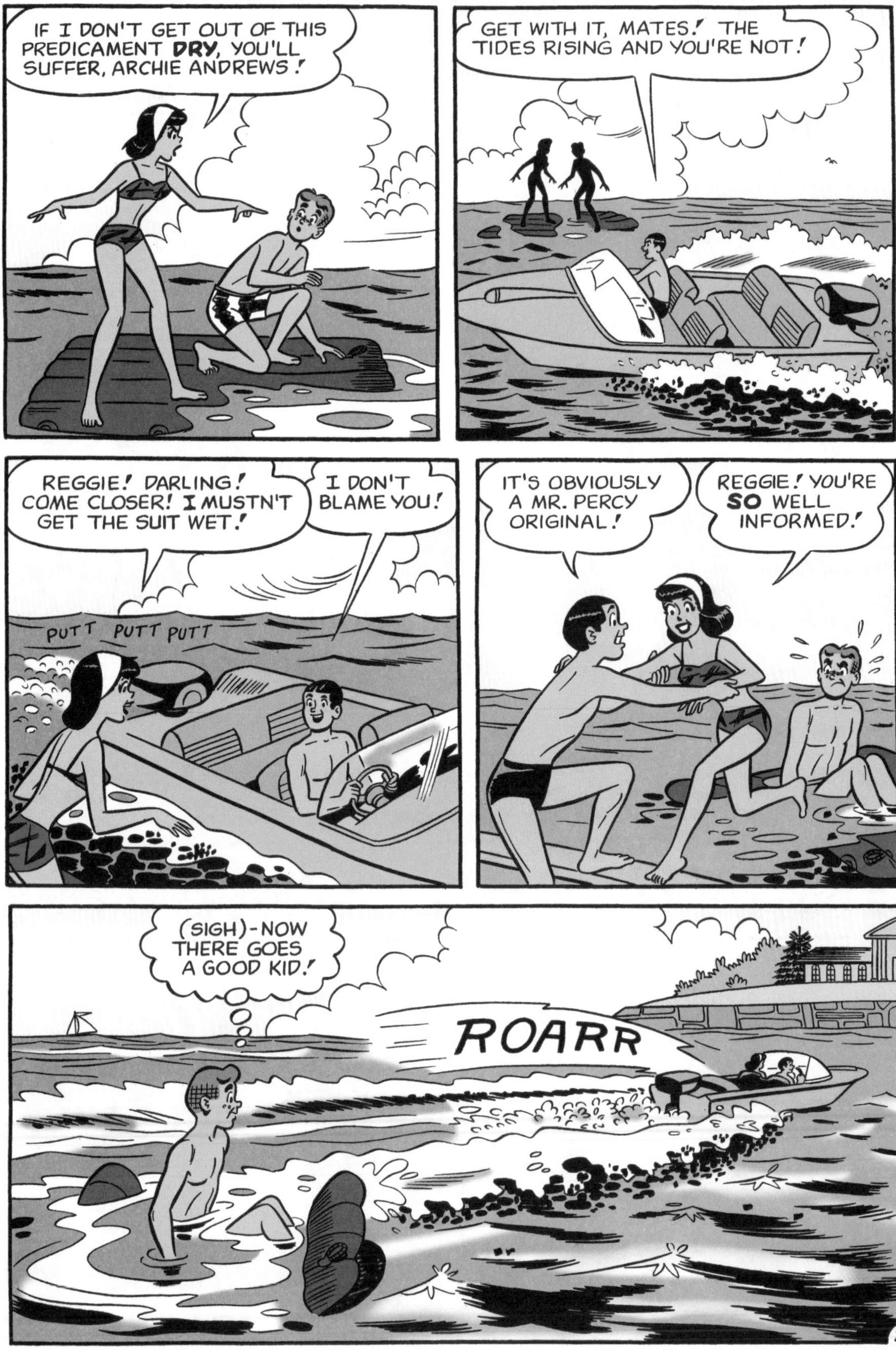
IF I DON'T GET OUT OF THIS PREDICAMENT **DRY**, YOU'LL SUFFER, ARCHIE ANDREWS!
GET WITH IT, MATES! THE TIDES RISING AND YOU'RE NOT!
REGGIE! DARLING! COME CLOSER! I MUSTN'T GET THE SUIT WET!
I DON'T BLAME YOU!
PUTT PUTT PUTT
IT'S OBVIOUSLY A MR. PERCY ORIGINAL!
REGGIE! YOU'RE **SO** WELL INFORMED!
(SIGH)-NOW THERE GOES A GOOD KID!
ROARR
2

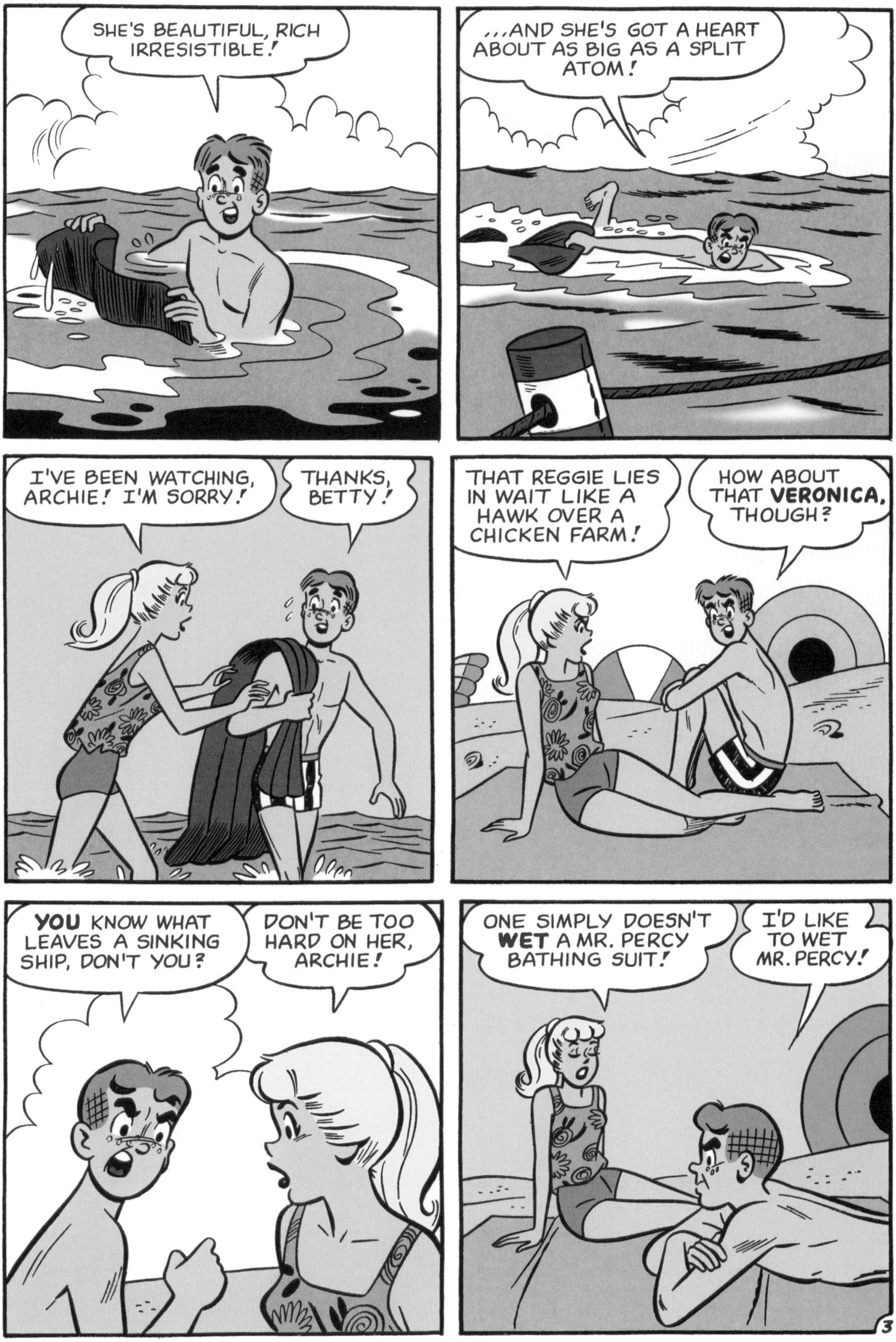
SHE'S BEAUTIFUL, RICH IRRESISTIBLE!
...AND SHE'S GOT A HEART ABOUT AS BIG AS A SPLIT ATOM!
I'VE BEEN WATCHING, ARCHIE! I'M SORRY!
THANKS, BETTY!
THAT REGGIE LIES IN WAIT LIKE A HAWK OVER A CHICKEN FARM!
HOW ABOUT THAT VERONICA, THOUGH?
YOU KNOW WHAT LEAVES A SINKING SHIP, DON'T YOU?
DON'T BE TOO HARD ON HER, ARCHIE!
ONE SIMPLY DOESN'T WET A MR. PERCY BATHING SUIT!
I'D LIKE TO WET MR. PERCY!
3

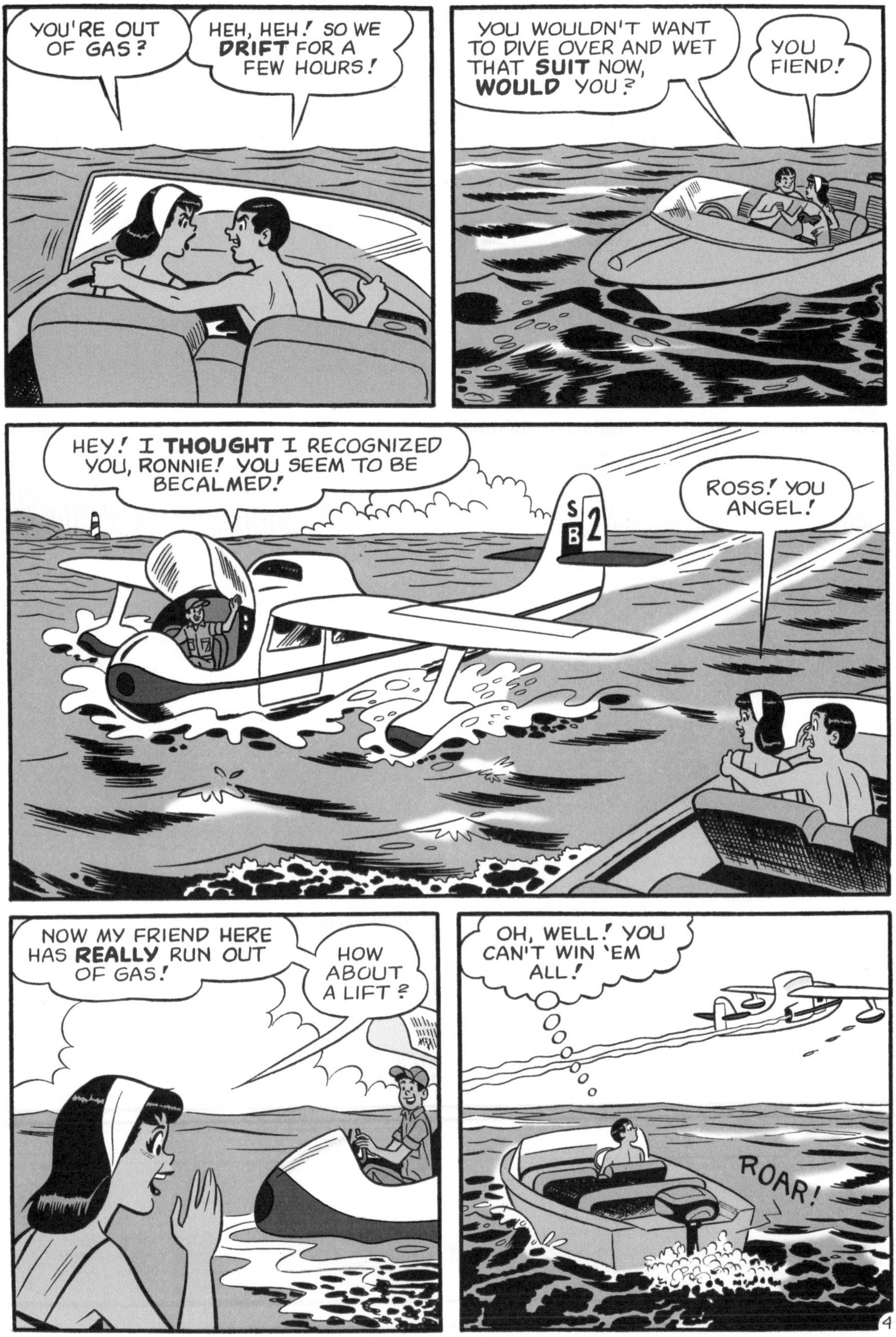
YOU'RE OUT OF GAS?
HEH, HEH! SO WE DRIFT FOR A FEW HOURS!
YOU WOULDN'T WANT TO DIVE OVER AND WET THAT SUIT NOW, WOULD YOU?
YOU FIEND!
HEY! I THOUGHT I RECOGNIZED YOU, RONNIE! YOU SEEM TO BE BECALMED!
S B 2
ROSS! YOU ANGEL!
NOW MY FRIEND HERE HAS REALLY RUN OUT OF GAS!
HOW ABOUT A LIFT?
OH, WELL! YOU CAN'T WIN 'EM ALL!
ROAR!
4

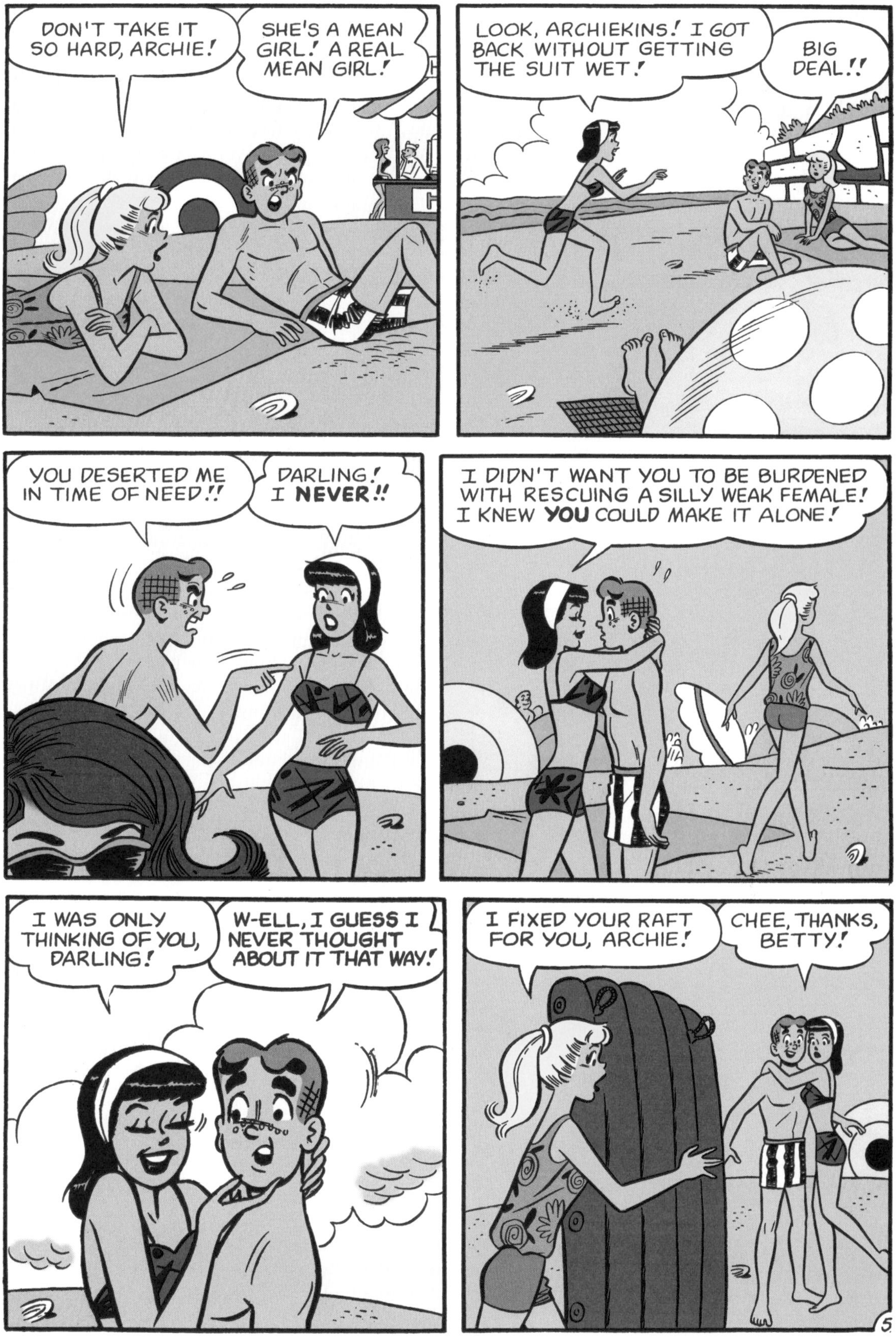
DON'T TAKE IT SO HARD, ARCHIE!
SHE'S A MEAN GIRL! A REAL MEAN GIRL!
LOOK, ARCHIEKINS! I GOT BACK WITHOUT GETTING THE SUIT WET!
BIG DEAL!!
YOU DESERTED ME IN TIME OF NEED!!
DARLING! I **NEVER**!!
I DIDN'T WANT YOU TO BE BURDENED WITH RESCUING A SILLY WEAK FEMALE! I KNEW **YOU** COULD MAKE IT ALONE!
I WAS ONLY THINKING OF YOU, DARLING!
W-ELL, I GUESS I NEVER THOUGHT ABOUT IT THAT WAY!
I FIXED YOUR RAFT FOR YOU, ARCHIE!
CHEE, THANKS, BETTY!
5

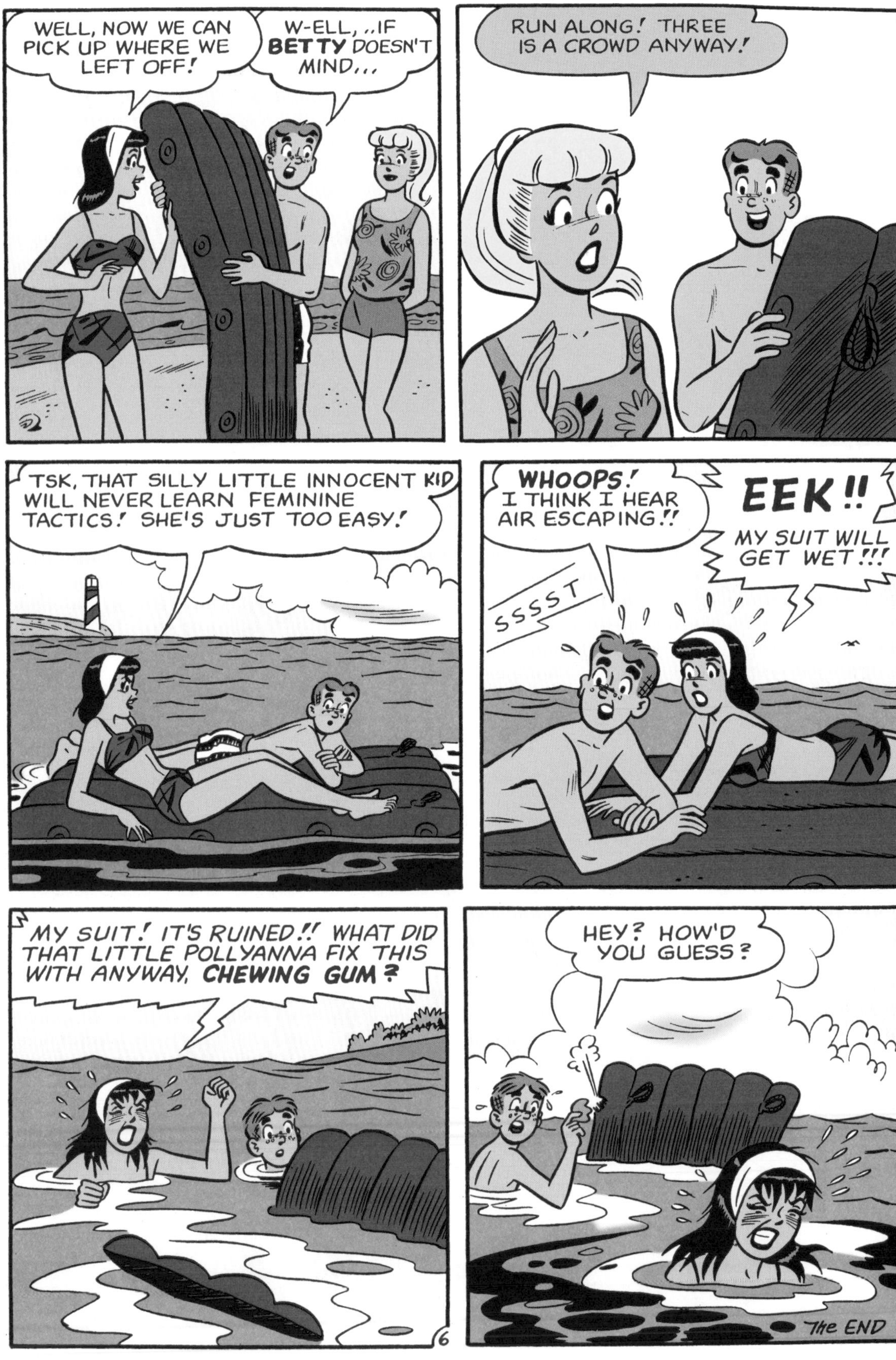
WELL, NOW WE CAN PICK UP WHERE WE LEFT OFF!
W-ELL, ..IF **BETTY** DOESN'T MIND...
RUN ALONG! THREE IS A CROWD ANYWAY!
TSK, THAT SILLY LITTLE INNOCENT KID WILL NEVER LEARN FEMININE TACTICS! SHE'S JUST TOO EASY!
WHOOPS! I THINK I HEAR AIR ESCAPING!!
SSSST
EEK!! MY SUIT WILL GET WET!!!
MY SUIT! IT'S RUINED!! WHAT DID THAT LITTLE POLLYANNA FIX THIS WITH ANYWAY, **CHEWING GUM?**
6
HEY? HOW'D YOU GUESS?
The END

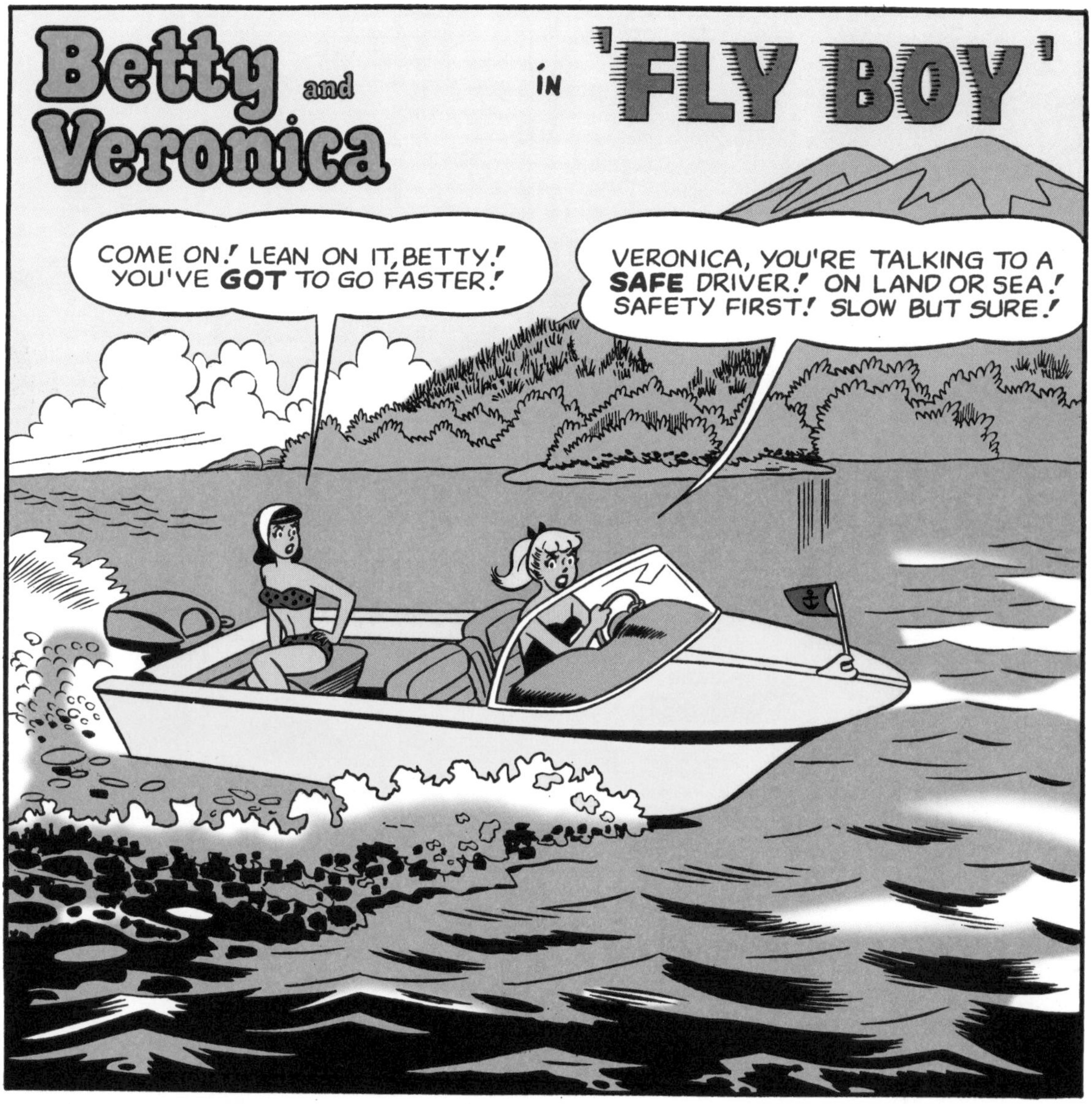
Betty and Veronica in 'FLY BOY'
COME ON! LEAN ON IT, BETTY! YOU'VE GOT TO GO FASTER!
VERONICA, YOU'RE TALKING TO A SAFE DRIVER! ON LAND OR SEA! SAFETY FIRST! SLOW BUT SURE!

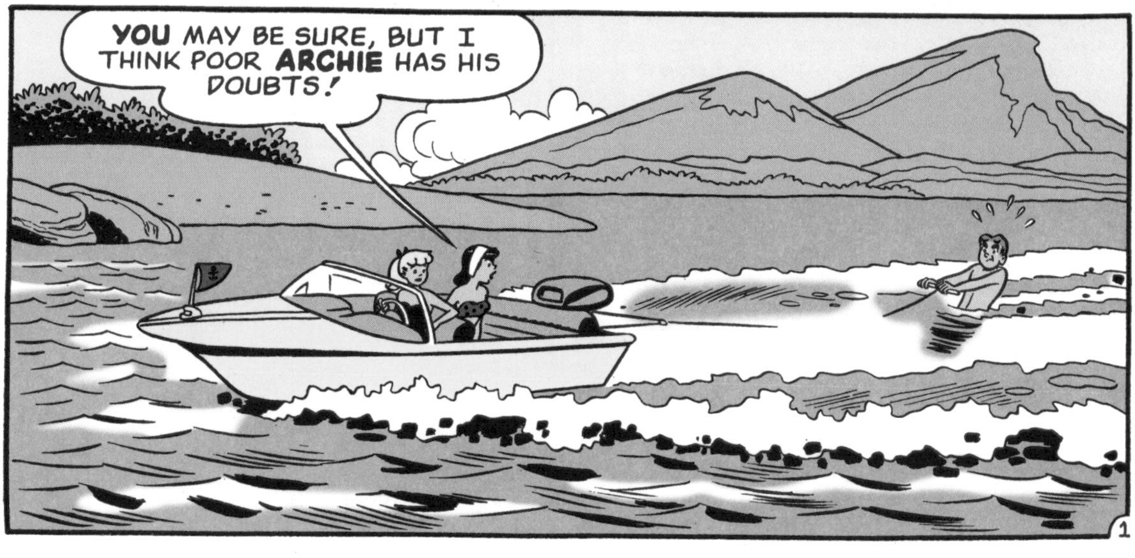
YOU MAY BE SURE, BUT I THINK POOR ARCHIE HAS HIS DOUBTS!
1

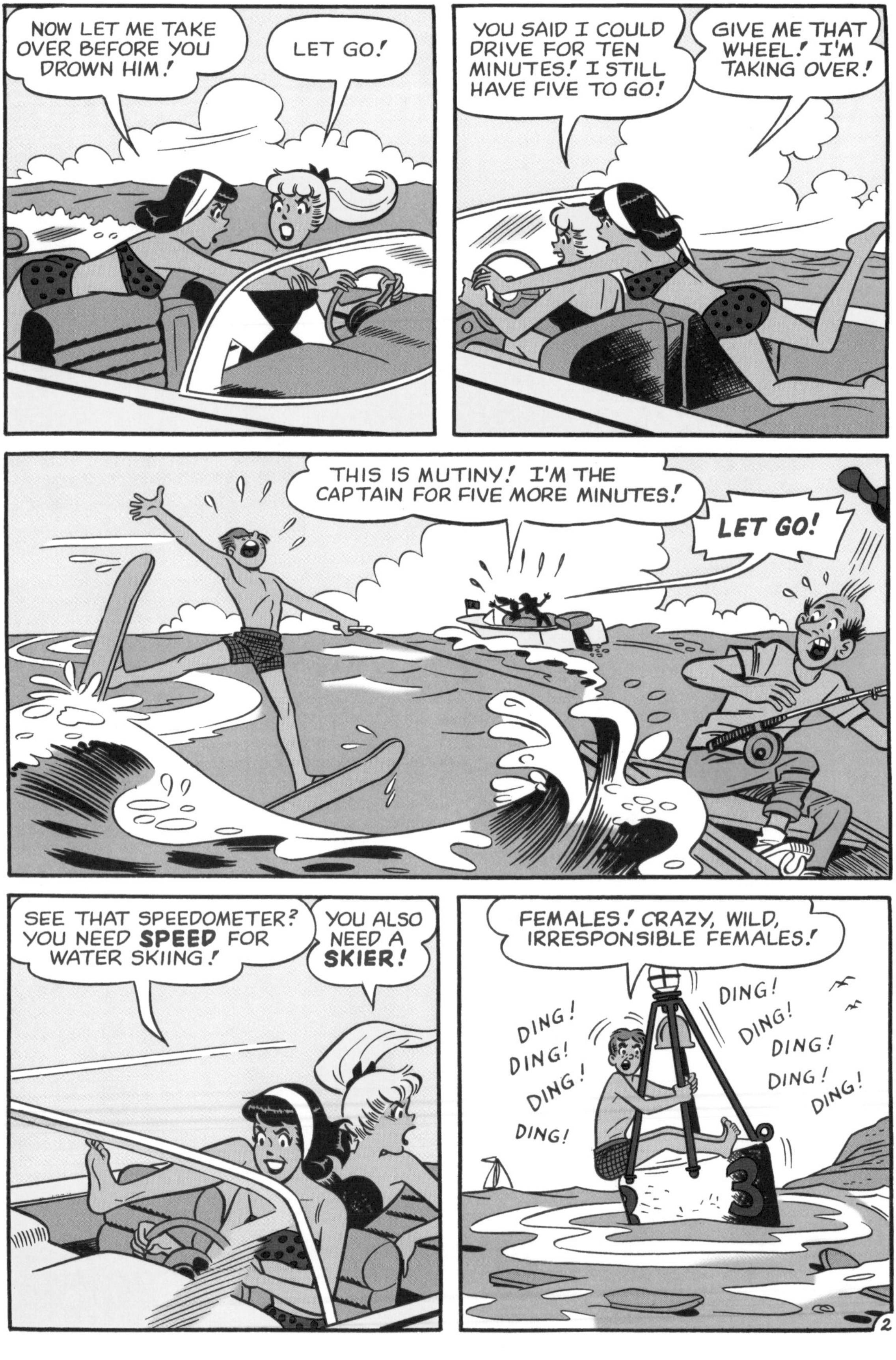
NOW LET ME TAKE OVER BEFORE YOU DROWN HIM!
LET GO!
YOU SAID I COULD DRIVE FOR TEN MINUTES! I STILL HAVE FIVE TO GO!
GIVE ME THAT WHEEL! I'M TAKING OVER!
THIS IS MUTINY! I'M THE CAPTAIN FOR FIVE MORE MINUTES!
LET GO!
SEE THAT SPEEDOMETER? YOU NEED SPEED FOR WATER SKIING!
YOU ALSO NEED A SKIER!
FEMALES! CRAZY, WILD, IRRESPONSIBLE FEMALES!
DING! DING! DING! DING!
DING! DING! DING! DING! DING!
2

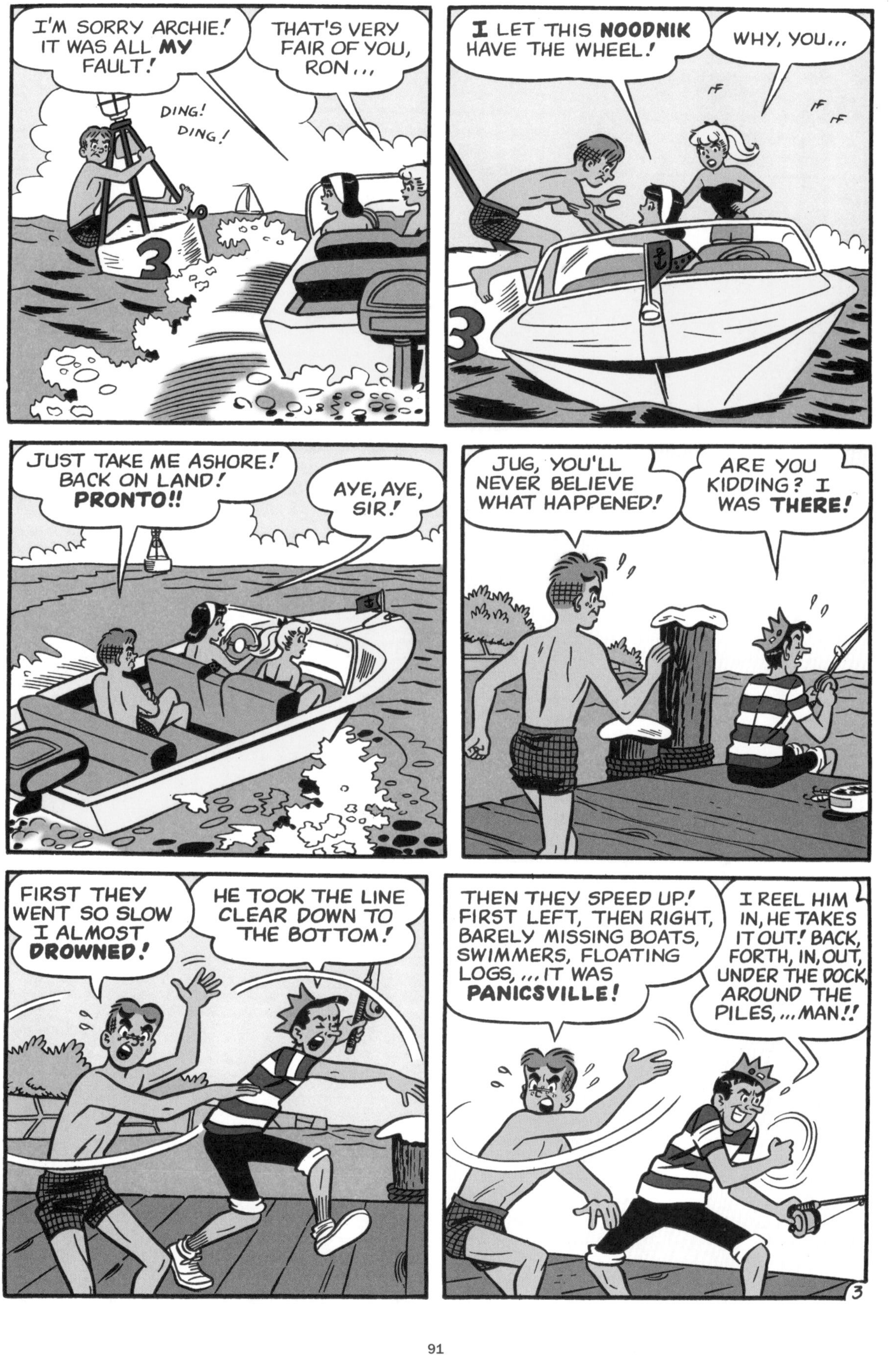
I'M SORRY ARCHIE! IT WAS ALL MY FAULT!
THAT'S VERY FAIR OF YOU, RON...
DING! DING!
I LET THIS NOODNIK HAVE THE WHEEL!
WHY, YOU...
JUST TAKE ME ASHORE! BACK ON LAND! PRONTO!!
AYE, AYE, SIR!
JUG, YOU'LL NEVER BELIEVE WHAT HAPPENED!
ARE YOU KIDDING? I WAS THERE!
FIRST THEY WENT SO SLOW I ALMOST DROWNED!
HE TOOK THE LINE CLEAR DOWN TO THE BOTTOM!
THEN THEY SPEED UP! FIRST LEFT, THEN RIGHT, BARELY MISSING BOATS, SWIMMERS, FLOATING LOGS, ... IT WAS PANICSVILLE!
I REEL HIM IN, HE TAKES IT OUT! BACK, FORTH, IN, OUT, UNDER THE DOCK, AROUND THE PILES, ... MAN!!
3

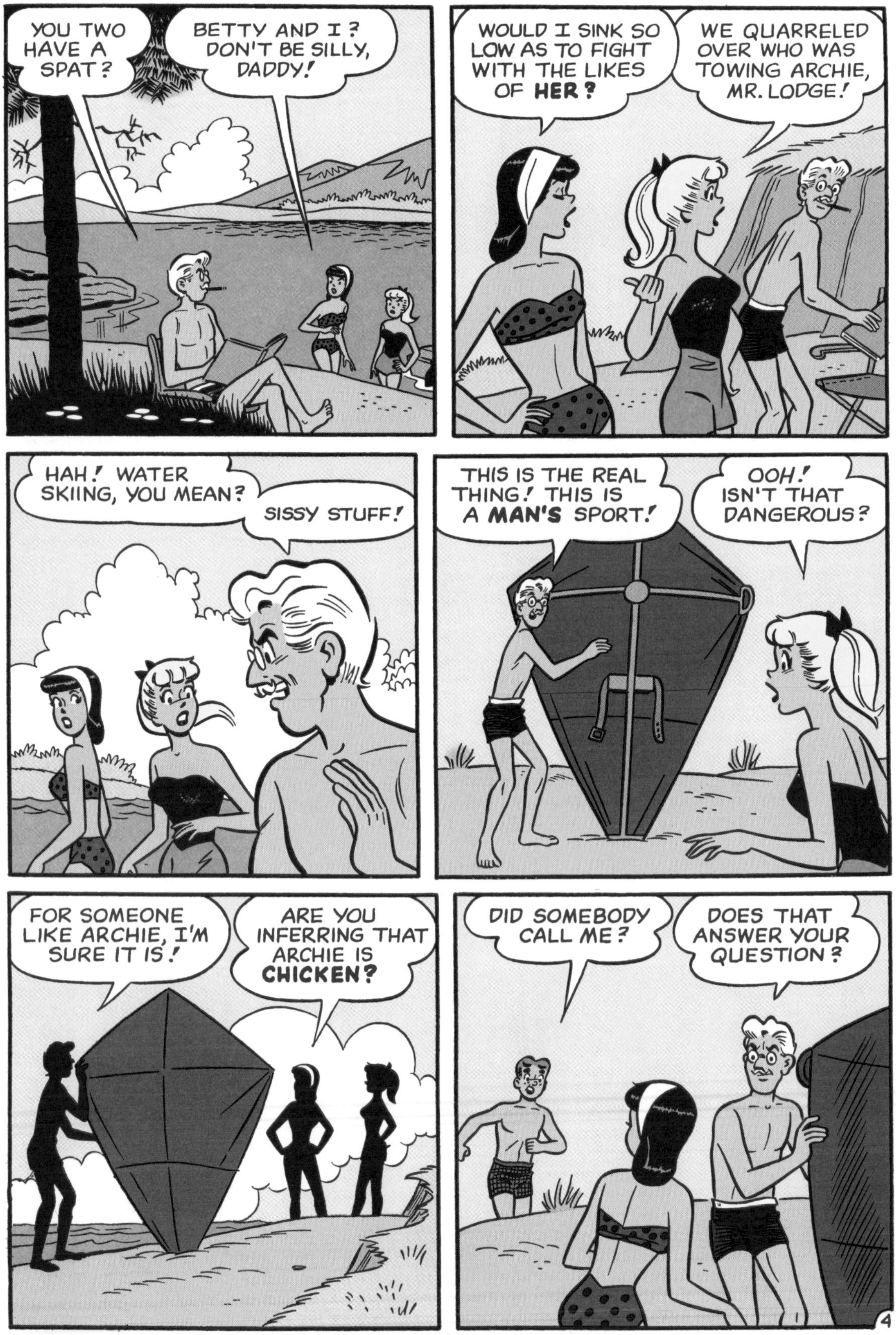
YOU TWO HAVE A SPAT?
BETTY AND I? DON'T BE SILLY, DADDY!
WOULD I SINK SO LOW AS TO FIGHT WITH THE LIKES OF HER?
WE QUARRELED OVER WHO WAS TOWING ARCHIE, MR. LODGE!
HAH! WATER SKIING, YOU MEAN?
SISSY STUFF!
THIS IS THE REAL THING! THIS IS A MAN'S SPORT!
OOH! ISN'T THAT DANGEROUS?
FOR SOMEONE LIKE ARCHIE, I'M SURE IT IS!
ARE YOU INFERRING THAT ARCHIE IS CHICKEN?
DID SOMEBODY CALL ME?
DOES THAT ANSWER YOUR QUESTION?
4

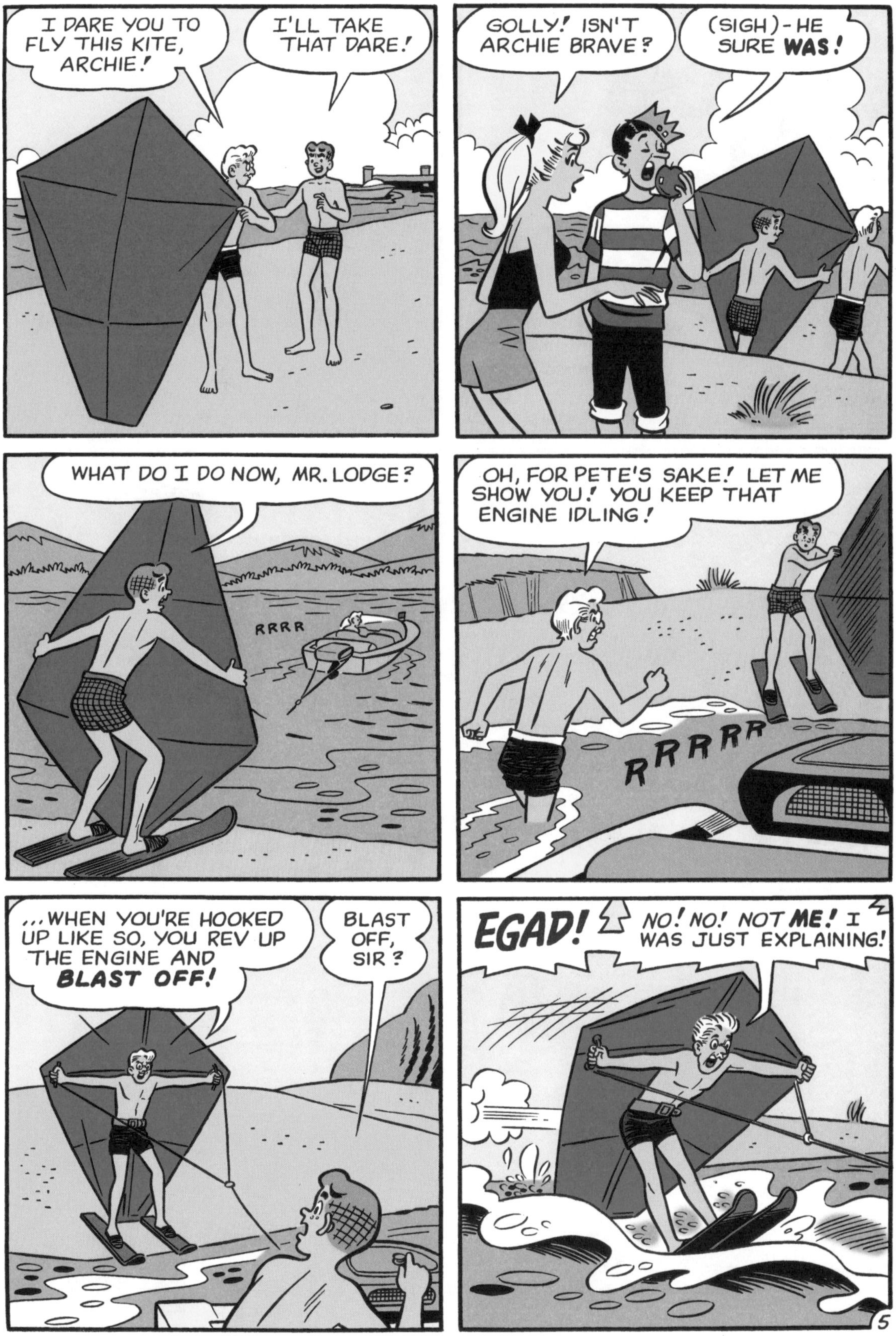
I DARE YOU TO FLY THIS KITE, ARCHIE!
I'LL TAKE THAT DARE!
GOLLY! ISN'T ARCHIE BRAVE?
(SIGH)-HE SURE WAS!
WHAT DO I DO NOW, MR. LODGE?
RRRR
OH, FOR PETE'S SAKE! LET ME SHOW YOU! YOU KEEP THAT ENGINE IDLING!
RRRRRR
...WHEN YOU'RE HOOKED UP LIKE SO, YOU REV UP THE ENGINE AND BLAST OFF!
BLAST OFF, SIR?
EGAD!
NO! NO! NOT ME! I WAS JUST EXPLAINING!
5

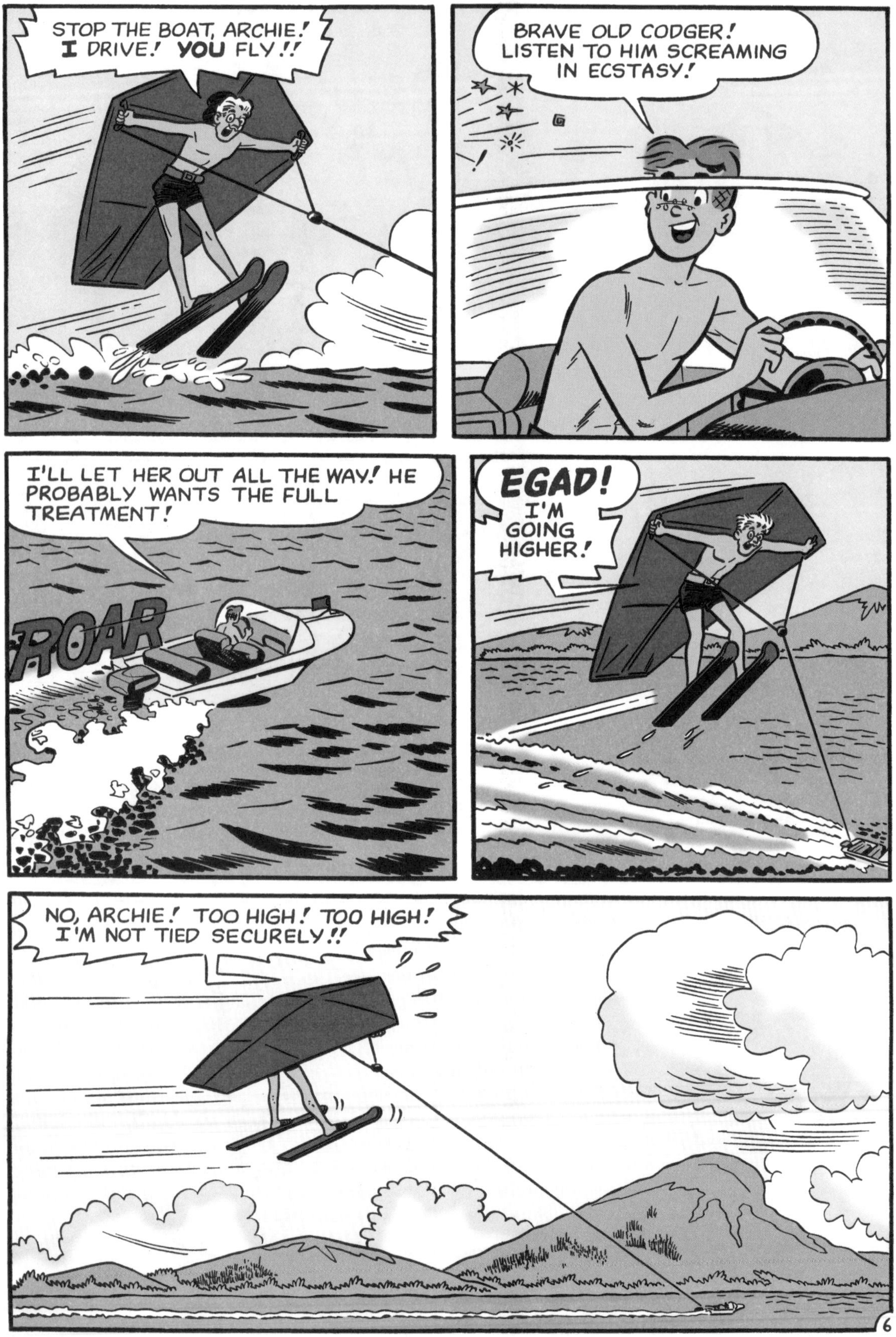
STOP THE BOAT, ARCHIE! I DRIVE! YOU FLY!!
BRAVE OLD CODGER! LISTEN TO HIM SCREAMING IN ECSTASY!
I'LL LET HER OUT ALL THE WAY! HE PROBABLY WANTS THE FULL TREATMENT!
ROAR
EGAD! I'M GOING HIGHER!
NO, ARCHIE! TOO HIGH! TOO HIGH! I'M NOT TIED SECURELY!!
6

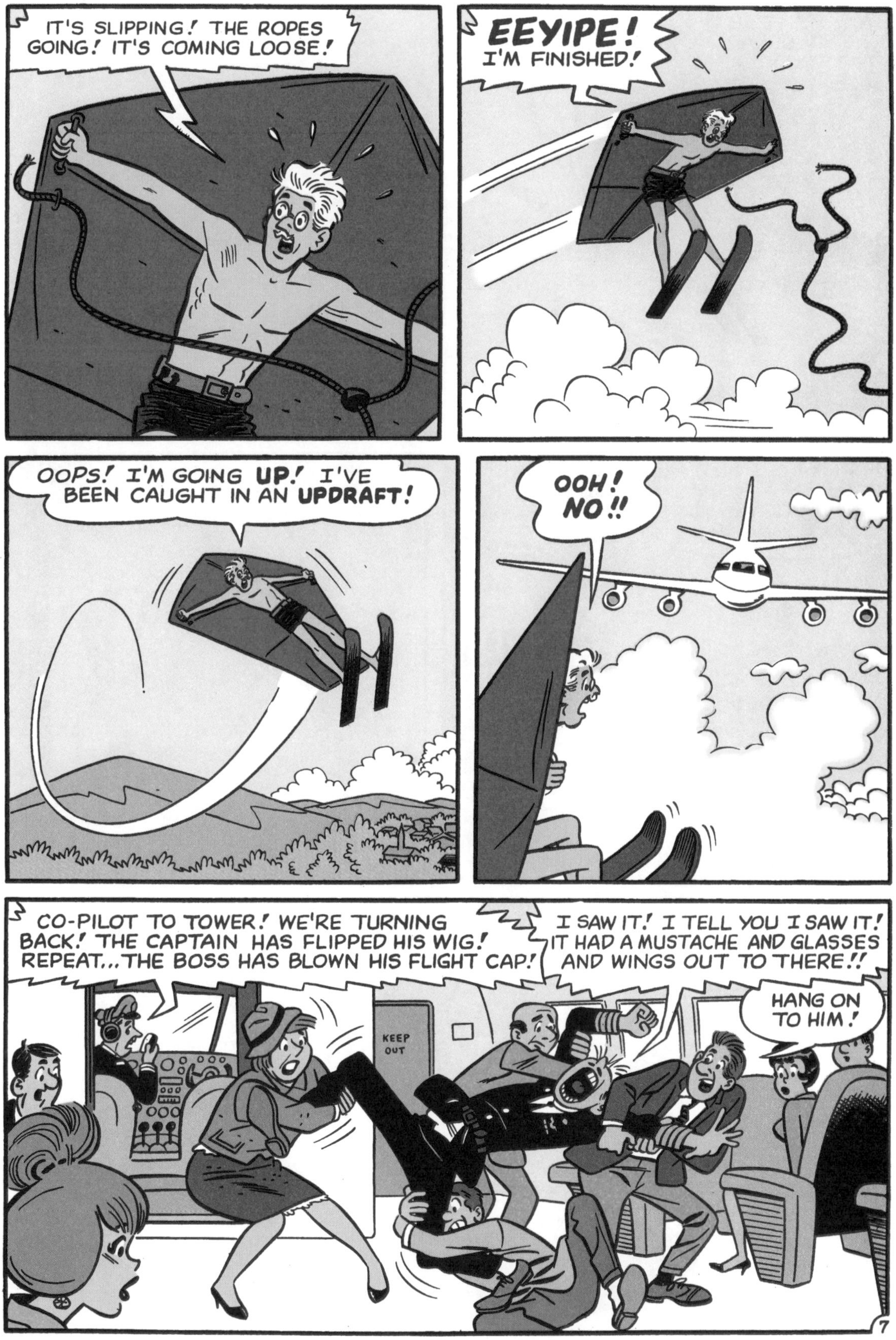
IT'S SLIPPING! THE ROPES GOING! IT'S COMING LOOSE!
EEYIPE! I'M FINISHED!
OOPS! I'M GOING UP! I'VE BEEN CAUGHT IN AN UPDRAFT!
OOH! NO!!
CO-PILOT TO TOWER! WE'RE TURNING BACK! THE CAPTAIN HAS FLIPPED HIS WIG! REPEAT...THE BOSS HAS BLOWN HIS FLIGHT CAP!
I SAW IT! I TELL YOU I SAW IT! IT HAD A MUSTACHE AND GLASSES AND WINGS OUT TO THERE!!
HANG ON TO HIM!
KEEP OUT
7

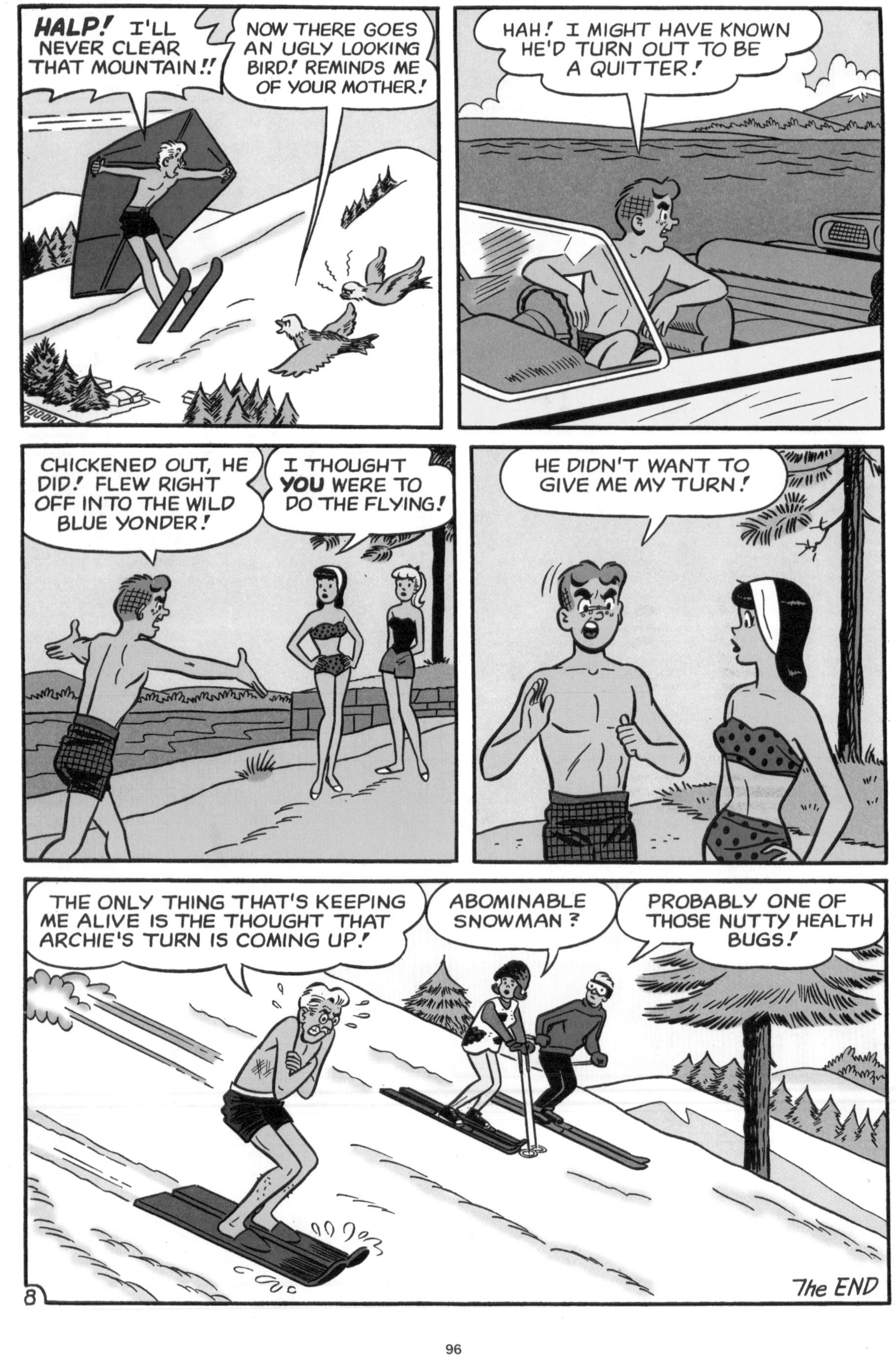
HALP! I'LL NEVER CLEAR THAT MOUNTAIN!!
NOW THERE GOES AN UGLY LOOKING BIRD! REMINDS ME OF YOUR MOTHER!
HAH! I MIGHT HAVE KNOWN HE'D TURN OUT TO BE A QUITTER!
CHICKENED OUT, HE DID! FLEW RIGHT OFF INTO THE WILD BLUE YONDER!
I THOUGHT YOU WERE TO DO THE FLYING!
HE DIDN'T WANT TO GIVE ME MY TURN!
THE ONLY THING THAT'S KEEPING ME ALIVE IS THE THOUGHT THAT ARCHIE'S TURN IS COMING UP!
ABOMINABLE SNOWMAN?
PROBABLY ONE OF THOSE NUTTY HEALTH BUGS!
8
The END